Acclaim for Twin Fantasies *by Opal*

4 stars! "Carew's devilish twists a⋯ ⋯he story moving from sad to suspense⋯ ⋯in the end. . . . The plot moves swiftly ⋯

⋯*antic Times BOOKreviews*

"Opal Carew brings erotic romance to a whole new level with *Twin Fantasies* . . . she writes a compelling romance and sets your senses on fire with her love scenes!" —*Reader to Reader*

4 stars! "Written with great style . . . *Twin Fantasies* is surely a must for any erotic romance fan, ménage enthusiasts in particular."
—*Just Erotic Romance Reviews*

4½ hearts! "*Twin Fantasies* has humor, angst, drama, lots of hot sex, and interesting characters that make for an entertaining read that you will have a hard time putting down." —*The Romance Studio*

"Opal Carew has given these characters [a] depth and realism. . . . *Twin Fantasies* is a thrilling romance, full of both incredible passion and heartwarming tenderness, and Opal Carew is an author to watch." —*Joyfully Reviewed*

"Super sexy and able to incite passionate emotions." —*Romance Junkies*

"Whew! A curl-your-toes, hot and sweaty erotic romance! I did not put this book down until I read it cover to cover. . . . I highly recommend this one."
—*Fresh Fiction*

"*Twin Fantasies* is every woman's fantasy!"
—Bertrice Small, *New York Times* bestselling author

Swing

ALSO BY OPAL CAREW

Twin Fantasies

OPAL CAREW *Swing*

ST. MARTIN'S GRIFFIN ⚏ NEW YORK

This is a work of fiction. All of the characters, organizations, and events portrayed in this novel are either products of the author's imagination or are used fictitiously.

SWING. Copyright © 2007 by Elizabeth Batten-Carew. All rights reserved. Printed in the United States of America. For information, address St. Martin's Press, 175 Fifth Avenue, New York, N.Y. 10010.

www.stmartins.com

Library of Congress Cataloging-in-Publication Data

Carew, Opal.
    Swing / Opal Carew.—1st ed.
        p. cm.
    ISBN-13: 978-0-312-36780-0
    ISBN-10: 0-312-36780-5
    1. Group sex—Fiction. 2. Sex-oriented businesses—Fiction. 3. Resorts—Fiction. I. Title.

PR9199.4.C367S94 2008
813'.6—dc22

2007038544

10 9 8 7 6

To the three special men in my life:

Mark

Matthew

Jason

Acknowledgments

Thank you to my wonderful editor, Rose Hilliard, who gave me the vision for this story and who helped me make it the best book possible. Thank you to my agent, Emily Sylvan Kim, for helping me with a great many things so I could stay focused and productive. Thank you to my sister-in-law, Colette, for your insight and enthusiasm. Thanks to the members of ORWA (my local RWA chapter) for all your support. Thank you to my two sons, for being so understanding and supportive about all the time I spend writing and sometimes traveling. Finally, thank you to my husband, Mark, for being so incredibly supportive.

Swing

Chapter 1

"WOULD YOU COME TO A SWINGERS' CLUB WITH ME?" SHANE asked.

Melissa's stomach felt like it had dropped to her knees. She couldn't think of a single question he could have asked that would have shocked her more.

As she stared at him in silence, he leaned toward her, candlelight glowing in his eyes. The clinking of cutlery and plates, mellowed by the hum of conversation, swirled around them.

"Would you pretend to be my wife and come to a swingers' club with me?"

His repeating the words didn't make them any clearer. She just sat there and stared at him for a moment, stunned. Finally, she realized there wasn't any more. No "April Fool's Day!" No "Boy, look at the expression on your face. I got you that time."

And to think, when she'd sensed the hesitation in his voice moments earlier, she'd been worried he was going to ask her if she wanted to take their relationship to the next level. Not that she should have expected him to ask such a question, but she realized now that a small part of her had hoped that's where he'd been heading.

And that shocked her almost as much as his actual question.

Almost.

Für Elise chimed from her purse. Saved by the bell.

"That'll be Elaine. I had lunch with her and she asked me to babysit for a few days. She was going to call to confirm dates. It'll just take a second."

And give her a moment to get her head together.

As Shane watched Melissa rummage around in her purse, he took a sip of his imported beer from the tall, gold-rimmed glass. The aroma of fresh bread filled his nostrils as the waiter placed a basket of crusty rolls on the table.

Melissa was a doting aunt to those kids and a regular mother hen to both her younger sisters, Elaine and Ginny. Although both were grown women, Melissa still felt she had to take care of them, as she had been doing since she was sixteen when her mother had abandoned them.

Melissa flicked open the phone. "Hello?"

"Hi, sis. Oh, damn, that's the baby, can you hang on?" Elaine said.

"Sure, I'll wait."

As Melissa listened to the sounds of kids chattering and a baby crying on the other end of the line, she gazed at Shane. Classically handsome with a boyish charm, his wide smile revealed straight, white teeth. Her gaze caressed the broad line of his shoulders. Those shoulders could carry a lot of weight, and had certainly soaked up a lot of her tears over the years. He always held her with such warmth, usually in the brief hugs he gave her in greeting, but sometimes longer, when he knew she was troubled or hurting.

Right now she could imagine her hands running over that solid, muscular form, imagine his strong arms sliding around her, pulling her against his hard, masculine chest. Her gaze shifted back to his face . . . to his full, sexy lips, imagining them capturing hers.

"Liss? Something wrong?"

Her face blossomed with heat as she realized Shane was staring at her.

"No, sorry, I just got . . . distracted."

He grinned. "I'd love to know where that serious mind of yours wandered off to, because I've never seen your cheeks so red."

Her cheeks blazed hotter. She stroked her hair behind her ear and took a sip of her drink. "Well, never you mind. A girl is allowed some secrets, even from her closest friends."

Melissa hoped he hadn't guessed what she'd been daydreaming about. This was the first time, since they'd met at college, that they'd both been unattached at the same time while living in the same city. They'd gotten closer than ever over the past few months, sometimes even joking that Shane was her surrogate boyfriend. If only he knew how close that was to the truth. Melissa had always felt a flicker of attraction to him, but lately it had spiraled into a full-blown crush.

Melissa's hand shifted to her neck to toy with the diamond heart necklace Shane had given her last Christmas. She had struggled with accepting something so expensive, but Shane had insisted, pointing out that with the money he had it was about the same, proportionally speaking, as her spending twenty-five dollars on a gift for him, so it wouldn't be fair of her to turn it down.

"Sorry, sis, can I call you back?" Elaine asked, tiny Joey wailing in the background.

"Sure, that's fine." Melissa hung up the phone and laid it on the table. "She's going to call back."

She tapped her fingers on the table.

"So this club . . ."

A swingers' club. *He'd asked her to a swingers' club.*

"It's like . . . wife swapping?" she continued.

"It's really a resort, not a club."

"But we're not even a couple. Why would you ask me to go somewhere like that?"

"Because I'm planning on buying the resort."

"What?"

Shane realized this was going better than he'd thought it would. At least she hadn't said no yet. He really wanted to experience the resort firsthand and he couldn't do that as a single male. Melissa was the only woman he could reasonably ask to pose as his wife.

He could understand her surprise at his request. A few weeks ago, he would have been just as surprised as she was—until he'd had that conversation with Geoff, a new member of his golf club. After a few rounds of drinks and a long discussion about the low success rate of marriages today, Geoff had confided to Shane that he knew the secret to a long and happy marriage. He'd handed Shane a card for a swingers' resort in St. Haven in the British West Indies. Shane had been skeptical until Geoff pointed out that he and his wife had been going there since it opened five years ago, and to local clubs before that, and they had been happily married for over twenty years now.

Maybe this really was the secret to marital bliss. Who was Shane, with his multiply divorced parents, to decide he knew better? And even if it wasn't, it could prove to be a great investment. Either way, he had nothing to lose, and a great deal to gain.

"I think a place like this could allow couples to overcome the stagnation that occurs after years of sleeping with the same person and add enough spice and variety to their lives so that they could keep a happy and loving marriage going. If my parents had gone somewhere like that, maybe they wouldn't have divorced." Shane grabbed a roll and buttered it.

"I'm really not comfortable with the idea of going to a place like that."

"I understand, but there's an orientation session that allows newbies to take a look around with no pressure to join in the . . . activities. It'll only be five days, and you don't have to do anything you don't want to do."

She pursed her lips.

"It's really a beautiful spot. It's on a small island called St. Haven and it's—"

Her cell phone chimed again.

"Sorry, excuse me . . ." She flicked it open. "Uh-huh."

She grabbed her pocket calendar from her purse and flipped through the pages to April.

"The sixteenth? Yeah, that should be okay. How many days? Five." She jotted some notes in her planner.

"Where is this place?" She glanced at Shane then made some more notes. "Uh-huh. Sounds nice. Okay, I'll talk to you Sunday."

She glanced at Shane. "What was the name of that island again?"

"St. Haven."

"And the resort? Is it called The Sweet Surrender?"

"Yeah, how did you know?"

Her mouth compressed into a straight line. "Because that's where Elaine and Steve are going."

Melissa watched the road through the drizzle-coated windshield as the wipers *whoosh*ed back and forth. Thoughts of Elaine and that . . . resort . . . bounced around her brain. How could Elaine have let Steve talk her into going to a place like that?

Shane said he'd told Steve about his plans to buy the resort and that seemed to have given Steve ideas of his own. Melissa knew Steve and Elaine had been having intimacy problems, but they just needed to balance their love life with the kids. Granted, that wasn't easy with three young children, but going to a swingers' club was definitely not the answer.

Elaine was rushing into something she didn't understand. Melissa's only chance of convincing her to change her mind was to go to this place and learn as much as she could about it and about the kind of people who went there. Faced with the facts, surely Elaine would see reason.

Melissa sighed. At least Elaine had a husband to go home to. All Melissa had was an empty apartment.

Damn it. Earlier she'd been terrified that Shane had guessed the way she'd been feeling about him. Now, faced with going home to a lonely bed again, she realized how disappointed she was that he hadn't.

She was so comfortable with Shane. The thought of falling asleep in his arms, snuggled against his firm, muscular chest, sent warmth washing through her.

As she drove, images of Shane in his swim trunks from when they'd gone to the beach last summer—his sexy, muscular body gleaming in the sunshine—washed though her mind. Her insides tightened at the thought of him pulling her against him and kissing her, consuming her lips in passion. Her lips tingled as she imagined his mouth moving against hers, his tongue slipping inside. She sighed. Sharp pangs of need pulsed through her as she imagined his hands gliding over her body, stroking her breasts, then his mouth covering her nipple. It hardened and elongated at the imagined pull of his mouth, the swirl of his tongue.

Oh God, she should not be obsessing about Shane just because she'd been without a man for a couple of months. She shifted in the seat, feeling hot and damp. Good heavens, she needed a man.

She turned right onto her street, then pulled into her driveway. She grabbed her purse from the seat and dodged through the rain to the front door. She unlocked it and, as she pushed it open, she heard the phone ringing from inside. She kicked off her shoes and raced across the room, then snatched up the receiver.

"Hi, there." Shane's deep voice greeted her.

"Oh hi, I just got in the door."

"I figured. I wanted to make sure you got home okay. With the rain and all."

"Thanks." His caring gesture warmed her heart. "I'm glad you called. I wanted to talk to you about the resort. . . ."

"Liss, I'm really sorry that Steve—"

"No, that's not your fault. What I wanted to say is that I'd like to go. I need to learn more about it. I need to be able to talk Elaine out of going there and . . . information is power. The more I know, the more convincing I'll be."

"Okay. I . . . uh . . . went ahead and booked us in for next week, just in case you said yes. We'll have to leave next Wednesday."

She smiled. "And if I'd said no?"

"Then they would have been stuck with an empty room."

"Room? Just one?"

"Well, I can't go as a single man. I assumed we'd go as a couple, but they do allow single women, so if you'd rather go alone . . ."

The thought of wandering around a resort like that on her own, among the sex-hungry males . . . and females . . . who would frequent such a place sent shivers up her spine.

"There's no way I'm going alone!"

"Great. You've got a passport, right?"

"Right."

"And can you make a doctor's appointment this week?"

"Why? Do I need to get shots?" She cringed, hating the thought of a needle piercing her skin.

"No. The resort is very exclusive and requires medical testing for all its guests, to ensure they don't have any sexually transmitted diseases. I saw Dr. Lane today and he told me he could get my results back in time. If you go in this week, he can rush them both through."

Her stomach knotted.

"But I'm not planning on . . . you know . . . doing anything while I'm there."

"They don't know that."

She sighed. Of course they didn't.

"Okay. I'll call tomorrow morning." She grabbed the planner from her purse and jotted down a reminder. "Anything else?"

"Yes. It's probably not a good idea to mention that you work for a news station. It could make people nervous. Maybe you should say you're a freelance writer or something. Also, do you mind if we go as Mr. and Mrs. Woods? It's better if we don't use my name. I don't want anyone to figure out I'm the one interested in buying the place."

"Sure."

Mr. Shane Woods.

Thoughts of Shane at her side using her last name and pretending to be her husband sent her heartbeat racing, interesting possibilities flickering through her mind. The two of them in an intimate setting, acting as husband and wife. Tender touches, holding hands, a kiss on the temple.

"One room means one bed, right?" she asked.

"Uh . . . yeah. . . ."

Excitement danced along her nerve endings. She imagined being in that room now, Shane lying on the bed. Her hormones surged once again as she thought about undressing him, about exploring every plane and muscular bulge . . . every hard, masculine surface of that gorgeous body of his.

Her insides quivered as she realized she was about to do something very foolish.

Chapter 2

TY ADAMS SETTLED BACK IN THE GUEST CHAIR AS HIS BEST FRIEND Suzanne sat down behind her desk. Her face was drawn and she lacked her usual vivacious, cheerful demeanor.

"How bad is it?" he asked.

"I have to sell."

His eyebrows arched. Suzanne loved that resort.

She'd been born on the tiny island of St. Haven in the British West Indies while her father had been stationed there to build an airport, and she maintained dual citizenship even though her parents had returned to the States when she was two years old. Six years ago, she'd gone to visit the island for the first time as an adult and she'd fallen in love with the place. She'd gone back a year later to set up The Sweet Surrender resort and had been planning on moving there permanently in a couple of years.

"I don't understand. You've run two clubs here in Chicago and they're both extremely successful."

She slid a file across her habitually tidy, maple desk. He picked up the royal blue folder and flipped it open. Financial statements for the resort. A lot of numbers in the red. She seemed to be getting by on a thread.

"I don't know. It's a bit different, being a resort rather than a club. Maybe I was too ambitious with this project."

He closed the file and tossed it on the desk. It skidded toward her, stopping when it bumped against the large amethyst crystal cluster she'd bought in Brazil. She said it brought positive energy to her work space. If he didn't know her so well, he'd think her a bit flaky when she said things like that, but other than her quirky way of viewing rocks, she was the most levelheaded person he'd ever met.

"No way. You had it all planned out. You did your homework."

That's what he admired about Suzanne. She was self-reliant and competent in business. More than competent, having built her own business from the ground up, relying on no one, male or otherwise.

"Yes, but we hit a lot of bad luck. Equipment breaking down. Fewer guests than we anticipated. We're never running at capacity. We advertise more, but it doesn't make much difference."

"We" included Hal and Vanna, the couple she'd hired to manage the resort for her. She did the same at all her clubs. Swingers expected a couple to run the place, not a single woman. When she visited the clubs to check things out, she never let anyone know she was the owner.

"So your mind's made up?"

She nodded. "I had an agent by yesterday representing some rich client . . . wouldn't say who. He said he'd get back to me in about two weeks. That's why I asked you to come by." She leaned forward, her eyes intent. "Ty, I need a favor."

"Honey, whatever you want." He'd known Suzanne for ten years. She'd always been there for him. He would do anything to help her. "You want me to find out who the buyer is?"

That was right down his alley as a private investigator.

She shook her head.

"My agent knows the other agent. Says the guy usually suggests his clients send someone in to investigate when buying this type of business."

He smiled. "Suzie, I don't think there are many businesses like this one."

She smiled despite herself. "Yeah, well, I mean like a resort, hotel . . ." She shrugged. "Even a store. He figures they should see how the business is run, how guests are treated, that kind of thing."

"Makes sense." He leaned back in his chair, crossing his jean-clad legs.

"I figure that means he'll send someone out to the next orientation getaway."

He raised an eyebrow. "So you want me to go there and . . . ?"

"Identify who you think the investigator is and then keep an eye on him, while I make sure things run smoothly, and convince him that the place is a good investment. Which it is." She sounded only a little defensive.

Ty knew it must be breaking her heart having to sell what was essentially her baby.

"It just requires a little more capital than I have . . . ," she continued. "And a lot more luck."

Ty wondered what Suzanne intended to do to convince the guy. He knew she'd call Hal and Vanna to ensure everything was shipshape, but it *was* a swingers' club.

He gazed at Suzanne's high cheekbones, heart-shaped lips, lovely green eyes, then followed her long strands of wispy blond hair to her black, tailored wool suit jacket, open at the front revealing a red silk, low-cut top that draped softly over her generous breasts.

This was a resort for swingers, and Suzanne was very open about sex, so she might decide to treat this guy to some seriously erotic persuasion. Ty's groin tightened as he remembered the last time he experienced Suzanne's talents. Her mouth lapping over his nipples, then her hot, slick body swallowing his cock deep inside, her intimate muscles squeezing him tight. His cock rose at the memory.

She stood up and walked toward him, smiling.

"So what do you say? I know you've got cases, but I'll pay for your time and your airline ticket, of course." She sat on the desk in front of him. "Besides, it'll be fun."

Fun? Sharing a room with her? Sharing a bed with her? And with any other women at the resort who were interested?

That wasn't fun. It was a five-star erotic fantasy!

"Of course I'll do it. And I won't accept your money."

Suzanne smiled and kissed his cheek, then her hand slid down his chest and over his crotch. At the feel of her fingers, his erection strained tighter against his pants. He uncrossed his legs.

"I see you're excited about the idea."

She leaned forward to kiss him, her fingers gliding up his denim-encased cock.

The sound of his zipper releasing accompanied the loosening of fabric around his cock. Her fingers wrapped around him, setting his hormones raging.

"In your office, Suzie?"

"Gina knows better than to come in without knocking . . . and waiting for an answer."

She knelt down and drew his cock from his pants. His groin tightened at the feel of her feminine fingers encircling him. Then her hot mouth covered him and he groaned.

Suzanne loved the feel of Ty's familiar cock in her mouth. She loved Ty, in a friendly way. He'd always been there for her. Someone to talk to, to help in a crisis, and she'd done the same for him. She was one of the few people he'd let past his barriers to form a real friendship. Probably because he knew she would never demand anything of him. But mostly, because she accepted him exactly as he was. That was important to him. He'd had enough of being molded and forced to be something he didn't want to be—first from his demanding father, then from his controlling ex-wife, Celia.

Suzanne licked the crown of his wonderful penis, then sucked. He stroked her hair back from her face, his touch gentle and filled with affection.

"Suzie, you do that so well."

She drew him in deep, then slid back. She moved back and forth, stimulating his shaft with the tips of her teeth, then sucked and squeezed.

"Oh, sweetheart."

She could taste the pre-cum on her tongue as she swirled it around and over the tip of his cock. She loved his taste, and couldn't get enough of his hard, male flesh in her mouth. She ran her tongue along his length, then sucked him deep again. Her hands stroked under his balls and cradled them in her palms as her fingers curled around them.

Ty's hands clamped gently around Suzanne's shoulders and he drew her upward.

"Whoa, honey. I won't be able to hold on much longer—you're way too good at that—and I want to be inside you when I come."

She released him from her mouth, then slid off her jacket as he unfastened his belt and dropped his jeans to the floor. She tugged off her crimson camisole and tossed it aside, then snapped open the front-clasp on her red lace bra. His gaze locked on to her breasts and her nipples immediately thrust outward.

He tucked his hands under her breasts and stroked over the hard, needy nipples with his thumbs. Sitting on the edge of the desk, she sucked in a breath at the exquisite pleasure of his touch. She stepped closer and cupped his face in her hands, then kissed him. His lips, firm and sure, opened at the gentle pressure of her tongue, allowing it to slide into his mouth. His tongue greeted hers and they coiled in a sensuous dance.

He leaned forward and she felt her skirt shimmy upward as he tugged at the fabric. She unfastened his shirt buttons as he dragged her panties down to her knees. She kicked them off the rest of the way and leaned back against the desk.

"You are the sexiest woman I know."

She smiled, stroking his wavy, dark brown hair from his face.

"So you keep saying."

He tucked his hands under her knees and lifted them. She wrapped her hands around his delightfully huge cock and pressed it against her slick opening. He eased forward, impaling her slowly.

Oh, God, it felt wonderful having him inside her. His long, hard cock never failed to please her. Of course, the mutual respect and affection they shared enhanced the experience intensely.

He drove forward, filling her to the base of his generous shaft. She squeezed him, welcoming and encouraging. She wrapped her arms around him and nibbled on his earlobe.

"Come on, lover. Show me what you've got."

He smiled, gazing into her eyes as he drew back.

"I'll show you, all right, honey." He drove forward, sending a wild pulse of pleasure through her. "That's what you want, right?"

"Oh, you know it." She felt her body shaking from the intense need building within her. "Only you can hit just the right spot."

He swiveled his hips, stroking her vagina in a delightful way, then he pulsed in short strokes several times, then swiveled again. Waves of pleasure swelled through her.

His finger slid between them and stroked over her clit.

"Ohhhh . . . I'm going to . . ."

He flicked her clit, then stroked as he thrust in and out, deeper and harder.

"I'm coming." She knew he loved to hear her say that. He loved knowing he gave her pleasure. "Oh, baby, you're making me come."

She wailed in ecstasy, clinging to his shoulders as he rode her through the rising tide of bliss. She continued to moan, caught up in exquisite pleasure, even after he erupted inside her.

They clung to each other, panting. She leaned against his chest, enjoying the strength of his arms around her.

His ex-wife had been a total idiot to let someone as sweet and sexy as Ty slip through her fingers. If Suzanne had been his wife, she'd never have let him go.

It would be great having Ty with her at the resort . . . spending several days . . . and nights . . . together.

Sadness oozed through her. Even though it would be the last time she ever went there. Because she'd just talked Ty into helping her sell her dream.

A warm, ocean breeze caressed Melissa's face as she stepped out of the cab and breathed in the scent of exotic tropical flowers. A bellman collected the luggage onto a cart, then led her and Shane into the air-conditioned lobby. She glanced around, taking in the large potted plants, shiny marble floors, and floral upholstered furniture. The place had a nice, airy feel. She glimpsed an inviting view of white sandy beach and rolling ocean waves out the glass doors along the back of the hotel.

She clung to Shane's hand as they approached the front desk to join the short line to check-in. To avoid making eye contact with any of the four people in front of them, she glanced toward the doors, watching the traffic outside.

The doors slid open and a couple entered, dragging wheeled luggage behind them. The man's gaze met hers and he smiled. Her gaze darted away, but not before noticing how extremely handsome he was. A true hunk. His gaze returned to his companion and Melissa watched him cross the lobby to the other check-in line. Tall, with dark, wavy hair, almost black, that curled around his collar. He wore faded jeans and a blue shirt. His wife was blond, tall, with a perfect figure. Her tan, as well as her long legs, were shown to advantage in a short white skirt, while her white cotton camisole stretched over her generous—and obviously bra-less—breasts.

The first couple in line finished checking in and Melissa and Shane moved up. She glanced at the other line again. As the blonde spoke to the woman in front of them, the hunk glanced at Melissa again. When he caught her looking his way, he smiled, a glint of interest in his eyes.

Oh, my heavens! The guy's going to think I'm interested. Slowly, she dragged her gaze away. Damn, she didn't want to give him the wrong impression. This place was going to be tricky. Everyone was a potential sexual partner, married or not.

She toyed with her pendant, her fingers stroking the diamonds that formed the heart.

"Okay, let's go."

At Shane's voice, she glanced up to see him smiling at her as he held a key card envelope in his hand.

She picked up her large travel purse, tucked the strap over her shoulder, and followed him to the elevator where the bellman waited for them with their luggage.

As they rode the elevator, she felt uncomfortable, certain the bellman kept staring at her from the corner of his eye, yet she never actually caught him doing it. Then again, it was probably just her nerves. She kept wondering what he thought of her. What kind of woman came to a place like this? Maybe he wanted to make a pass at her. After all, he believed she was here looking for sex with men other than her husband. Maybe he would suggest the three of them get it on right now!

Her spine grew rigid, dreading an embarrassing proposition. But the elevator dinged, indicating they had arrived at their floor, and the bellman delivered their bags to their room, accepted Shane's tip, smiled at her as he wished them a wonderful vacation, then left. Nothing more.

Melissa collapsed on the nearest chair, barely noticing the stunning view of the ocean outside their tenth-story window, and breathed a sigh of relief.

Then she noticed the large, king-sized bed—the only bed in the room—dominating the space.

Not that the room wasn't large. In fact, it was huge. The light cream-stained wooden furniture with antique gold fittings set off the sage green walls nicely. A spacious couch with a matching chair in a tropical floral print, faced a patio door leading to a large balcony, which framed the gorgeous view of palm trees, a white sandy beach, and the turquoise ocean beyond.

But that bed loomed in front of her. She glanced at it, then at Shane, who leaned over to pick up her large suitcases from beside the bed, giving her a lovely view of his tight buns. A twinge of awareness vibrated through her, while her stomach knotted in dread as to how this day would end.

Would there be an awkward "what do we do now" when it came time for bed? Or would he take her in his arms and kiss her, then *whoosh* her off to heaven? On that bed.

"Liss, you want a drink? You look like you could use one."

"I . . ."

He glanced at his watch.

"Wait, never mind. We'd better get going to dinner." He tugged off his beige linen jacket and hung it over the back of the desk chair. "I'll just change my shirt first."

He unfastened the buttons on his shirt and tugged it off, revealing his thick, muscular arms and well-defined abs. She'd seen his bare chest many times when he'd been in a bathing suit, but this was different. They were in a hotel room. He was changing clothes, even if just a shirt. She licked her lips as she watched him, wanting to run her hands over his tanned, taut flesh, to feel those muscles rippling beneath her fingertips.

He smiled at her. "Aren't you going to change? Remember we're going to the orientation meeting, then there's a party after. You brought that great black dress, right?"

"Oh, that's right."

She hurried to her suitcase and snapped it open, then sifted through her belongings until she found the dress. She scurried into the bathroom, then leaned back against the closed door, glad for the moment alone.

Good heavens, how would she ever survive five days here when she had nearly had a panic attack just coming up the elevator, then freaked out at the sight of a king-sized bed because Shane might seduce her? Not that it would take much convincing on his part. Her barriers seemed to be dissipating by the second.

No, it wasn't being alone with Shane in this room that worried her the most. It was all the predators she'd be facing in the resort. Her spine tingled in dread at the prospect of walking among them, like a kitten surrounded by a pack of wolves. She could almost see their glinting eyes and drooling mouths.

She'd been a fool to come here.

∽

She was the one. Ty was sure of it.

Melissa Woods.

He'd seen her in the lobby when he and Suzanne had first arrived at the resort. She'd appeared nervous and out-of-place. That in itself wouldn't have been enough to convince him—any new arrival to a club like this might act that way—but there was something more. Honed instinct, an instinct he'd learned to rely on in his line of business, told him she was hiding something.

He watched the woman, with her pert little nose, full sexy lips, and wavy ash-blond hair caressing her shoulders, as she listened to Vanna, the hostess, outline the etiquette at the resort. Woods wore an alluring black dress, cinched in at the waist, which revealed an enticing glimpse of cleavage and plenty of long, shapely leg. Although she fit in completely with the other wives, something in his gut told him she wasn't here for a weekend of sex.

Which was a damned shame because a weekend of sex with her was a hell of an exciting prospect. His body tightened in response to the thought of dragging that voluptuous body against his, her tight nipples pressing into his chest as his tongue invaded her soft, sweet mouth.

But he was sure she was the one he'd been hired to watch.

She glanced his way and their gazes caught. He found himself staring into her soft blue-green eyes, the color of the ocean, and he smiled. She was certainly an attractive woman. Maybe in this case business could be mixed with a little pleasure. Her face glowed red and she curled her fingers around her husband's hand as she glanced away again.

Annoyance built in him as he watched her hand clinging to her husband's. Why did so many women feel they needed the protection of a man? Ty preferred a woman who could stand on her own two feet. Unlike his mother, who'd been needy and unable to take care of herself . . . or her son. She couldn't protect herself, let alone Ty as a child, from his abusive father. She had let her husband walk all over her because of some warped belief that she'd needed him. That he would take care of her.

This woman clung to her husband in the same way he'd seen his mother do a thousand times. Yet it was clear to Ty that Melissa Woods and her husband were not in love. They shared an affection, he could see that, but the chemistry—some sense of belonging together—was missing.

"Be sensitive to others," Hal, the host, said. "Always ask, and remember, 'no' means 'no.'"

"Also remember"—Vanna flipped her long, raven hair over her shoulder and smiled—"that it is perfectly acceptable to sit back and watch." She winked. "But believe me, participating is much more fun." A few nervous giggles twittered around the group.

Melissa glanced at the clock, carefully avoiding the gaze of the darkly handsome man who'd been watching her. The same man she'd seen in the lobby earlier. Her heartbeat accelerated as his disturbing gaze slid down her body, then rested on the swell of her breasts before continuing down to her crossed legs. She forced herself not to shift in her chair.

She tightened her grip on Shane's hand. Shane smiled at her, then turned his attention back to the auburn-haired beauty with emerald eyes a few chairs away. If Shane had been her real husband, she would have been jealous at the way he flirted with the other woman, but he wasn't her husband. Still, she *was* a little jealous, but she reminded herself that she and Shane were just good friends, despite their attraction for each other.

His flirting made their role here appear more real. She should be doing the same thing, but there was no way she was going to have sex with a stranger.

She intended to play the "I just want to observe" card a great deal, and by *observe* she meant the rituals, not others having sex. No one should be surprised, since Hal said that it was quite common for newbies to take a few days to open up.

She toyed with her necklace and chanced a quick glance at the dark stranger, who had introduced himself as Ty Adams, as he whispered something to his blond, blue-eyed, aerobic-instructor-perfect wife. The problem was, Melissa sensed that this guy, with the midnight eyes that could chip away at a woman's resolve, would view a newbie like her as a challenge. And she had the impression that whatever challenge this man took on, he pursued with a vengeance.

"Now I suggest," Hal said, "that you all take a look around the resort. There is a welcome dance in the ballroom. Feel free to talk to the other members and ask questions. Everyone is very friendly." He grinned. "There are various bars and," he winked, "specialty rooms available. These are outlined in the orientation booklet. And you can always take a dip in the pool or soak in one of the four hot tubs—bathing suits optional, of course."

Melissa glanced at the orientation booklet without really seeing it, trying to quell her uneasiness at the thought of naked people lounging around the pool doing who-knows-what and especially trying not to imagine what went on in the *specialty rooms*.

"One more piece of advice." Vanna smiled at them. "Don't stay with your spouse this evening. Practice experiencing the club and meeting other people on your own. If you have any questions, we'll be circulating around the club. Now, go have fun."

Everyone took that as a cue and stood up. Couples began milling toward the door.

"Do you want me to stay with you?" Shane's eyebrows rose.

Yes, she did. Desperately. But she couldn't hide behind Shane all week, and she refused to be ruled by her anxieties.

"No, they suggested we separate."

The thought of roaming around this place on her own filled her stomach with butterflies, but she was a big girl and she could handle it. Experienced patrons who were interested in newcomers would probably go to the ballroom. If she went to the bar, hopefully the patrons there would ignore her.

As Shane crossed the room, Auburn Hair smiled at him, her face lighting up. They chatted for a moment, she laughed, then he slid his arm around her waist and they slipped through the door.

Melissa noticed Mr. Dark Eyes standing by his wife's side as she chatted with Vanna. He smiled at Melissa. Calmly, she returned his smile then headed for the door, relieved when he did not follow her.

She returned to the lobby, then followed the signs to the lounge. Soft music flowed from the room. She walked straight to the bar, then sat on one of the high, wooden stools and ordered an orange and cranberry juice.

"So you're a virgin," a woman's voice said.

Chapter 3

MELISSA GLANCED AT THE LADY TO HER LEFT. "I BEG YOUR PAR-don?"

The slender brunette smiled, her green-eyed gaze taking in Melissa's black wrap-dress, her velvety high-heeled shoes trimmed with rhinestones, then returning to her face. Her red lips parted to reveal pearl-white teeth. She nodded to Melissa's name badge, with the little lipstick kiss symbol on the corner.

"That's what we call new members. Virgins."

"Oh." Melissa picked up her drink and churned the straw through the crushed ice, blending the orange and red juices. "Yeah, that's me."

"It's strange being at a place like this for the first time." She smiled, resting her elbow against the bar. "I've been a member for years. If you have any questions, just ask."

This was the perfect opportunity for Melissa to find out more about what went on here, which she needed to do to fairly evaluate the place, but she couldn't bring herself to ask. Not until she became more comfortable with the place. *If that ever happened.*

"Thanks." She took a sip of her drink.

"Sure, honey." She held out her hand. "Karen Smeed."

Melissa shook her hand. "I'm Melissa Woods."

A man stepped to the bar and Melissa cringed, fearing he was going to approach her, but he slid his arm around Karen's waist.

"Hello, sweetheart. I see you've made a new friend."

"Yes, Derrick, this is Melissa." Her voice took on a conspiratorial tone. "She's a virgin."

Melissa wished the woman would stop saying that.

"Really?" A smile spread across his rugged face and his eyes twinkled. "Isn't that delightful."

His hand slid higher and he cupped Karen's breast. Melissa's breath caught and she kept her gaze on Karen's face, trying valiantly to ignore the way Derrick's fingers circled over her breast and how the nipple rose to a clear outline through the thin fabric. Karen arched forward, forcing her breast fully into his hand.

"This man knows how to work a pair of tits."

Melissa's hand went to her necklace as she gazed around and noticed a few people glancing their way. Her face heated.

"We'd love you to join us, Melissa." She rested her hand on Melissa's arm.

Melissa stiffened at the woman's touch.

Suddenly, she could imagine her little sister Elaine sitting here, alone and uncertain, this lewd couple propositioning her while Steve was off chasing other women. Protective urges catapulted through her, followed by a determination to make Elaine see reason.

"Derrick is very good with virgins. I can just watch or . . ." Her fingers stroked along Melissa's arm. ". . . Join in. There's nothing like a good licking from another woman, don't you think?"

"I, uh . . ." Panic overwhelmed Melissa. She wanted to pull away but she couldn't.

"Ah, never tried it." She squeezed Melissa's arm in encouragement. "Well, that's what this place is about. Trying new things." She smiled wickedly. "And talking about new things, if you want to invite your husband along, you could try two men at the same time. You've never felt real pleasure until you've had one cock in your cunt and another up your—"

"Melissa, there you are."

Melissa jumped at the voice and the hand clamping simultaneously on her shoulder. She glanced around and came face-to-face with Ty Adams.

"I told my wife about your proposition and she would love for you to join us." Ty held out his hand and she grabbed it like a lifeline. As he drew her to her feet, he turned to Karen. "Sorry to interrupt, but Melissa and I have a prior engagement."

Disappointment crossed the woman's face, but she smiled sweetly. "Of course. Maybe later, Melissa."

Melissa just stared at her dumbfounded as Ty gently tugged her away from the bar. She followed him across the room, then out a door to a patio beyond. She sucked in a breath of fresh air. The rolling waves of the ocean serenaded them as they walked beneath the glittering cascade of stars in the black sky.

Finally, Melissa regained her composure and stopped in her tracks.

"Wait a minute. I'm not going to join you and your wife—"

He waved her words away. "I know that. I just thought you could use some rescuing."

Her back stiffened. "I didn't need rescuing."

She became intensely aware that her hand was still nestled in his, but pulling it away would draw too much attention to the fact.

He shrugged. "If you say so."

She glared at him, but then realized she really hadn't handled herself well.

What had come over her? Shock, most likely. She had suspected people were as brazen as Karen and her husband in a swingers' club—that's one of the reasons she didn't want her sister anywhere near a place like this—but Melissa really hadn't anticipated being approached in such a bold manner.

Damn it, the man *had* helped her out of a difficult situation. She should at least be gracious about it.

"Thank you," she said, the words strung tight.

Usually, she was the one taking care of others—her sisters anyway. It was a strange feeling to have someone else looking out for her. As she walked along beside him, she realized it wasn't altogether a bad feeling.

"Apparently, Karen can be hard to escape once she's set her sights on you," he said.

For the first time, she realized how comforting his hand felt wrapped around hers. Tendrils of warmth coiled up her arm into her body and spiraled downward. She remembered Karen's breast, pointed and aroused, Derrick's fingers curling over the tip of her nipple. Melissa's nipples peaked, longing for a man's touch. This man's touch, which made no sense at all. Wanting Shane's touch—that she understood. She'd wanted to make love with Shane for a long time. But this man was a stranger. This man was a lecherous husband who frequented swingers' clubs in search of lewd sex with other men's wives.

Actually, he was a newbie, the voice of reason reminded her. Just like her. That meant he hadn't done this before either. The difference was, Melissa wasn't really a swinger. She'd come here to find out what the club was like so she could look out for her sister.

This guy was here for the sex.

And Melissa damned well wouldn't be the one to give it to him!

People laughed nearby, then Melissa heard a splash.

"The pool must be close." Melissa glanced to the right and saw a clump of bushes. Probably on the other side.

"Do you want to check it out?"

She nodded and headed toward it, then suddenly remembered the swimsuits-optional rule. She slowed, but he kept going. She peered around the bushes and there was a beautiful free-form pool with a waterfall at one end. Colored lights reflected on the falling water and people reclined around the edge of the pool, several floating in the aqua water.

To Melissa's relief, all of them wore bathing suits. Not a naked breast, or any other private body part, in sight.

"There's a hot tub over there." Ty pointed beyond the pool to a tub that seemed carved from stone.

"It's lovely."

As they passed another set of bushes, farther from the building, she caught sight of a second hot tub. She sat down on a wooden bench by a flowering bush, enjoying the warm night air and the smell of the ocean. Ty sat down beside her.

There were two women and a man in the hot tub, and another man lounging on the side. As Melissa watched, one of the women, tall with short blond hair, stood up and Melissa realized the woman was topless.

The man slid his hands around her waist and drew her onto his lap. In shock, but unable to tear her gaze away, Melissa watched him cup her breasts. The woman moaned as her head lolled back, resting on his shoulder.

The other woman, a brunette, slid in front of the couple. The man released one breast, then slid his hand down his partner's stomach and into the water. Melissa could guess its destination. The brunette leaned forward and sucked the free breast into her mouth. The blonde moaned, then squirmed a little. The man on the side of the pool drew his cock from his bathing suit and stroked the long, hard flesh.

Melissa's gaze remained glued to the scene, despite her embarrassment, which was made worse with Ty sitting beside her. Melissa's nipples hardened and intense need ached within her. All she could think about while watching the man's hands circle over the woman's breast, her nipple thrusting outward in eager arousal, was that she wanted a man's hands on her breasts, too.

The blonde arched and moaned. Clearly, the man's hand toyed with her clit. Melissa wanted to feel a man touching her clit, nuzzling it with his tongue, sucking it into his mouth. She imagined Shane crouching in front of her, easing her legs apart, leaning toward her. At least, she tried to make it Shane, but the handsome stranger, Ty, kept replacing him.

The ache within her intensified. She'd love to rest her hand on Ty's leg and stroke upward. To wrap her fingers around his growing cock, then draw it free and pump it until he cried for mercy. She'd love to shed her dress and part her legs, inviting him to feast on her slick flesh.

The blond woman in the hot tub groaned. The man lifted her from his lap and sat her on the edge of the tub. She was totally naked, and definitely a natural blonde. He dropped his face between her thighs. The man on the side of the tub sucked on one of her breasts and the brunette sucked on the other. The blonde groaned with pleasure, then the pussy-eater stood up, his erect cock bobbing up and down. He wrapped his hand around it and placed the tip against her opening. He slid forward and she cried out.

The other man and woman released her breasts, then kissed each other. He lifted her from the tub and laid her on the stone edge, while the other man thrust into the blond woman. The second man shed his bathing suit. The brunette opened her legs, and wrapped them around him as he lowered himself onto her. His cock entered her in one swift stroke, then he thrust deep.

"God, yeah. Good and deep, honey," she urged.

He thrust in and out as she moaned her approval. The first couple, fucking fast and furious now, moaned and grunted. The blonde wailed, clearly in orgasm as he thrust faster and faster. He grunted again and collapsed against her. The other couple continued for another few minutes before they, too, reached orgasm.

Melissa felt herself dripping. She wanted a cock so badly, she was tempted to reach over and grab the closest one.

"Feel like a dip?" Ty asked.

His voice startled her and her gaze locked on his. Humor danced in those dark, midnight eyes.

Oh God, he knew she was turned on. She was sure of it.

Embarrassment flashed through her. She lurched to her feet and strode toward the building. He followed her, keeping up with her easily with his long-legged stroll.

She dashed in the nearest door, then walked down the carpeted hallway, following the sound of music and laughter. Anything to get away from the relative solitude of the patio, his knowing gaze, and the questions that might follow.

She entered a room full of people seated at tables. A man inside the door offered her a piece of paper. She grabbed it and continued into the room, then negotiated her way through the press of people. She sat down at the first empty table she found. Ty followed her, waving away the paper they offered him. He sat down beside her.

"You probably shouldn't have taken that." He nodded to the paper in her hand.

"Why not?"

"Hi. My name's Mindy. What'll you have?" An attractive waitress in a low-cut black top and short skirt stood beside the table.

"Piña Colada, please." Melissa glanced at the paper and noticed two numbers handwritten on it.

"Whatever's on tap." Ty smiled at the waitress and Melissa had to stamp down a disturbing lance of jealousy.

Which was absolutely ridiculous. If anyone should be jealous, it should be his wife. Not that anyone should feel jealous. Especially not Melissa. She sucked in a deep breath. Oh God, she was going over the edge.

Ty leaned back and crossed his long legs. Melissa noticed the movement of muscle under the dark gray fabric. Her gaze glided upward, over his thigh, resting briefly on his crotch before it careened away again, but not before her swirling hormones kicked in, sending her barely recovered heart rate into hyper-drive once again. She shifted her gaze back to the relatively innocuous piece of paper. What was it about this man that sent her so off kilter?

"This is a game room and those numbers represent activities."

"What kind of activities?" Melissa asked once the waitress left.

"I think we both know what kind."

The blood drained from her face as she stared at the offensive slip of paper in her hand. Of course she did. *Damn.*

The waitress returned with their drinks and placed a fancy glass garnished with a pineapple slice and a maraschino cherry on a tiny sword in front of Melissa and a tall, frosty mug of beer in front of Ty.

Melissa stared at the digits in red ink trying to fathom their hidden meaning.

"There are two numbers," Melissa pointed out.

"One is probably a person."

Someone she was supposed to . . . do something sexual with. Her hand started to shake. She grasped her heart pendant and stroked it.

She glanced around and realized most people were staring in the same direction. She followed their gaze and noticed a couple across the room, the woman's dress open, revealing her large breasts, and the man sucking on them.

A buzzer sounded.

"Time," a man with a microphone said.

Oh, God, she couldn't stay here.

She took a gulp of her Piña Colada and pushed her chair from the table, ready to flee yet again.

"Now," the announcer said, "we have a special treat. A virgin has joined the game."

A spotlight shone on Melissa and she froze. Oh God, this couldn't be happening to her.

"I know there are many of you ahead of her, but I don't think we should make her wait, do you?"

The crowd broke into applause, all of them staring at her. Escape was impossible now. But she couldn't stay here and perform a public sexual act.

Ty's gut clenched at the trapped look in Melissa's eyes and how her hands shook uncontrollably. For the second time since they'd met, protective instincts rose to the surface with an earth-shattering roar, which disturbed him.

The first time had been when he'd seen that Karen woman and her husband hitting on her. Melissa had tried to hide it, but Ty had seen her apprehension. Her back had stiffened, her expression had frozen into a polite smile, and she'd glanced around like a trapped animal when the guy had pawed at his wife's breasts. Ty had swooped in to save Melissa from her predicament then and he knew he'd do it again now. Would she give him grief for his efforts, like she had the last time?

Damn it. As exciting as the prospect was to see her involved in some erotic scenario, he couldn't stand to see her so vulnerable, and outright frightened. He had to do something to help her.

The announcer gestured to the band and a drum roll sounded.

Building his voice to excite the crowed, the announcer said, "Number twenty-two. This is your lucky night."

While a waiter drew an empty chair in front of Melissa, a tall, blond tennis player type stood up, a broad smile splitting his face. Sending a feral glare at the other guy, Ty lurched to his feet and claimed the chair. Blondie stopped in his tracks.

"Are you twenty-two?" the announcer asked the blond.

"No, I am," Ty declared.

The blond man held up his slip. "I have the number here."

Ty sent the man such a ferocious glower, the man froze.

"I am twenty-two." Ty's tone discouraged any contradiction. The other man reluctantly returned to his seat.

"Well, it seems we've found our virgin's lucky partner," the man with the microphone announced, a sly grin on his face.

The waiter leaned in to whisper in Melissa's ear and pointed to a list on the wall. Ty noticed the number fifteen written in large red digits under twenty-two. He glanced at the chart. Fifteen. Oral sex.

Melissa stared at the chart, then at Ty. Panic glazed her eyes.

He leaned toward her.

"Look, just pretend you're doing it and I'll go along, then we can get out of here."

"I, uh . . ."

"You can try to explain to them instead."

Melissa glanced around at all the hungry faces, waiting for her to do something. She could stammer her way out of here, or run out and look like a complete idiot. How could she stay here the rest of the weekend if she did that? She didn't want to look like a fool.

He took her hand and drew her forward, then stroked her hair.

"Use your hair to hide what you're doing. It'll look totally natural."

She nodded, then crouched down in front of him. She dragged her nail down the line of his zipper so it sounded like she'd unzipped it. She leaned forward and pretended to take his member out.

Unfortunately, a part of her wanted to do it for real. She could imagine sliding her hand into his fly and wrapping her fingers around his smooth flesh, the iron rod cushioned by the kid-leather skin solid within her grasp. She curled her hands, one over the other, holding his imaginary erection. She bobbed her head up and down, imagining the heat of it in her mouth, her lips gliding over his hot, hard flesh. She could feel his growing bulge beneath her lower hand and her vagina clenched.

Would he mind if she drew him out for real, if she sucked his long, hard cock deep into her mouth? She bobbed up and down and he groaned, acting the part of a man receiving a great blow job.

Oh, man, she wanted him in her mouth. His fingers stroked around her head, caressing the back of her neck. He groaned, then jerked a little, pretending to climax.

Ty could barely hold himself back, the thought of her lovely, rose lips pulsing over his cock so enticing he nearly lost it then and there. But he held back. He strategically thrust his left hand out, knocking over her drink. He palmed a little of the white foam as she pretended to zip him up again. The feel of her fingernail gliding up his zipper brought him close to the edge again. As she sat up, he curled his right hand around her head and brought her face to his for a kiss. Her lips tasted as sweet as he thought they would. She stared at him, seeming a little dazed. He was sure she was as affected by the pretense as he was. He stroked her cheek with his other hand, smearing a little of the foam from his palm onto her lips and chin.

It looked exactly like evidence that she'd brought him to climax.

The crowd cheered louder. The sight of the white foam on her delicate lips, like semen, made Ty even harder. He dragged her into his arms and kissed her soundly, licking the semen—uh, foam—from her mouth, then thrusting his tongue between her lips. Her tongue curled over his, then stroked his lips. He drew back and stared into her eyes, astounded by the deep longing he saw there.

Chapter 4

GOOD GOD, TY WANTED TO DRAG HER AWAY AND MAKE WILD, passionate love to her right now. He drew her from the chair and planted her in front of him, then leaned close to her ear.

"Stay in front of me," he cautioned. "They'll wonder at the sight of my huge hard-on, after what you supposedly just did for me."

She nodded and led the way from the room.

Once in the hallway, Melissa lurched forward and raced for the outside door, adrenaline still flooding through her. He slowed, pulling back on her hand, and she ricocheted into his arms and another heart-stopping kiss. His lips merged with hers—hot, full and masculine—passionately drawing her into a sweet haze of longing. She melted against him, succumbing to the erotic deluge. Her arms slipped over his broad shoulders and around his neck.

She was so turned on. More than she'd ever been. And this man—so convenient . . . so *available.*

But no, it was more than that. There was something about *this man,* something that drew her passions like the moon drew the tides. From the very first moment she'd laid eyes on him, she'd recognized it, even if she hadn't allowed herself to acknowledge it.

Until now. And now she wanted him desperately.

His hands pressed against her back, drawing her tighter against his body, her breasts crushed against his solid chest. His tongue slipped into her mouth and curled around her lips, a delicate, silky touch. She felt faint at the exquisite sensations careening through her.

His hand slid to her lower back and drew her tighter still. She could feel the bulge of his erection pushing against her. Her womb contracted in silent invitation and her folds grew slick. She wanted to arch her pelvis up, to open to him right here and now.

And that shocked her to the bone.

She stiffened in his arms. After a moment's hesitation, he released her.

"Sorry," he mumbled.

She nodded at the single word. "I guess we both got carried away."

He folded his hand around hers. "Come on. Let's go find your husband."

She nodded. Shane would help her find her grounding. As Ty led her into the ballroom, she hesitated.

"You know, I doubt we'll be able to find him. He's probably . . . you know . . . with someone."

"Don't give up so easily."

He eyed her speculatively and she wondered what he thought of her—a woman who would happily let her husband go off with another woman. Which reminded her that he'd done the same with his wife.

They crossed to the bar and Ty gestured her to a stool, then strode to the other end of the bar and asked the bartender a few questions. The bartender waved over one of the waitresses and, after a short conversation with her, the bartender consulted a video screen behind the bar.

Melissa wondered at how this man seemed so intent on taking care of her. A part of her wanted to resist, to flaunt her independence and seek Shane on her own. After all, she had been looking after herself for a long time. Yet another part of her, a part long hidden inside, reveled in the warmth she felt at having someone look out for her. Care for her.

She had done without a mother for so many years. Her mom had left when Melissa was only sixteen and she'd taken on the care of the household and the day-to-day upbringing of her younger sisters—ensuring they got their homework done, making the meals, managing chores around the house. Helping them come to terms with the loss of their mother.

Melissa had done the caretaking, never receiving it. Her father had been so busy working and trying to cope with raising three daughters as a single parent, he'd focused on the younger two, knowing Melissa could take care of herself. In fact, he'd depended on her. She'd never resented it, but sometimes, late at night when the world was quiet, she had wished she could be just a teenager again.

A moment later, Ty returned to her side.

"He's in the Mariposa room, on the second floor."

Again, she followed him out the door, then up the curved staircase from the lobby. The Mariposa room stood at the end of the grand hallway to the left. Melissa headed for the double doors, but Ty wrapped a hand around her waist and steered her to the left.

"Over here." He led her to a single door down a side corridor.

Quietly, they entered a small room with eight theater-style seats. It looked like a small, private balcony in the back of a theater, but facing a dark curtain only a yard or so away.

"He's not here," Melissa said. "Are you sure they said the Mariposa room?"

"This isn't the Mariposa room." Ty pushed a button on a control panel at the side of the room and the curtains parted. *"This* is the Mariposa room."

The parting curtains revealed a window looking onto a room. Inside the room, were several people, all naked.

"Oh, my." Melissa sank into a chair.

Ty sat beside her, gazing at her in concern.

She couldn't bring herself to look directly at the people, but beyond she could see that the walls were mirrored . . . reflecting more images of the naked people.

"There are other viewing rooms behind those mirrors."

"Other people are watching?"

"Watching. Possibly lost in their own activities. The viewing rooms are private. I've booked this one for the next two hours so no one will interrupt us."

"But—"

"I didn't think you'd want other people to come in while you were watching this."

Her eyes narrowed. "And why would I want to watch?"

"Because that's your husband."

Melissa's gaze shifted to where Ty pointed.

There was Shane, fully naked and fully aroused.

He sat on the edge of the huge bed in the middle of the room, a woman kneeling in front of him. His cock slid in and out of her mouth as she lovingly stroked his balls.

The sight of Shane naked, a sight she'd longed to see for so many years, mesmerized her. His muscular frame and bronzed skin glowed in the soft light of the room. She wished the woman would move away so she could see his cock, full and erect, for the very first time.

"Would you like me to get you a drink?" Ty asked.

She nodded, her gaze never straying from the lips gliding along Shane's cock. She relaxed a little once the door closed behind Ty, relieved to be alone with her thoughts, and her disturbing need to watch Shane in his sexual display.

Her breasts ached as her nipples pushed against her clothing, seeking escape. Behind the woman pleasuring Shane, a man stroked her buttocks and thighs, while another man, with long hair drawn back into a ponytail, sat on a chair to the right with a woman on his lap. He caressed her breasts while she toyed with his raging hard dick. The man behind Miss Lips drew her ass in the air, so she was on her hands and knees while sucking Shane. The man behind her crouched down and leaned forward to lick her slick opening.

The door opened and she felt Ty sit down beside her. He handed her a drink, which she sipped, and coughed because it was rum and Coke. She hadn't expected alcohol, but then she took another deep sip.

Warmth from the liquor washed through her, as her vagina tightened at the sight of one man licking Miss Lips and Miss Lips sucking Shane. Melissa took another sip.

The licking man shifted onto his knees. His cock, at least nine inches of hard male flesh, sprang forward. He grasped his cock in his hand and aimed it for Miss Lips's exposed slit, like an arrow going for a bull's-eye. She glanced over her shoulder and smiled, Shane's cock left exposed and naked in her hand.

What a glorious cock it was! Melissa savored her very first sight of Shane's wonderful male member. As big around as the woman's wrist . . . and long! Bigger than either of the other two men's, and it curved slightly.

Suddenly, it disappeared again as Miss Lips swallowed him deep into her mouth. The man behind her thrust forward. Melissa's vagina clenched. The couple in the chair stroked each other as they watched with focused attention. Her hand stroked up and down his shaft while his fingers disappeared between the moist lips between her legs.

Melissa's hormones swelled within her, threatening to burst into a blaze of reckless behavior. Melissa watched in sheer fascination as one man thrust in and out of Miss Lips and Shane's cock slid in and out of Miss Lips' mouth. Melissa imagined her own mouth gliding along his long, hard cock.

She became extremely conscious of Ty's long, lean leg brushing hers. Suddenly, it was Ty's cock she imagined in her mouth. A naughty image of both Shane and Ty sitting in front of her, cocks at attention, shimmered through her brain, her mouth watering to pleasure both of them, then ride them for all she was worth. Her cheeks burned.

The woman began to gasp and the man behind her thrust faster.

"Come on, honey," he urged.

She released Shane's cock from her mouth, pumping it with her hands.

"Oh, yeah, baby," she pleaded. "Make me come."

The man's hand slipped around her and dipped into her pussy. She wailed, then sucked Shane deeper. Shane's face contorted and he jerked a little, clearly coming in her mouth. Miss Lips released him as she wailed, louder and louder as she came to orgasm. The man withdrew from her and turned her to face him. They embraced and kissed lovingly.

The other couple stood up and the second woman slid into Shane's arms.

"Now it's my turn, lover." She kissed him, then laid on the bed, her legs wide open.

Shane, still stiff and ready for action, prowled over her. He leaned forward and kissed her enormous breasts, giving each one loving attention. Melissa desperately wanted to slide her hand inside her top and tweak her hard, aching nipples. Instead, her fingers reached for the heart necklace at her neck and she twirled it back and forth.

"Oh, darlin', that's lovely," the woman staring up at Shane said, "but what I really want right now is that cock of yours deep inside me."

Shane smiled. "Whatever you say, sweetheart."

He positioned the tip of his cock at her opening, then pushed forward.

"Oh God, yes. Give me that huge thing."

Shane thrust into her, again and again. She arched against him, her legs wrapped tightly around him. The man Shane's current lover had been with laid down beside them and Miss Lips climbed on top of him, sinking his cock inside in one swift motion, then she laid down on top of him, her buttocks high in the air. To Melissa's surprise, the third man, stroking his cock, kneeled behind her. He placed his erection against her ass and, slowly, pushed inside her.

Melissa's heart lurched in excitement. The woman had two cocks inside her!

Melissa's wide-eyed gaze slid to Ty, who watched the scene beside her, then flicked away again. She couldn't help picturing herself lying on that bed with Shane inside her from behind and Ty approaching her, ready to slide his cock inside her.

She took another sip of rum and Coke, trying to push away the wanton . . . uh, unwanted . . . images.

The woman with the two cocks began to move. Melissa tried to imagine how the two cocks moved inside her, stroking her insides, filling her so full of masculine sexual power. Oh, God, what would that feel like?

Ty leaned in close. "Are you jealous?"

Without thinking, Melissa nodded.

"A little," she said absently, wishing it was her between the two men, but one Shane and one Ty. She gulped some more of her drink, then realized she'd finished it.

Shane and his lover rolled over and the woman bounced up and down on him, her breasts bobbing in a mesmerizing fashion.

Melissa's breathing accelerated. She had to stop her hand from grasping Ty's knee and sliding up that muscular thigh of his. She desperately wanted to grab his cock and stroke it until it was so hard he couldn't stand it, then mount him and ride him until they both screamed in ecstasy.

She clenched her hands around the arms of the chair. Oh God, if this went on much longer, she couldn't be responsible for her actions.

Shane groaned his release and slumped back. The woman on top of him kissed him, then pushed herself away, Shane's spent cock sliding free. She shifted beside the other three, who moved in unison, undulating to their passionate groans and sighs. She stroked the naked buttocks of the man on top, then slid downward, until she stroked his balls. He thrust harder and Miss Lips moaned. Suddenly, all three of them gasped in orgasm, their faces contorting in wild, unimaginable pleasure. After a few moments, they slumped to the bed, then disentangled themselves. Miss Lips kissed the man who'd been fucking her pussy and the other woman kissed the ass man.

The lights in the viewing room turned on and Melissa realized Ty had moved to the door and flicked the switch. Shane glanced up and stared right at Melissa.

"With the lights on in here, he can see through the mirror," Ty explained.

Shane smiled and waved, then gathered up his clothing and pulled it on.

A moment later, he entered the room.

"Hey, Liss. Did you enjoy the show?" He glanced speculatively at Ty.

"It was . . . interesting."

"If you'll excuse me," Ty said, "I'll leave you two alone." He disappeared out the door.

Shane watched him go, then gazed questioningly at Melissa's face.

"So, did you and he . . . ?"

"No, of course not," Melissa replied a little too sharply.

"Liss, is there some problem?"

At the perplexed look on his face, she sighed and shook her head.

"No, I'm sorry. I just . . . you know I won't just do . . . stuff with a stranger."

He slumped into the chair beside her. "You know, you could let yourself loose and try something new. It wouldn't hurt to be a little wild every now and again."

She glanced at his familiar, loving face and thought the only wild she'd like to get right now was with him. Guilt slid through her at the wayward thoughts she'd had only moments ago that included Ty. But that had happened in the heat of the moment. It was some kind of transference, or something like that.

Shane stood up and held out his hand.

"You look exhausted? Do you want to go back to the room?"

She nodded. That was the only place in this whole resort she would feel settled. And where she knew she wouldn't run into Ty Adams again and have to deal with the disturbing feelings he triggered in her. She picked up her glass and remembered it was empty.

"Maybe just one more drink."

He sniffed the glass.

"Rum and Coke? That's not like you." He smiled. "I approve."

Shane slid his arm around her waist and they headed for the bar.

Ty rode the elevator alone. His hand stroked over his cock, thinking of the sexy scene he'd just witnessed in the Mariposa room. Remembering Melissa sitting beside him, clearly turned on, watching. A clear outline of her nipples had been visible through her dress and he'd longed to stroke them, to suck them.

His reaction to that woman confused him. She wasn't the type he was usually drawn to. She was sexually inhibited, uptight, and . . . married.

A knot twisted his stomach at the fact she'd been jealous of her husband with the other women. She'd clung to that diamond heart around her neck—probably a gift from him—like a lifeline. Maybe Ty had been wrong about her and her husband not being in love. At least, about *her* not loving him. Ty could read people and the guy, although clearly holding a deep affection for Melissa, didn't love her.

Hell, here he was at a swingers' resort, where every woman was fair game, married or not, and his dick had settled on the only one he couldn't have. The woman's rigid thinking wouldn't allow her to relax and enjoy the resort, therefore she wouldn't be open to a fling with him.

In fact, the woman wasn't here to enjoy the resort at all. If his instincts were correct, she was here to do a report on it to Suzanne's potential buyer. What bugged him most was that clearly she hadn't even arrived with an open mind. His gut told him she didn't intend to give a balanced report—she intended to condemn the place, which would make Suzanne's sale fall through.

But, damn it, that didn't stop him from wanting her.

He rubbed his cock, feeling it straining against the confines of his jeans. He arrived at his floor and the elevator door opened. He could prowl the resort looking for an available female, but most were already occupied—and he didn't really like having sex with strangers.

He strode down the hall and slid his key card into the slot. As he opened the door, he heard soft moaning. He turned to leave, realizing Suzanne was probably *entertaining*.

"Ty, wait."

At Suzanne's voice he stopped, doorknob in hand.

"Don't go."

He turned around to see her strolling toward him, totally naked. His cock jumped at the sight. She took his hand and led him forward.

She leaned toward him and murmured, "I know you've been busy with work this evening, so I thought you should be rewarded with some R and R."

She led him farther into the room and he realized another woman sat on the upholstered armchair. Naked. Her long, dark hair cascaded around her pert breasts, accentuating the hard nipples pointing toward him, and the large, dusky rose aureoles. He smiled as his cock pushed painfully against his fly. A movie played on the television, showing an erotic scene between two women.

Two women. His cock throbbed at the thought of Suzanne and this stranger stroking his body, sucking his cock, letting him bury himself inside each of them. Hearing them cry out in ecstasy.

"This is Greta," Suzanne said, smiling.

Greta stood up and walked toward him.

"You're right, Suzanne. Your husband is gorgeous," she said with a trace of a German accent, which Ty found incredibly sexy.

Maybe the idea of sex with a stranger wasn't such a bad idea. Of course, now that he knew her name, she wasn't technically a stranger.

She stroked his cheek, then took his hand and settled it over her lovely breast. His breathing accelerated as the soft, round flesh conformed to his hand, the nipple pressing into his palm. He squeezed gently, then stroked.

She stepped away from him, then took Suzanne's hand and led her to the bed. The two sexy, naked women sat down on the side of the bed and Ty settled in the chair, still warm from Greta's sexy body. Suzanne stroked Greta's breasts as Greta nuzzled Suzanne's neck, kissing downward until she reached a large, taut nipple and licked it. Suzanne moaned. Ty stroked the bulge in his pants. Greta sucked Suzanne's nipple into her mouth and her hand slid down Suzanne's stomach then disappeared into her golden curls. Greta eased Suzanne onto her back, then parted her legs. Her head dove down between Suzanne's thighs and she began feasting.

"Oh, yeah," Suzanne encouraged.

Ty tugged down his zipper and freed his cock, then grasped it in his hand and stroked, a sense of urgency building within him. His cock wanted hot pussy right now, but his mind wanted to watch and enjoy these two women pleasuring each other.

Greta licked and sucked on Suzanne's clit and Suzanne arched, moaning and pinching her own nipples. She gasped, then wailed as an orgasm overtook her. Ty squeezed the base of his cock, stopping the sudden urge to ejaculate.

Greta turned to him. "Bring that huge cock over here, Ty."

Ty moved to the bed and lay down beside Suzanne. Greta grasped Ty's cock and stroked.

"Oh, yeah. That's what I need." He throbbed in her hand. Thoughts of Melissa wound through his hormone-ridden brain. *Damn.* As sexy as Greta was, what he *really* needed was Melissa's hand wrapped around him. At the thought of her slender fingers encircling him, his cock grew even harder.

"Poor man is close to bursting," Greta said.

Suzanne shifted onto her knees and the two women urged him to the center of the bed, then began kissing his nipples and stroking his body. Electric pleasure jolted through every nerve ending. He imagined Greta's hot, damp tongue was Melissa's as it stroked the length of his cock, followed by Suzanne's moist lips stroking the other side of his rod. He moaned at the incredible sensation.

The two of them wrapped their mouths around the sides of his shaft and stroked up and down in unison, then Greta slid up and over his cock, gliding down and taking him deep into her throat as Suzanne licked his balls. She nibbled lightly, then drew them into her mouth.

He jerked and, unable to hold back, flooded Melissa's—no, Greta's—throat with his semen as he burst into an intense orgasm.

His two lovers laughed, then Greta climbed over him, settling her hot pussy on top of his spent penis. She shifted forward and back while Suzanne slid up behind her and stroked Greta's breasts. In no time, his cock swelled. Greta continued to stroke it with her gliding, wet pussy and Suzanne kissed Greta's neck. Both women watched him, smiling, their eyes sultry and full of mischievous, sexy allure.

Greta leaned forward until the tip of one breast stroked his cheek. He captured her hard nipple in his mouth and ran his tongue over the pebbled surface, then sucked her deep inside. Oh, man, how he'd love to suck Melissa's breast into his mouth, to feel her hot, wet pussy caressing his cock.

Greta gasped, her pelvis gliding faster over his hard cock. She lifted her body and he slanted his cock upward to nuzzle her hot slit. She pushed down on him, capturing his cock inside the hot sheath of her vagina.

As she rode up and down on his cock, Suzanne kissed him on the lips, then settled her pussy over his face. He pushed his tongue into her slit and rolled it around, stroking inside her.

"Oh, you know how I love that." She sighed as she shifted slightly, giving him access to her clit.

He sucked it into his mouth as Greta pounded up and down on him. Suzanne moaned and Greta began to wail. Ty's groin tightened and he wrapped his hands around Greta's hips, helping her bounce up and down as he sucked and cajoled Suzanne's clit. Suzanne screamed as her orgasm flooded through her, her pussy vibrating on his mouth. At Greta's moans and the way her pussy contracted around him, he could tell she had started to climax. Suzanne, finally sated, sighed and slid away. As he watched Greta's face contort in exquisite pleasure, his cock erupted inside her, sending semen flooding into her. He pivoted his pelvis and her moans blossomed into loud wails of intense pleasure as she hit the second wave of orgasm.

Suzanne stroked Greta's stomach, then slid her finger over Greta's clit. Greta's eyes widened.

"Oh God. Yes. YES. YES!!!!!"

She pounded up and down on Ty, her voice growing hoarse with her moans, until finally she flung her head back and wailed at the top of her lungs. Oh, God, he'd love to hear Melissa cry out like that. To know he'd made her come.

Greta's movements slowed and she settled down on Ty's chest and nuzzled her head under his chin. He cuddled her close, his cock still buried deep inside her. Finally, she gave him a kiss, then slid off.

"That was great." She smiled and grabbed a pile of clothes from the floor and started pulling them on. "If you two want company again, just let me know. Maybe next time my husband, Bob, can join us."

Ty watched in appreciation as she headed for the door. Even though his cock was totally drained, and this woman before him was well-proportioned and incredibly sexy, all he could think of as he watched her sensational ass sway back and forth was how he wished it was Melissa's ass and, if it was, how much he'd love to sink his now growing cock into it.

$\sim$

Melissa sat at a table as Shane ordered her another rum and Coke.

"Hello, again."

Melissa blanched as she turned to see Karen Smeed standing beside her. Not because she might have a problem escaping the woman but, after watching Miss Lips take on two men, Melissa was worried she might be *tempted* by Karen's proposition.

"Oh hi, Karen," she said. Karen's husband was nowhere to be seen, but Melissa didn't doubt he'd show up.

Karen, drink in hand, sat down beside her. "So where's your handsome— Oh . . ."

Shane placed Melissa's drink in front of her and smiled at Karen.

"Hello." He sat down beside Melissa.

"Hello, there." Karen turned a half grin on Melissa. "Why, you've been a busy girl this evening."

Melissa took Shane's hand and stood up, tugging him with her. "Yes, and if you'll excuse us, I intend to get busy again."

She grabbed her drink and dragged Shane from the room. He chuckled as they strode along the corridor toward the elevator, the ice cubes in their drinks tinkling against the glass.

"Do you realize what she'll assume you mean? About getting busy?"

The elevator doors opened and she pulled him inside. As the doors closed behind them, she slid her free arm around his waist and pulled him close.

"I know exactly what she's thinking." She pushed herself to her tip toes and pressed her lips to his chin and nuzzled, then slid to his mouth. At first, he remained motionless, then his free arm slid around her and he pulled her closer. The sweet sensation of his mouth moving on hers burned through her. Her drink spilled and she lurched back. Dark liquid trailed down the leg of his beige dress pants.

"Oh, Shane, I'm so sorry."

He tugged her close, capturing her lips again.

"I don't care about that," he murmured, releasing her lips briefly. "This is the only thing I care about."

He intoxicated her with another kiss. He curled his hand around her head, cradling it gently while his lips seduced her mouth. She breathed in his crisp, tangy after shave—so familiar and masculine. The essence of Shane.

This is the only thing I care about. His words delighted her, but she couldn't help wondering if he meant kissing or, more realistically, sex . . . or if he meant kissing *her* . . . and having sex with *her.*

The elevator doors opened at their floor and he linked his hand with hers and drew her down the hall to their room. Once the door closed behind them, he took the drink from her hand and plunked it on the dresser beside his own, then swept her into his arms for a hair-raising, blazing five-alarm kiss.

Every thought dropped from her mind like lead weights, leaving her free to float in the delightful, cloudlike euphoria of his touch. His lips caressing hers, his tongue slipping sweetly into her mouth, his arms crushing her against his hard, muscular body.

A heaven she had long dreamed about but never quite imagined being this sweet.

His lips drew away and she whimpered.

"Liss, are you really sure?"

Chapter 5

"HMM?" MELISSA'S EYES OPENED.

Shane's deep, blue eyes, full of concern, gazed into hers.

"Are you sure? I don't want to ruin what we have."

A mix of deep emotions washed through her. She stroked his cheek, delighting in the feel of his slightly whisker-roughened skin.

"You won't." She stroked his sandy, blond hair, then kissed him, hungry for his lips.

He cupped her face with both hands. "Promise I won't lose you as a friend."

Shane had had family problems growing up. Both his parents had divorced several times, and she knew her friendship gave him a sense of stability.

She nodded. "I promise. I'll always be your friend." And so much more, she hoped.

Their lips met again and this time, with a blazing passion. Melissa felt the sparks sizzle through her, setting her body on fire.

Her nipples became impossibly hard, thrusting into his chest, demanding attention. She tugged the tie holding her dress fastened, releasing the bow. She drew back and pulled the dress open, then dropped the garment from her shoulders. As it pooled at her feet, his face filled with awe.

Shane stared at Melissa, clad in only a sheer black lace bra, skimpy panties, a garter belt, and black stockings. The sweet, delicate scent of her perfume filled his senses. He longed to hold her close. To breathe her in and take comfort in the curves of her body. Even though he'd just been with two women, the powerful yearning for Melissa still coiled from deep within

"You are incredible." For so long he had wanted this woman—his friend, his confidante, and now, soon to be his lover.

Her hard nipples pushed at the delicate fabric of her bra. He stroked under her left breast, then dragged his finger over her nipple. She sighed, a soft wispy sound that set his blood on fire. He dipped down and licked over the lace, feeling her hard nub through the fabric. Impatient, she tugged the fabric down, baring her dusky pink nipple to his sight.

His cock throbbed at the sight of it. Everything about her was so beautiful. He licked her nipple, feeling her aureole pebble under his tongue. She tasted like warm honey—hot and sweet. His fingers dipped under the lace to find her other nipple as he sucked this one into his mouth. She moaned softly. Her fingers flicked the tab at the front of her bra and it popped open. He peeled it away, staring at her two perfect globes of soft, womanly flesh.

"Melissa, you are so beautiful. My God, why did we wait so long?"

"Because fate worked against us." She stroked his temples and kissed him. "But we don't have to wait any longer."

Her tongue slipped into his mouth. She tasted minty, with a hint of rum.

She planted her hands on his chest and backed him up until he felt the bed behind his calves, then he sat down. He caressed her generous breasts reverently, then sucked one into his mouth again, swirling his tongue around and around her sensitive nipple, reveling in her desperate little gasps.

Soon those gasps would turn to moans as he brought her to orgasm. Tonight he would touch her, taste her . . . explore her body in intimate detail.

If he could last that long.

He released her nub and smiled. She hooked her fingers into the waistband of her tiny panties and pushed them downward, then stood up again, placing her pert naked little pussy right in front of him, framed by her black garter belt and stockings.

"Oh, sweetheart, I want you so badly," he said.

She stroked her hand over the growing bulge in his pants.

"Mmm. I can feel that." She knelt in front of him. "Now let me see it."

She dragged down his zipper, then her hand slid inside his pants. At the feel of her delicate fingers encircling him, he sucked in a breath. It felt *so* good. She drew him out, exposing his solid length.

Soon he would feel what it was like to make love to Melissa. He would sink into her hot body like he'd dreamed of doing so many times.

Melissa stared at Shane's long, hard cock, mesmerized by the sight. She stroked his substantial length, delighted by the feel of the rock-hard flesh gliding between her hands. She leaned over and licked the tip, tasting the salty pre-cum oozing from the tiny hole. This proof that he wanted her excited her no end. She wrapped her lips around him and slid her mouth over the head of his cock, then swirled her tongue around the ridge under the crown.

"Oh, Liss, that feels wonderful."

Yes, wonderful. She'd wanted to share this intimacy with him for a long time.

Encouraged, she took him deeper, opening her throat and sucking him all the way in. She curled her hand around his balls, stroking them gently.

"You're moving so fast, sweetheart."

"I got so turned on watching you with those women." Her vagina clenched at the memory. Oh God, she wanted his cock inside her, stroking the length of her vagina.

He tugged open his shirt and she stroked her fingers over his hard little nipples, then shifted to suck one into her mouth, loving the pearl hardness against her tongue, while her hand stroked his cock, keeping it warm. His chest, so firm and muscular under her hands, rose and fell at an increasing rate.

"Okay, you've seen me, now I want to have a good look at you."

He tugged the bedspread back, revealing the white sheets, then grabbed her waist and drew her onto the bed. She stretched out on the satiny linen, her insides melting at the look of awe in his simmering blue eyes as he knelt beside her. He removed one of her stockings, then the other. The delicate feel of his fingers gliding along her legs as he rolled each stocking downward sent wild tingles rushing through her. He unhooked her garter belt and tossed it aside, then positioned himself over her. His large, warm hands encompassed her breasts.

"These are incredible."

He leaned forward and kissed one nipple, then sucked it deep into his warm, moist mouth. She gasped at the electric sensation. He released her nipple and it ached in the cool air. His warm hand covered it as he switched to her other nipple and kissed and licked it with the same sweet deliberation. He smiled at her, then kissed down her chest and over her stomach, sending tingles erupting along her nerve endings. She sucked air rapidly into her lungs.

He nuzzled her navel, then kissed across her hip. She parted her legs in invitation, desperate for him to invade her slick flesh, but he kissed around, then down her thighs. She arched upward, trying to coax him there, but he ignored her and kissed her inner thighs, stroking the soft, sensitive flesh with his fingertips. Kissing and licking, until her breathing became frantic little gasps. He stroked up her thighs, then she moaned as she felt his finger glide along her incredibly wet, slippery slit. He followed with his tongue, then eased her folds apart and pressed his mouth against her. She gasped as he pushed his tongue against her clit, then spiraled it in circles. His fingers slipped inside her, moving in the same rhythm as his talented tongue.

Desire pelted through her, swirling higher and higher. He drew his tongue away and smiled.

"You are definitely ready for me."

"I've been ready for you for years."

He grinned. "Well, it wouldn't be fair to make you wait any longer."

As he placed the tip of his erection at her opening, she realized this was finally happening. She was making love with Shane. Elation whispered through her as he slowly eased inside. At the feel of his rock-hard cock gliding into her depths, her heartbeat accelerated and she almost came on the spot.

Her legs wrapped around him. He pulled back, then glided forward again.

"Oh, Liss. You feel incredible."

He pulled back and thrust again and she moaned. A blissful euphoria swept through her as his cock drove in and out, plunging her to
heaven.

She wailed.

"Oh God, Liss. I love being inside you. You're so silky. So sweet."

He drove in hard and deep. She clung to him, riding the rising
waves of pleasure.

"Oh, Shane. I'm going to come."

"Yes, Liss. Come for me, honey."

He drove harder and harder, pushing her closer to the brink . . .
closer . . . then she careened off. In wild free fall. Into an ecstatic state
of bliss.

As she wailed her release, he groaned and his semen spurted into
her. Warm and wet, filling her with his heat.

He leaned forward and kissed her. She smiled, holding his muscular, broad-shouldered body close to hers.

"That was wonderful."

"Honey, it's not over yet."

His finger slid between them and found her clit. He glided in and
out of her again, this time adding a little spiral. Fireworks sparked
from her clit, flaring through her whole body, triggering a new orgasm. She gasped and moaned as he drove deeper and faster and the
orgasm built, exploding through every part of her until finally her insides erupted into a cataclysm of bliss.

She flopped back on the bed. The combination of Shane's warm
generous nature as a lover and their close friendship had made this the
deepest, most profound lovemaking experience of her life.

"That was amazing," she murmured, pushing the hair back from
her eyes.

"You were amazing." He kissed her then pulled her against his body and cuddled her close.

She sighed, then fell asleep in the warmth of his arms.

~

Melissa clung to him. Oh God, she needed this man. Why had it taken her so long to find him? How had she lived without him, and the pleasure only he could provide, for so long?

Her entire body seemed to contract. She gasped, then moaned with his thrusts. An overwhelming, tortuously sublime, reeling pleasure blazed through her, searing every nerve of her body.

He thrust deeper and harder. Faster and with more enthusiasm. Her pleasure increased until her consciousness expanded beyond time and space. She became pleasure in its most basic form. Pure bliss.

"Oh, Ty."

~

Melissa catapulted awake.

Oh my God. Guilt flushed through her as she realized here she was, in Shane's arms, *dreaming about another man*!

She glanced around at Shane's handsome, beloved face on the pillow beside her. Last night, they'd made love for the first time ever. An event she had dreamed about for years. And as soon as it had happened, she'd dreamed about Ty Adams. A man she'd just met. A man who would have casual sex with other women even though he was married. A man she could never, ever love.

Yet, in the dream, she'd felt so totally smitten with him.

Stupid dream!

She snuggled closer to Shane, taking comfort in the warmth of his arms around her, and the solid mass of his chest against her cheek.

Gazing at his classically handsome, familiar face . . . a face she'd known and loved for years . . . she wondered how she could have dreamed of Ty Adams. Shane was the one she wanted to be with.

He wrapped his arms around her, drawing her tight against his hard, broad chest. As she snuggled against him, his chest hairs tickling her nose, she realized that in Shane's arms she felt safe and cherished.

This is where she wanted to be. Not with Ty Adams. That dream was just an aberration, triggered by the wild goings-on in this crazy place. It didn't mean anything.

So why then did she feel so guilty?

"Mmm. Hi, there, sweetheart. Sleep well?" His murmured words caressed her cheek.

"Uh . . . yeah. Great."

His sea-blue eyes opened a little wider and he focused on her.

"Melissa, what's going on?" He propped himself up on his elbow. "Are you having regrets?" His expression grew taut. "Damn, I was afraid—"

She darted forward and covered his mouth with hers, stopping his stream of words. Then she toppled him backward and climbed over him, keeping him in a passionate lip-lock. She thrust her tongue between his lips, swirled it around, then released his mouth.

"Does that feel like a woman having regrets?"

"No." He smiled but his blue eyes grew pensive as he stroked her hair. "So what does this mean exactly? With respect to our relationship."

She perched her head on her elbow.

"Well, we're still friends," she assured him, purposely hedging around his question.

"And lovers?"

She smiled and stroked down his chest, the coarse hairs tickling her palm, then over the firm ridges of his stomach. "Are you trying to hint you'd like another tumble?"

His hand clamped over hers, stopping its downward progress.

"Liss, I want to know. Was this just because we're here . . . at this resort?" His strong, warm hand wrapped around hers. "There are a lot of . . . stimulating activities going on around here . . ."

She drew away, holding the sheet to her naked chest. Tumultuous emotions somersaulted through her. Emotions she did not want to examine too closely.

"Are you asking if I just slept with you because you're convenient?"

"I know you wouldn't want to have sex with a stranger."

Her stomach tightened. "So you think I just used you?" Anger blazed through her. "Because I was horny?"

"Liss, it's okay. I understand, and I don't mind being there for you. I've had friends with benefits before—we just need to be careful not to let our emotions get involved."

Her fist clenched around the white cotton sheet.

"Don't worry, you can keep swinging with the wildlife around here." She bolted from the bed, tugging the sheet with her, ignoring Shane's fully exposed, naked body. "I don't have any claims on you."

She stormed toward the bathroom. As soon as she'd closed the door behind her, she leaned against it and sucked in a deep breath, her heartbeat hammering in her chest. Why was she so angry?

Maybe because what he says is partly true.

Last night, she had been confused, her hormones reacting to seeing Shane in that mini-orgy. Confused about the excitement she'd felt seeing the woman making love with two men at the same time. Disturbed by how close she'd come to grabbing onto Ty Adams and making a total fool of herself.

I know you wouldn't want to have sex with a stranger. I've had friends with benefits before. That's what Shane had said.

Although she'd love to convince herself last night had been about pursuing a loving, intimate relationship with Shane, which she'd longed to do for quite a while, it wasn't true. Last night had been about fleeing an onslaught of disturbing sexual desires—including Ty Adams.

Melissa hugged the fluffy beach towel to her chest as she walked across the hot, stone patio toward the pool. The sun, still low on the horizon, set the sky alight in soft pinks and mauves. The sound of the surf rolling along the beach and the salty breeze caressing her face did nothing to distract her from the blazing guilt escalating within her.

How could she have used Shane like that? Then, after having the greatest night of her life in Shane's arms, how could she have dreamt of loving Ty Adams? No, *making* love with Ty. Actual love had nothing to do with it.

No one was at the pool at this early hour. Melissa dropped her towel on a lounge chair and walked down the steps into the water. It felt a little cool on her calves. She waded deeper. As the cool water caressed her breasts, a little shiver rushed down her spine and her nipples blossomed beneath her turquoise bikini. She swam to the deep end and treaded water. Her eyelids drifted closed as she allowed the sounds of the birds twittering in the trees, mingling with the soft breeze and the ocean rushing over the sand then rolling away again, to wash her mind free of troubling thoughts.

"Good morning."

Melissa opened her eyes. A statuesque blonde stood by the side of the pool, her trim, yet well-endowed figure showcased in a floral wrap top, plunging low in front.

The aerobic-instructor-perfect blonde who had been on Ty Adams's arm. This was Ty's wife.

She dropped her towel on the chair beside Melissa's, then unfastened the tie at her waist and slipped off the top. She wore only a bikini bottom beneath. As she walked down the steps of the pool, her bare breasts—perfect full, round globes—bounced slightly. The nipples puckered as she stepped deeper and deeper into the water. Finally, she swam toward Melissa, then tread water beside her.

"It's a lovely time for a swim."

Melissa had to force her gaze to the woman's face rather than watch the bobbing breasts visible under the water.

"Um . . . yes. Quiet."

"My name's Suzanne. I was in the orientation meeting with you. I'm a virgin, too."

Not bloody likely. It was difficult to believe this woman had ever been a virgin. She exuded too much raw sensuality.

"Yes, I remember," Melissa said.

"So, are you enjoying the resort so far?"

"It's definitely been . . . interesting."

Suzanne's brow furrowed as she watched uncertainty cross the other woman's face. This did not sound good. Ty had told her he was sure this was the woman who would report to the buyer interested in the resort, and if she didn't enjoy herself here, she would probably give a negative report. Suzanne really needed this sale. She had to find a way to make this woman come to a positive opinion.

"It is pretty overwhelming," Suzanne said, hoping to prompt more conversation.

"Yeah, no kidding."

Melissa swam to the edge of the pool. Suzanne followed her, then rested her hand on the tiled deck so she didn't have to keep treading water.

"Did you go to the welcome party last night?" Suzanne asked.

"Briefly."

"Didn't you enjoy it?"

"It's not that. I guess it's just not my kind of scene."

As Suzanne watched Melissa, she realized there might be a different explanation for the woman's unease.

"Honey, you look troubled. Are you here because your husband pushed you into it?"

She'd seen it many times. Wives who came along because their husbands pressured them, telling them it was the key to spicing up their marriage, when in reality, they just wanted permission to chase tail. It always angered her that these susceptible, unconfident women had to put up with such psychological abuse from boorish, uncaring, self-centered husbands.

This woman *might* be here as a spy for the buyer, but Suzanne didn't know that for sure. She might be one of those sad, uncertain wives. Either way, she seemed to be hurting right now. Suzanne could sense it.

"No, we both wanted to come."

Suzanne didn't believe her. It was clear that she was totally out of her element here.

"I heard that your husband took part in one of the viewing rooms last night. You knew about that, right?"

Melissa's stomach churned. Did Suzanne know Ty had been with Melissa at the time? If so, was she jealous?

Suzanne rested her arm on Melissa's shoulder.

"Honey, do you feel betrayed by your husband?"

Betrayed? She thought about the fact she'd made love with Shane last night—for the wrong reasons—then been in Ty's arms in her dreams.

"No, I feel I've betrayed him." Damn, why had she said that?

"Oh, honey. You shouldn't feel that way. Whatever you did, and with whom, it's all right. Everyone who came here did it with the intent of having sex with someone else."

Suzanne slipped her arms around Melissa and pulled her into a hug.

"It's okay."

The woman patted Melissa's back, but rather than being soothed, all she could think about were Suzanne's large, firm breasts pushing against her bare skin, one tight nipple pushing against her arm.

"I didn't actually do anything with anyone."

"Come on, honey. I heard that you did oral sex on my Ty in the numbers room."

Chapter 6

MELISSA STIFFENED AND PULLED AWAY. SURPRISED, SHE FOUND Suzanne still smiling warmly.

"Don't look so worried. It's fine with me." Suzanne laughed. "I hope you enjoyed him."

Melissa shook her head. "Did he tell you . . . ?" She paused, not quite sure what to ask. *Did your husband tell you a strange woman pretended to suck his cock while a roomful of people watched?*

"No, he didn't tell me. One of the other newbies did. But relax. It's not a problem. Really."

Melissa would have been more comfortable if Ty had told Suzanne it had been a pretense, but from his point of view, why should he? Suzanne clearly had no problem with it.

This was all so strange. Melissa simply couldn't understand these people.

"Look, honey. I've met some people here. Members who've been coming for a long time. Why don't you come have breakfast with us and you can talk to them? Find out about their experiences and how they handle the swinging lifestyle."

Melissa nodded. This was exactly what she needed for her research.

∾

Suzanne stepped from the pool and dried off. Melissa had gone ahead to her room to change.

"There's one gorgeous sight."

Suzanne smiled at Ty, stepping from between the trees. He was the gorgeous one, in his moss-green bathing suit, his broad chest and arms bulging with muscles, his abs tight and well-defined.

His gaze caressed her naked breasts like the soft breeze of the ocean. She stroked her hands up her ribcage and beneath her breasts, lifting them slightly.

"Are you talking about these?"

He stepped behind her and wrapped his arms around her.

"Definitely." He cupped her breasts in his big, masculine hands, and gently caressed them. Her ripe nipples rubbed against his palms, pushing out, hardening.

She leaned back against him, feeling his muscular chest against her bare back. "If you start something, you'd better follow through."

He nuzzled her neck, sending tingles careening through her.

"Whatever you say."

Still holding one happy breast in his hand, he slid his other hand down her stomach then dipped inside her thong. He stroked her silky curls, then one finger slid over her mound and into her wet slit.

"Oh, honey. You know what I like." She parted her legs to give him better access.

He slid one finger inside, then two, stroking and pulsing inside her.

They heard voices—two men talking—and Ty started to slip his hand away, but Suzanne flattened her hand on top of his, preventing its escape.

"Don't stop."

A moment later, two men appeared at the top of the steps to the patio. They stopped, taking in the scene with Ty and Suzanne. Suzanne smiled at them, then leaned her head back on Ty's shoulder. The men continued down the steps, both pairs of eyes on Suzanne. Ty pushed his finger deeper inside her, then started to thrust. The men sat where they had a full-frontal view of Suzanne. One began stroking his crotch. She felt her whole body flush in excitement. These men watching her, getting turned on, Ty stroking her, wanting her.

Ty's thumb brushed across her clit and she moaned. She was so close, ultra-turned on with the combination of physical stimulation and being the intense focus of several horny males.

An orgasm crashed through her like wild surf hitting rocks, intense, raging pleasure pounding through her. She slumped against Ty, then turned in his arms and kissed him. She led him to the pool's edge and urged him to sit down, legs draped over the edge. She slipped into the water and slid her fingers into his bathing suit, then wrapped them around his lovely big cock. She pulled it out and smiled at it, then licked the crown. His cock pulsed in her hand. As she wrapped her lips around him, then glided downward, the other two men moved closer, sitting on either side of Ty, several feet away.

Suzanne loved Ty's big cock. It was friendly and familiar. She dabbed the little hole with the tip of her tongue, teasing, tasting the salty pre-cum.

The other men had pulled out their cocks and begun to pump them.

Suzanne slid her mouth off Ty's rod and she tipped her head toward one of the guys and raised her eyebrows. Ty smiled indulgently and nodded.

"Why don't you two fellows move in closer," she suggested, smiling seductively.

Their faces beamed as they moved closer to Ty. Suzanne sucked Ty deep, then bobbed up and down a few times. Keeping her left hand wrapped around him, she shifted to the right and wrapped her free hand around the tawny-haired man. His cock was average length, but broad. She stroked him.

He grinned at her touch. When she leaned forward and swallowed him into her mouth, he groaned. She bobbed up and down. He hardened within her mouth.

She released him and moved to the other man. She stroked Ty with her right hand while she pumped the dark-haired man with her left. She licked his cock head then swallowed him deep.

Moving from one lovely cock to the next, she bobbed up and down on each of them, Ty getting double attention being in the middle. As she sucked on the dark-haired man's cock, he tensed.

"Sweetheart, I'm close," he said.

She stroked his balls and he groaned, then spurted into her mouth. She released him, smiling, then moved to Ty. She licked and swirled her tongue up and down, then sucked hard. She switched to the tawny-haired man. By the tensing of his body, she could tell he was close, too. She sucked him off until he released his load into her mouth as well.

As she returned to Ty, the satisfied men slipped into the water and came around behind her. They stroked her breasts and caressed her ass while she sucked on Ty. They drew off her bottoms. Then one slipped his fingers inside her vagina, and the other slid a finger into her ass. The feel of their fingers stroking inside her sent her pulse rising.

She licked Ty's balls, then nibbled gently with her lips as the heat stole through her. The intensity, like steam in a pressure cooker, built to an amazing level. She sucked Ty deep inside and bobbed up and down, her hand fondling his balls as the other men fondled her. One man ducked under the water and a second later, she felt his mouth cover her clit and suck. She exploded in orgasm, still sucking on Ty. He exploded in her mouth, groaning loudly.

Suzanne slid off Ty's member and smiled up at him. He bent down and kissed her tenderly.

The other man had come up for air and both of them came round to kiss Suzanne.

"I hope you guys don't think you're finished." Suzanne pushed herself onto the edge of the pool and ran over to grab one of the foam mattresses by the beach house a few yards away. She dropped it by the pool and lay down, spreading her legs wide.

The men glanced at each other and, in unspoken agreement, decided Ty would go first. He kneeled on the foam and kissed her, then shifted downward to kiss her breast. Tawny Hair kissed her other breast.

"Oh God, yes." She loved the feel of two men kissing her breasts. Both nipples covered by hot man-mouth. Ty released her breast and the third man took over. Ty pressed the head of his cock to her vagina, then thrust inside in a long, sturdy stroke. She clamped around him. He thrust in and out, stroking her vagina, filling her with his solid length. Rock-hard cock thrusting into her. Excitement rippling through every part of her.

"Ty . . . Oh God . . . yeah . . ."

Pleasure tore through her, shattering in its intensity. She clung to the two male heads sucking her breasts. The men watched her face contort in bliss as she careened to heaven, and back again.

Ty slid from her pussy and Dark Hair shifted to his knees in front of her. His cock nudged her opening and he slid inside. He thrust in and out as Tawny Hair pumped his own cock while watching them. Ty smiled and stroked her hair as she plummeted into another orgasm.

Next, Tawny Hair entered her and she squeezed him with her inner muscles. His cock stimulated her vagina in wild and wonderful ways as he swayed his hips from side to side as he plunged inside her. Ty and Dark Hair stroked her breasts lightly and, within moments, she catapulted into yet another orgasm. Finally she collapsed, sated, on the mattress.

The men tucked their cocks away and, Ty helped her to her feet. Each of them gave her a long, warm hug, then kissed her. Her two new friends waved as they continued to the beach.

Suzanne noticed the time on the tall, stone clock tower across the patio. Eight fifty.

"Ty, I'm meeting Melissa for breakfast so I have to get a move on. I'm going to introduce her to some people, hopefully make her a little more comfortable with the resort. Would you do me a favor?"

"Of course."

"I'll get Maurice, the maître d', to call you when we leave the restaurant. I need you to give me . . . oh, twenty minutes . . . then call me on my cell phone."

"What have you got up your sleeve?"

She glanced at the clock again. She had arranged to meet Melissa in ten minutes. She was afraid if she was late, she might lose this opportunity.

"Just call me and I'll explain later."

Melissa followed Suzanne into the dining room. Bright sunlight filtered in from the tall windows overlooking a fantastic ocean view. A light stream of people wandered along the boardwalk at the edge of the white, sandy beach beyond.

The maître d' led them past a buffet of fresh tropical fruits, eggs, breakfast meats, breads, pastries, and other assorted treats. He stopped at a table in the corner of the restaurant with windows facing both the ocean and a lovely patio garden. A smiling couple sat at the table. The man rose and pulled out a chair for Suzanne as the maître d' held Melissa's chair, then shifted it forward as she sat down.

"So nice of you to join us, Suzanne." The woman smiled, her gaze falling on Melissa. "Who is your lovely friend?"

"Giselle, Armand, this is Melissa. She's another virgin."

Melissa's back stiffened. What had she gotten herself into?

Armand, a tall man in his late thirties smiled at her. He was very attractive, in a debonair way, with his dark brown hair flowing back from his face in thick waves, his fine physique showcased in a gray silk shirt that tapered at the waist, setting off his broad shoulders.

"So nice to meet you, Melissa."

Oh, heavens, he had the merest trace of a French accent. It was sooo sexy. He took her hand and kissed it, brushing lightly over her knuckles with his full lips. Tingles rippled through her.

"So, Melissa, how do you like the resort so far?"

"It's quite beautiful. A lovely spot."

Suzanne leaned toward Giselle. "She's a little overwhelmed by the goings-on here. I thought it might help if she could chat to you two, so you could share the benefit of your experience."

"Of course, Melissa. We'd be happy to answer any questions you have."

Giselle's pert nose crinkled with her bright, friendly smile. Melissa felt her tension ease a little.

Giselle's hand stoked over Armand's. Melissa was struck by the physical contrast between the petite auburn-haired woman with tight curls framing her emerald green eyes, set off by her creamy skin, and her tall and tanned, dark-haired husband. They certainly made a handsome couple.

The waitress stopped by the table and poured coffee for Melissa and Suzanne. Once she'd gone, they went to the buffet and filled their plates.

As they ate, they chatted about innocuous things like the weather and the beautiful view. Once they'd finished, the waitress stopped by and cleared away their dishes and refilled their coffee cups. Melissa had been avoiding asking them anything about the club, but finally she took a sip of her coffee, sucked in a deep breath, and forged ahead.

"Giselle, how long have you been coming to the resort?"

"This place? Only a couple of years, but we've lived the lifestyle for over a decade. That's what you really wanted to know, isn't it?"

The lifestyle. That's how swingers referred to what they did.

"Yes, it is."

Armand slid his arm around Giselle's waist. He smiled at her like golden sunshine on the ocean, and she basked in the light of that smile. They seemed very much in love.

"So why do you do it?" Melissa asked, quite puzzled.

"Why, honey, that's simple." She patted Melissa's hand. "To keep our sex life exciting."

She glanced at Armand. How could it not be exciting with a hottie like him?

"But you can do that with fantasies and—"

"Sure, but you must have been there already. You can only go so far with a fantasy. Armand and I . . ." She gazed adoringly at her husband. "We tried them all. But being a harem girl, or rodeo cowboy, or whatever gets your jets going . . . only takes you so far. Adding a new sexual partner to your bedroom activities, well . . ." She grinned wickedly. "That's absolutely explosive."

"But going off with another man . . . and don't you get jealous knowing Armand's with another woman?"

"Oh, we don't do it like that." Armand's sexy French accent set her hormones sparking. "We invite one person from a couple into our bedroom and we all make love together."

Melissa's eyes widened. "You mean, three of you? Together?"

"Well, we've tried four . . . two couples," Giselle answered, "but so often it winds up with two couples side-by-side making love, and what Armand and I want is to be involved together. That's the point of the whole thing for us."

Armand stroked his wife's hand. "Not that the other ways are wrong. They're just not right for us."

"Are the people you . . . sleep with . . . always women?" Suzanne asked, then sipped her coffee.

"Most often." Armand smiled broadly, revealing straight, white teeth. "But I do like watching another man pleasure Giselle. I like having her sit on my lap while I stroke her breasts and watch another man slide his—"

"Armand." Giselle playfully smacked his hand. "You'll scare them."

Melissa could imagine Armand's long, masculine fingers curled over Giselle's generous breasts, while another man kneeled in front of her and, to her dismay, excitement trickled through her. In fact, she started to imagine Armand's hands on her breasts while he whispered sweet, French nothings into her ear.

"So you always share the experience," Suzanne commented. "That's nice." She smiled. "It's good that you know what you like."

"And that's another thing." Armand smiled, revealing straight, white teeth. His blue eyes glinted, like sunlight reflecting on the water on a bright, summer's afternoon. "We have to like the other person. We get to know them and only go for it if we hit it off."

Armand's gaze captured Melissa's and she sat mesmerized. God, but he was a sexy man.

"And we like *you*."

Chapter 7

MELISSA'S BREATH LOCKED IN HER LUNGS.

Armand turned his gaze to Suzanne. "*Both* of you."

"Yes, we do," Giselle added.

"Would either of you—?" Armand continued.

"Or both of you?" Giselle winked.

"Like to join us?" Armand asked.

Melissa's fingers wrapped tightly around her cup as she waited for him to finish the sentence. *In the pool. For lunch. On a plane to Lithuania.* It didn't matter. Anything.

But she knew very well what they wanted her to join them in doing. Her lungs ached with the need for air. She released her breath very slowly and drew in another.

"I . . . uh . . ."

Suzanne patted her hand and turned to Armand.

"That's a very sweet offer. I don't think Melissa is quite ready for that, but I would be delighted."

Melissa's eyes widened. Well, what did she expect? As much as she and Suzanne had hit it off . . . as much as Melissa considered her a *normal person* . . . Suzanne was here at a swingers' resort. She was here to have sex with people besides her husband. She was here to have sex with strangers.

"I have a great idea, though. Melissa is really nervous about this whole thing, so why don't we let her watch?"

Melissa gasped. "What? No, no." Her head shook back and forth like a bobble head gone wild. "I can't do that."

Suzanne squeezed her hand.

"Sweetie, look. You didn't just come here to ask questions, right?"

"I didn't?"

Suzanne's eyebrows dipped in confusion as she stared at Melissa. Damn, she'd blow this whole thing if she wasn't careful.

"I mean, no, I didn't."

"Well then?"

"We'd be happy to have you watch." Giselle sent her a smile filled with welcome.

"I just don't think I'm ready yet."

Suzanne grabbed her hand and pulled her to her feet.

"Come on. You just need to jump in."

Melissa felt herself swept along the hallway toward the elevators, Armand and Giselle, their hands joined, following along behind them. Two couples chatting by the bar sent them a knowing glance. Suzanne pushed the elevator call button and the doors whooshed open. Moments later, they exited the elevator on the fourth floor and Giselle led them down the carpeted hallway.

Melissa caught sight of herself in the mirror over one of the hallway tables. Her eyes wide and filled with consternation, her shoulder length hair caught back in a ribbon, her demure white camisole revealing shoulders tinged pink showing the beginning of a tan—she didn't look anything like a footloose, fancy-free, hot-to-trot swinger. How had she wound up being swept up to a room with a couple and another woman intending to have sex?

Melissa—a voyeur. It didn't make sense. And yet, an odd excitement built inside her. At first, she thought it was just anxiety, but now she could feel it boiling inside her. Thinking about how Armand would kiss Giselle, then Suzanne. How Suzanne would strip off her blouse and Armand would stare at her large, round breasts. Armand would touch them . . . and kiss them. Maybe Giselle would kiss them, too. Armand would undress and reveal his big cock—it would be long and hard, maybe curving upward.

And Melissa would watch this all from across the room. Like she had watched the couples in the hot tub last night.

They stopped in front of a door and Giselle used her key card to open it. She swung the door open to reveal a large, stunning room with two huge king-sized beds. The colors and fabrics used were the same as in Melissa's and Shane's room—sage-green walls, tropical floral print, and whitewashed furniture—but this room was bigger. They stepped inside and Melissa noticed a large area by the windows that accommodated a full sitting room with a couch and two upholstered chairs. This would be a great place to entertain. It was clearly set up to accommodate more than one couple, for a few hours, or even overnight.

Giselle pointed to the leftmost bed and panic welled up inside Melissa. Had Giselle forgotten Melissa was not going to participate?

"You curl up right there, honey. You can relax and enjoy yourself while you watch."

Melissa sucked in a breath, her tension level decreasing a little knowing the woman wasn't suggesting that Melissa get involved.

Suzanne plumped up the bed pillows and set them in an upright position, comfortable for sitting on the bed. She patted the bedspread.

"Honey, you'll be fine here."

Reluctantly, Melissa kicked off her shoes and sat on the bed, then leaned against the pillows.

Armand took Giselle into his arms and kissed her.

"I love you, my sweet."

"Mmm. I love you, too."

Melissa watched them in fascination. They seemed like such a happy couple. She just couldn't understand why they'd come to a place like this. *To stay happy*, a nagging little voice said, but she ignored it. It was a ridiculous idea.

Armand turned to Suzanne and smiled at her. She stepped forward, then stroked his shoulders. He drew her into his arms and kissed her. She sighed softly. The way their mouths moved against each other, Melissa could tell they were sharing tongues. French kissing with a Frenchman. Armand's mouth shifted to Suzanne's neck and she sighed deeply. She began to unfasten the buttons of her blouse. Three pairs of hands made quick work of releasing them, then she slipped the garment off her shoulders and let it flutter to the floor.

Her breasts stood proud and full in a lovely, pink bra, the soft, round swell of her flesh straining at the lace. Giselle released the hooks at the back while Armand kissed along Suzanne's collarbone. Suzanne dropped the straps from her shoulders then sat down on the bed as she drew the cups from her breasts.

Giselle stroked up and down Suzanne's back, watching the bra slip away. Suzanne's dark, dusky nipples stood rigid. Armand sat down beside her and ran his thumb over one hard nub. Giselle ran her hand over Suzanne's ribcage then cupped her other breast. A moment later, both husband and wife feasted on Suzanne's nipples. Suzanne fell back on the bed and moaned, a soft, delicious sound.

Melissa was embarrassed watching but, at the same time, she was getting turned on. She felt her own nipples harden and, as she watched Armand's tongue quiver over one of Suzanne's lucky nipples, she wanted to slide her hand under her top and stroke her own.

Giselle unfastened the button on Suzanne's jeans, then unzipped them. A moment later, Suzanne wriggled out of them as Armand pulled them down over her hips then discarded them on the floor. Suzanne wore only a pink thong and she looked amazingly sexy, especially with two pairs of hands, masculine and feminine, stroking her from shoulder to ankle.

Armand kissed and licked her breasts lovingly while Giselle kissed her calves, then stroked behind her knees, eliciting an excited gasp, as she kissed the inside of her lower thighs.

"Oh, my God, that feels wonderful." Suzanne sucked in a breath as Armand pulled her nipple deep into his mouth, then he kissed up her chest and took her lips in a passionate kiss.

"What do you want, my sweet Suzanne?" he asked.

"Well, I wouldn't mind seeing you naked," she replied.

Melissa leaned forward a little, her gaze gliding along his lean, masculine physique. *Me, too.* She imagined his shirt dropping to the floor, then his pants slipping away, revealing strong, muscular thighs. As his briefs lowered, his cock, strong and proud, would angle forward from his body, ready to thrust into Suzanne. Then Giselle. Then Melissa, if she wanted him to. And right now her pussy drenched at the thought.

His lips turned up in a devilish smile and he stood up. He unfastened his belt and, as he unzipped, an electronic melody sounded.

"Oh, that's my cell." Suzanne sat up. "I'm so sorry. Ordinarily, I'd just ignore it, but that's my sister's ring and . . . I really have to take it."

She bounced up and darted to her purse, lying on the chair across the room, then snatched the phone out.

"Hello, sis?" She listened. "Uh-huh . . . Yes, of course. I'm not alone right now. Let me call you back in two minutes . . . It's okay, honey. Two minutes."

She closed the phone and plunged it back into her purse.

"I'm really, really sorry about this."

"Is everything okay?" Giselle asked.

Suzanne collected her clothes from the floor and started pulling them on.

"My sister. She's having some problems with her husband. She really needs to talk to me." She bit her lip. "I'm so sorry. I don't mean to leave you here like this."

"Don't worry. We understand," Giselle said. "Family comes first."

Armand nodded.

Suzanne's gaze shifted to Melissa. "I'm sorry, Melissa."

Melissa shifted forward and sat up.

"That's okay."

"No, you stay," Giselle insisted. "You came here to watch and you can watch Armand and me."

"That's a great idea," Suzanne agreed as she tugged on her shoes.

"Sure," Armand added. "I bet you've never watched a couple make love before. In real life."

Melissa shook her head. She didn't want to admit that she'd seen Shane and the other people making out in the viewing room last night, but that wasn't technically watching a couple. It was more an orgy. Then there was the hot tub. But neither of those situations involved her sitting in the same room watching a couple. This felt much more personal.

"Great. That way you're still pushing your comfort level."

"I think I should just go."

"Come on, honey. This is less than you already agreed to." Suzanne smiled encouragingly. "Don't back out now."

Trapped, Melissa pushed herself back on the bed, eyeing Giselle and Armand nervously. Armand's pants hung open, revealing snug, black briefs beneath.

Suzanne leaned forward and kissed Melissa on the cheek. Strangely, it felt warm and comforting. She watched as Suzanne strode to the door and sent her one last smile before she exited and closed the door behind her.

"We know you're nervous, Melissa, but just relax and do what comes natural. If you want to get undressed, or touch yourself, feel free."

Melissa felt her cheeks flame at the suggestion.

"If you want to join us, that's fine with us. Whatever you want to do."

She wanted to leave, but that ship had already sailed.

Armand drew Giselle into his arms and kissed her. She wrapped her arms around him and, as though dancing a slow dance, she turned them around and then eased Armand to a sitting position on the bed. Slowly, she drew the hem of her T-shirt upward, revealing lightly tanned flesh. She flashed one of her bra-clad breasts, then the other. Armand stroked his fingertips along her ribcage, then slid them over her full breasts. Giselle tugged off the shirt and tossed it across the room.

Melissa watched as Armand's thumbs glided over and over her nipples. He tugged the blue lace downward, revealing her hard, dark rose nipple. He sucked it into his mouth and she gasped. She unfastened the bra, still groaning at his exquisite maneuvers on her breast, then disposed of it. His hand cupped her other naked breast and he gently squeezed it in a pulsing motion.

Melissa's own nipples stood at full attention now, wanting to be introduced to Armand's experienced hands . . . and his mouth. Giselle moaned again as he sucked her other nipple into his mouth. Oh God, how Melissa longed to feel his hot, wet mouth on her. Her hand found its way under her T-shirt and up to her nipple and she tweaked it.

Giselle slid her hands under Armand's shirt and, from the motions under the cloth, Melissa knew she was tweaking his nipples, too. He tugged off his shirt and cast it aside. His penny-sized nipples hardened under her busy fingers. She slid her hands downward, over his tight abs, then over the hem of his tight, black briefs, the fabric straining against his erection.

Melissa leaned forward, longing to see his long, hard cock. Her elbow knocked the table and a book dropped to the floor.

"Oh, I'm sorry." She hopped off the bed and grabbed the book.

She now stood right beside Giselle and couldn't help but stare at Armand's crotch, mesmerized by the sight of the head of his cock peering out the top of his briefs.

Giselle smiled. "You want to see it, honey?"

"What?" She blinked, trying to push herself to go back to her own bed, but her feet wouldn't budge.

"You want to see my husband's long, hard cock?"

Melissa nodded.

Slowly, Giselle peeled back the black briefs, releasing his marvelous, purple-faced penis to Melissa's sight.

Armand stood up and Giselle pulled his jeans and briefs downward until he could just step out of them. He stood there, his long cock jutting forward, needing a woman's touch.

Giselle took Melissa's hand and drew it toward Armand.

"Touch it," Giselle urged.

"No, I couldn't."

Giselle kneeled in front of him and kissed the tip of his cock, then she licked it like a lollipop.

"I think he'd really like you to touch him."

Melissa glanced to Armand.

He smiled his encouragement. "Yes, I absolutely would."

Giselle took Melissa's hand and drew it toward Armand.

"I don't know."

Melissa hesitated, her fingers a breath from his member. The giant cock twitched.

Giselle leaned close to Melissa. Giselle's naked breasts brushed against Melissa's arm as she murmured, "You do want to touch it, though, don't you?"

Involuntarily, Melissa nodded.

Giselle drew her hand the rest of the way and Melissa felt hot, hard flesh, smooth as kid leather, against her fingertip.

Oh, it was heaven.

Giselle released her hand and Melissa stroked a single fingertip the length of him. His face contorted in pleasure and a sense of power surged through her. She stroked her finger along the underside of his cock head and he groaned.

Melissa sank to her knees, knowing she had to taste that marvelous cock. She lapped at the tip of him, then opened her mouth as she slid her lips over him, then cradled his head in her mouth while she glided her tongue around his shaft, right under the crown.

"*Mon Dieu,* that feels *incroyable.*"

Giselle eased Melissa's camisole off and stroked around the bottom of her bra. Melissa's breasts ached to be free. Giselle unfastened the hooks and the bra released. Melissa dove down on Armand's cock, swallowing the whole thing into her throat, then drew back. Giselle's hands cupped Melissa's bare breasts.

Her delicate fingers stroked over Melissa's nipples as Melissa released Armand's cock on a long moan. Armand took her arms and drew her onto the bed. Giselle climbed in behind her.

Armand leaned in and captured her lips. His full, sexy mouth moved on hers and her sensitized lips pulsed with pleasure. His tongue swept over her lips then plunged inside her mouth. She met his with enthusiasm.

"You are incredibly sexy," he murmured.

"That is so true," Giselle added as she tugged Melissa's skirt downward, followed by her panties. Armand laid her on the bed and a second later his hot mouth covered her nipple, just as she'd longed for when she'd watched him with Suzanne. Suddenly, the pleasure doubled as her other nipple disappeared into Giselle's mouth. Intense pleasure swept through her. As they tugged and sucked, licked and kissed her nipples, she thought she'd go insane with bliss. Her vaginal muscles contracted and she thought she might come then and there.

Armand kissed down her stomach, over her navel, then around to her inner thighs. She arched her pelvis upward as she felt the tremors quake through her body. She wanted him to touch her.

He smiled. Clearly knowing her need, his fingers stroked upward and teased over her curls. She sucked in a breath.

"That feels great, doesn't it, honey?" Giselle murmured in her ear. "I bet you'd love him to touch your pussy."

His fingers stroked her moist flesh. Lightly. Sending trembling pleasure shooting through her.

Giselle gently nipped Melissa's earlobe, her fingers twirling and squeezing her hard, sensitive nipples.

"You want him to lick you. To drive your pussy crazy with his mouth."

Melissa nodded.

He leaned forward and licked her slit. She gasped. His big tongue slid through her folds and found her clit, then dabbed at it.

"Oh God, yes."

He sucked and cajoled while one finger slid inside her, then another. Vaguely, she realized it was Giselle's fingers, not Armand's, but she didn't care as waves of pleasure swept through her.

"Oh God. Oh yes."

"Look at her, Armand. She's coming." Giselle's excitement fed Melissa's and she wailed as an intense orgasm blasted through her.

As she caught her breath, Armand slid sideways a bit and she realized Giselle lay beside her. Armand's hand stroked his wife's thighs and he covered her pussy with his mouth.

"Oh yeah, baby. Oh, that's so good."

Giselle's face contorted in pleasure and she arched her body. Melissa's gaze fastened on her hard nipples. They looked so beautiful. And needy.

Melissa reached out and touched one. Just a light graze.

"Oh yes, Melissa. Please. More."

A streak of pleasure shot through her at being wanted like this. She leaned over and touched the tip of her tongue to Giselle's nub.

"Oh . . . yes . . ."

Bolder, Melissa covered the whole nipple, drawing it fully into her mouth. The aureole pebbled against her tongue. She sucked deeply.

"Oh . . . yeah, yeah, yeah . . ." The last ended in a squeak then Giselle wailed long and loud.

Melissa watched her face as she came. It was beautiful in its bliss. Almost angelic.

Giselle's eyes opened and she smiled at Melissa.

"Thank you, honey. That was really nice." She stroked Melissa's cheek.

Giselle shifted, sitting back against the cushions, then Armand slid Melissa between Giselle's open legs. Now Giselle was behind her and Armand in front of her. Giselle's hands covered Melissa's breasts and stroked them. Electric joy rippled through her.

"Do you want more, Melissa?" Armand leaned toward her, his big cock sliding along her inner thigh.

"Yes," she whispered.

His cock nudged her wet opening and she felt faint with need. In a moment, that huge cock would drive into her.

Giselle stroked and squeezed her nipple with one hand and stroked her hair back with the other. Armand leaned forward and kissed her, a gentle caress of lips on lips.

"I want you," she murmured. "Make love to me."

The words shocked her. Here she was making love to another woman's husband, right in front of her. Actually, on top of her. Still, she couldn't turn back now. Her need was too great.

His big cock nudged her tender flesh, then slid forward an inch, burying the tip inside her.

"Oh yes," Melissa sighed.

"Oh baby, drive that cock of yours into her." Giselle stroked her husband's cheek and he kissed her.

He pushed forward a little more, burying his cock head fully inside. Melissa squeezed her vaginal muscles, loving the feel of his invasion.

"More. God, give me more."

He smiled, kissed her briefly, then drove in hard. She gasped, delighted at the feel of his big cock stretching her.

"She likes that, honey," Giselle exclaimed. "Look at her face."

He kissed Melissa again, then smiled at her.

"Yes, it's a lovely face. Especially so full of pleasure."

He drew back, then thrust forward again.

Giselle plucked at Melissa's nipples. Armand thrust again. Soon he thrust in and out, faster and faster, driving her to the edge of ecstasy. He tucked his hands under her thighs and lifted, changing the tilt of her pelvis. Suddenly, she exploded with pleasure.

She wailed as electric bliss erupted through her. He thrust again and again, then jerked forward and held her tight to his body. She felt hot liquid fill her.

They collapsed in each other's arms. A moment later, they rolled sideways, Armand spooning her. Giselle curled in front of Melissa. Melissa's hand crept around Giselle's waist and she relaxed in the warmth of their affection, soon drifting off to sleep.

Ty hung up the phone. He didn't know why that minx Suzanne had wanted him to call, then pretended he was her nonexistent sister, but he was sure she knew what she was doing. He returned to his e-mail. He was waiting for his assistant to send him an update on the agent who represented the potential buyer for the resort. He had every faith Ashley would find out who it was.

Soon he heard the *blip* of the lock and the door push open. Suzanne sauntered in, her face a little flushed.

"What's up?" he asked.

Chapter 8

SUZZANE GLANCED AT HER SHINY DARK PINK FINGERNAILS. "That call I had you make? It was to pull me away from a ménage à trois. Me and a couple."

Ty's eyebrows arched upward. "And why would you want to be pulled away?"

She sat down beside him, smiling in supreme satisfaction. "To leave Melissa alone with them."

His groin tightened. "Melissa? With them *who*? Do you mean Melissa and Shane were the couple?"

"No. Me and a couple. Melissa was watching."

Watching? His breath caught. He didn't know why the thought turned him on so much. She'd watched several couples last night. A damper on that scenario, though, had been that one of them had been her husband.

Earlier that evening, seeing her watching the couples in the hot tub had been pretty hot. Of course, Melissa participating would have been even more of a turn-on.

"You wanted me to pull you away so she'd take your place?" he asked.

"Now you've got it."

The image of Melissa stretched out on a bed, a man fondling her breasts, a woman licking her pussy, pulsed through him.

"Do you think she went for it?" The words came out a little hoarse.

"She was teetering on the edge, but I'd wager this whole place that she did."

Suzanne sighed and he realized she probably felt that's exactly what she'd done.

"That was a great idea. That'll really get her involved and enjoying herself."

Suzanne stared at him with naked vulnerability in her eyes.

"Ty, what if I made a big mistake? What if she goes for it and hates it . . . or, worse, feels overcome with guilt?"

He took her hand.

"Don't worry, Suzie. I'm sure this whole thing is going to work out fine. Melissa seems to be enjoying the place. I'm sure she'll write a great report for her employer."

Suzanne trailed her fingertip over his knuckles.

"If she's even the one."

Ty shrugged.

"If she isn't, then it doesn't matter, right?"

She smiled. "I guess you're right."

She stood up and walked to the chair by the window, then settled in with her book.

He turned back to his e-mail. A new message had come in from Ashley.

You were right, boss. Melissa Woods was lying about her background. Almost everyone else checks out, though I still have to track down information on a couple of people. Including Ms. Woods's husband. See the attachments for detailed information.

Melissa and her husband had both raised flags. That was suspicious. Shane Woods had said he was self-employed—a consultant. That could translate to "unemployed." He'd send Ashley a reply suggesting she check out unemployment insurance for him, but she was probably on top of it.

Ty clicked on the first attachment Ashley had sent, which contained photos of each of the orientation guests. He scrolled down until he came to Melissa's picture. Her wide blue eyes stared at him from her lovely oval face, her golden blond hair cascading to her shoulders. This was definitely his Melissa Woods.

His. Damn it. Why did that sound so appealing?

"What are you working on, Ty?"

He glanced over his shoulder at Suzanne. "I found out that Melissa Woods isn't who she claimed to be."

"Really?"

He heard Suzanne rise from her chair and move across the floor. She leaned beside him, peering at the screen. He tried to ignore her soft breast brushing his arm.

He clicked on the second attachment and glanced down the text until he found Melissa's name. She was not a freelance writer as she'd claimed during the introductions at the orientation meeting. She worked for Lion, a major television network based in Chicago.

"Melissa works for a TV station?"

"So it seems."

"So she's not the investigator?"

"It doesn't look like it." Ty shook his head. "But I don't like the fact that she lied about who she is."

Suzanne opened her bag and retrieved a red bikini. "Who do you think the investigator is?"

He tugged his gaze from the sexy sight of Suzanne shedding

her clothes and tucking her voluptuous breasts into the small red bikini top.

"It could be her husband," he said absently as he returned his attention to Ashley's email.

"Really? Well . . . maybe I should spend some time with *Mr.* Woods."

Farther down the document, Ty found a brief description of Melissa's job. She was a researcher for the news department and one of her duties was to recommend stories for their weekly exposés.

"You know, in case he's the one."

His gut clenched. He watched their broadcasts regularly. Their exposés were hard-hitting and thorough, and generally well balanced, but he remembered the occasional piece where they played on the emotions of the audience, whipping them into a frenzy of outrage and moral superiority.

The hair on the back of his neck rose. This could be worse than he had thought.

Anger simmered through him as he remembered the one exposé they'd done on strip clubs a couple of years ago. Their report had made it look like the places were all thinly disguised brothels when, in fact, the management of most of them had very strict rules protecting their dancers. Suzanne's cousin, Kiki, a young single mother, used to work at one of the clubs they targeted, until it closed down as a result of their biased reporting. Kiki had enjoyed an excellent salary and days at home with her two young children until the Lion report outraged the community and forced the club to close.

That report had kicked Lion's ratings through the roof. Maybe Ms. Woods was looking for a new slant on an old theme, trying to paint Suzanne's clubs with the same wash of immorality.

"Ty?" Suzanne's insistent voice broke through his thoughts, as her hands ran over his shoulders.

He glanced at her. The red bikini bottom hugged her hips and accentuated her long, sexy legs, while the top pushed her bosom together, forming a deep crevasse between the ample globes.

"I suggested that I should watch Melissa's husband in case he's the investigator, but you were so engrossed in that e-mail that you didn't hear me. Is there something wrong?"

He couldn't lie to her, but he didn't want to alarm her.

"I want to keep an eye on Melissa Woods."

"Well, of course you do." She grinned. "She's gorgeous and you'd love to get her into bed."

He couldn't deny that, even though he wished it weren't true. Not now that he'd found out what kind of sleazy trick she was trying to pull.

Her smile faded when he didn't join in her joke.

"Tell me what's going on, Ty. What do you think she's up to?"

"She's doesn't seem like the type to come to a swingers' resort."

"That's true. She's more resistant than most beginners, and she doesn't seem like one of those wives dragged here by her husband."

"So why would a woman who works for a news network and is so uncomfortable with the idea of swinging come here this weekend?"

Suzanne's eyes widened. "You think she's going to do a story on us?"

He realized he'd said too much. There was no reason to get Suzanne all upset about something that was just a theory on his part.

"Probably not, but I believe in being cautious."

His fear was that she was doing research for an exposé that would not only trash Suzanne's reputation and make it impossible to sell the resort, but would force her other two clubs to close down as well.

The thought of Melissa maligning Suzanne and destroying all she'd worked so hard for sent spikes of anger through Ty.

~

"Melissa? Sweetie?"

Melissa opened her eyes at the woman's voice, slightly disoriented. A face—Giselle's—smiled down at her.

Naked images of this woman, and her oh-so-sexy husband, shot through Melissa's brain. She bolted to a sitting position, then suddenly realized she was naked herself and grasped for the blanket someone had covered her with.

Oh my God. What have I done?

"You can stay as long as you like, Melissa, but I just wanted to let you know that Armand and I are going to the beach. Will we see you at dinner tonight? There's that big show."

"Uh . . . sure."

She watched the two of them exit the room, then she scooted off the bed and grabbed her clothes, which someone had laid neatly on the second bed. She pulled them on, then sat on the upholstered armchair by the window, gripping the armrests.

How had she let herself get so carried away? She'd gone to bed, not just with a stranger, but with a couple. A man, *and a woman.*

She stood up and walked toward the door. She caught sight of her pale face in the mirror and looked away.

Oh God, this place definitely had a very bad effect on people.

Melissa followed the hallway back to the elevator and rode it up to her floor. Once back at the room, she opened the door, peering inside to see if Shane was there. No sign of him. She raced to the shower and washed thoroughly, soaping every part of her and rinsing, then soaping again. As she brushed out her hair, clad only in a big, fluffy white towel, she saw Shane in the mirror, standing in the doorway. She turned around, clinging to the towel tucked around her bosom.

"Hi." He smiled but she sensed his tension.

Damn. She'd treated him horribly this morning, storming off in a huff, when all he'd wanted to do was figure out what she wanted.

"Shane, I'm so sorry. It was all my fault. Last night, it . . . was so strange and . . ."

He rested his hand on her shoulder.

"It's okay, Liss. I shouldn't have talked you into coming to this place. I should have known it would make you uncomfortable."

"It's not your fault. I just feel bad that . . ." She glanced away, wrapping her arms around herself. "Shane, when I kissed you last night, I was confused . . . overstimulated . . ."

"Horny?"

Her gaze jerked to his face. At the sight of his lips curled up in a half grin, her aching jaw muscles eased. She smiled, too.

"Sure, horny. But I don't want you to think that what we did last night didn't mean anything to me. It was . . ." How could she describe the deep sense of intimacy she'd felt in his arms and the spectacular heights of ecstasy he'd shown her?

"I know. I rocked your world." His amused expression grew serious as he took her hand. "Honey, whatever your reason for making love with me last night, I'm thrilled. And if you want to use me as your boy toy while we're here . . . I'm fine with that." He kissed her knuckles, sending tingles quivering along her arm. "On the other hand, I think this could take our relationship in a new direction to become something deep and meaningful, and I don't want to screw that up, so if you want me to curtail my activities here and be a one-woman man, I will."

Melissa couldn't believe it. Shane was willing to give up any man's idea of paradise—being with all the hot, sex-hungry women he wanted—for her. She squeezed his hand, smiling. What a great guy.

But the fact that she'd made love to Shane last night, then Armand *and his wife* this afternoon, showed that not only was *she* not a one-man woman, she couldn't even keep to one lover at a time. It hardly seemed fair to spoil Shane's fun.

"Shane, I think you should enjoy the resort—and the women—as much as you want." She couldn't believe she'd just said that. This place was definitely having a weird effect on her. "When we get back home, we can have a long discussion about where we want our relationship to go."

He smiled, his gaze gliding down her body.

"And these women you recommend I enjoy while I'm here." He traced his finger along the edge of her towel, over the swell of her breast. Goose bumps blossomed across her chest and over her shoulders. "Does that include you?"

Her insides tightened and, despite having just spent an hour trying to forget about anything having to do with sex, she couldn't think of anything but.

She shifted toward him. "Well . . . I am your wife."

He stepped forward and drew her into his arms. His lips, so sweet on hers, teased, then his tongue slipped inside her mouth. Soon their tongues tangled and danced as she found herself fumbling with his belt, then tugging down his zipper. He drew the towel open and fondled her breasts, sending electrifying need from her nipples to her groin.

She slipped her fingers around his erection and pulled it free of his pants. He backed her to the wall and pressed her tight against it while he leaned in to capture her nipple within the warmth of his mouth. He sucked and dabbed with his tongue. She clung to his head, raking her fingers through his hair.

"Take me now, Shane."

He smiled. "A little anxious, are we?"

She squeezed his cock and pumped.

"I want you inside me."

His finger slid along her slick pussy and his eyebrows rose.

"Wow. You really do. Well, sweetheart, how can I ignore an invitation like that?"

His cock nudged her slit, then slowly eased inside. She groaned at the delicious invasion. He tucked his hands under her butt and lifted her, changing the angle of his cock inside her. Then he started to move. She wrapped her legs around his waist, which pulled him deeper.

She sucked in a breath. Waves of heat washed through her immediately. She couldn't believe how close she was. He ran his finger over her clit.

"Oh, Shane. I'm going to come right now."

He thrust deep, then kept on thrusting, banging her against the wall. She barely noticed the cold tile against her back as blissful euphoria swept through her, carrying her on a surge of pleasure.

"Oh my God. Yes, yes, YEESSSS!" she wailed, clinging to his shoulders.

He stiffened and held her tight, spurting inside her. She clamped her legs tighter around him, pumping him with her vaginal muscles, milking every drop from him.

He held her against the wall for several moments, her face snuggled into the warmth of his neck. Finally, he kissed her cheek. "Liss, you've turned into a wildcat."

He eased her to the floor.

She picked up the towel and wrapped it around herself, suddenly shy of being naked in front of him. Still naked, Shane followed her into the bedroom, where she dressed, her back to him allowing a little modesty without feeling ridiculous. After all, she'd just demanded he bang her against the wall, then wailed like a cat in heat.

She could feel his presence behind her, sense him watching her pull on and fasten each article of clothing. Fully dressed, she turned around. He stood there, heedless of his nudity, his cock half-erect, still watching her.

"God, you're sexy." He stepped forward and drew her into his arms, then kissed her. "With or without clothes."

He nuzzled her neck. If he kept that up, she'd soon be *without clothes* again.

"Aren't you getting dressed?" she asked.

He grinned and eased away from her. "Okay, I get the hint."

He leaned over to open a drawer, exposing his exceptionally tight rear end. She wanted to lean forward and cup it, then stroke the hard, round flesh. He stood up, red swimming trunks in his hand, then pulled them on.

"There, is that better?"

A little less stimulating, but not better. She already missed his long, hard cock.

Oh man, she was turning into a sex maniac.

"Going for a swim, I take it."

"That's right. Want to join me? I met some people earlier and they're waiting for me by the pool."

Women or men friends? she wondered. An image of Suzanne in the pool this morning, her bare breasts bobbing in the water, skittered through Melissa's brain. Would Shane be swimming with partially-naked women? Or maybe totally naked? Would he make love with one? Or more?

He had already shown last evening in the viewing room that he was willing to participate in sexual activities with more than one person. She was sure he wouldn't mind indulging in a little sex by the pool.

Images danced through her head . . . of lounging by the pool, her breasts bared to the tropical sun . . . taking whatever came her way, hopefully, in the form of tall, dark and handsome. The temptation was overwhelming and all too persuasive, throwing her totally off balance.

"I . . . uh . . . no, I think I'll just stay here and read."

He tucked his key card in the pocket of his trunks and gave her a kiss on the cheek.

"Okay, I'll see you in a couple of hours. I'll be back in time for the dinner and show tonight. It should be a fun evening."

Once he'd gone, she slumped on the bed. Her attitudes about sex, her body, relationships . . . were all in a mess right now. She wanted things she'd never wanted before, she felt things she'd never allowed to surface. Fantasies pushed their way through her mind. Like being fucked by Ty Adams. Karen Smeed's words trickled through her head.

You've never felt real pleasure until you've had one cock in your cunt and another up your . . .

Ass. That's what she'd been going to say. Melissa had never had anal sex, let alone two men at the same time. Of course she hadn't. Before this, she'd been a normal woman, not some sex-craving maniac.

Images of Ty Adams shimmered through her brain. She could imagine his cock gliding into her, stroking her vagina, then her leaning forward and Shane sliding his cock into her from behind. The thought of two large cocks stuffed inside her, moving inside her, stroking her insides, sent thrills through her. She remembered the woman in the Mariposa room with Shane, when the two men had fucked her at the same time.

Melissa's finger found her clit and she twirled and dabbed, imagining

Ty and Shane fucking her silly. It took less than a minute before she exploded in another orgasm.

~

As Melissa and Shane entered the large dining room, she noticed Suzanne smiling and waving at them. She was with Ty, Giselle, and Armand at a table for six.

"Melissa, why don't you and your husband join us?" Suzanne's eyes twinkled at Shane, so handsome in his classic black tuxedo. "Your name is Shane, right?"

Shane took her hand and kissed it. "My pleasure. Suzanne?"

She nodded, a slight flush on her cheek.

"Shane and Melissa, this is my husband Ty."

Melissa felt a prickle dance down her spine as the focus of Ty's charcoal eyes, glinting coldly, locked on her then flicked away. Dismissive, with none of the charm and friendliness of the previous evening.

Her hand drifted to her diamond heart necklace and her fingertips traced around the edge.

"Melissa, you already know Giselle, and her husband, Armand."

Shane shook hands with each of them. Giselle and Armand both sent Melissa warm smiles and Melissa flushed a little as she clung to Shane's hand. He must have noticed but didn't even blink.

A waitress came around with a bottle of red wine, filling their glasses. Soon after, the serving staff brought their salads. Everyone chatted amiably over dinner, though Melissa noticed that Ty managed to totally ignore her without being obvious about it. While they ate their dessert, a decadent triple-chocolate cheesecake, an announcer stepped onto the small stage with a microphone.

"Before everyone breaks after dinner for the gambling part of the evening, I'd like to enlist your help. We'd like several volunteers to take part in our show this evening. I promise, it will be a lot of fun. Now who's game?"

A couple of hands went up.

"Don't be shy, now." A couple more hands went up. "I'd really like to see some of our virgins take part."

Giselle nudged Melissa's elbow.

"You go, Melissa."

"No, I don't think so."

"That's a great idea," Suzanne added.

"Why don't you go?" Melissa asked. "You're a . . . new person, too."

"I tell you what. I will if you will."

Melissa clamped her lips tight. Why had she opened her mouth?

Shane leaned close to her. "Why don't you, Liss? It would be good for you to try something new."

Something new? She'd tried plenty new in the past twenty-four hours.

Ty's gaze fell on her. A look of challenge in those dark eyes bored through her.

He didn't think she'd do it. He thought she was too much of a wuss.

She lifted her head and pushed back her shoulders, then thrust up her hand.

One of the resort staff, holding a clipboard, proceeded to the table.

"Two volunteers here," Melissa said to the young man with the clipboard.

"Oh, I'm sorry, ma'am, but we only need one more. Are either of you a virgin?"

"We both are," Suzanne responded.

"I can only take one of you."

"I'm sorry, Melissa," Suzanne said. "I said I'd go with you, but . . ." She shrugged helplessly.

"No, it's fine. I'll go anyway," Melissa said, the memory of Ty's challenging gaze goading her on. She stood up and followed the man.

As they approached the other volunteers collecting at the side of the stage, Melissa started having second thoughts. She leaned toward her recruiter.

"This thing onstage . . . Will I be expected to take part in any . . . uh . . . sexual activity?"

"Not if you don't want to."

She let out a sigh of relief.

"I don't."

He took her name and jotted it down on his sheet of paper along with a note beside it, then pointed to the other volunteers following the announcer backstage.

"Go with them to wardrobe. You'll be set up with a costume and given instructions."

Chapter 9

TY STARED AT THE FIFTY ONE-THOUSAND DOLLAR BILLS IN HIS hand. Auction dollars.

"You want to win as many of those as you can." Suzanne tucked hers in her evening bag.

"Wouldn't you rather I keep an eye on Melissa?"

The two of them walked toward the gaming area alone. After dessert and coffee, Giselle had headed for the ladies' room and Shane and Armand for the bar.

Ty still kicked himself for the way he'd behaved when Melissa had joined them at the table this evening—succumbing to his anger at the thought she was here to expose Suzanne's club as something degenerate. He'd never let his feelings show in a professional situation before. It had something to do with the fact that he liked Melissa Woods—and he really didn't want her to be a bad guy.

"That's just it," Suzanne continued, "you need to win enough money to buy her."

His eyebrows arched up. "Come again?"

"Because she's a virgin participating in the show, she is chosen as the grand prize for the auction."

"Why?"

She glanced around at the others swarming to the gaming tables.

"You'll see. Right now, go get all the money you can. Then you'll have her for the rest of the evening."

The thought of *having* Melissa for the rest of the evening sent his cock rising. Despite his anger at her and his uncertainly about her purpose here, he wanted to *have* her. Again and again.

According to Suzanne, Melissa had joined in the ménage à trois as Suzanne had hoped. In fact, it had been the couple they'd sat with at dinner tonight. Giselle had told Suzanne that Melissa had thoroughly enjoyed herself.

If she had enjoyed that, Ty had a plan that was sure to convince her to push her limits even further. And the further she pushed them, the more likely she was to become a convert. Even if she didn't embrace the lifestyle, how could she throw aspersions on the place if she'd been participating in the sexual activities herself?

"How much do I need?"

"Hard to say exactly. Five million should be enough. You can go to the blackjack tables," Suzanne continued, "but we've found that a lot of the female guests aren't that interested in gambling, so if you can find a way to get their auction dollars, you'll probably wind up ahead."

Ty raised an eyebrow. "What do you suggest?"

She eyed him speculatively.

"Well, you are one of the best-looking guys here. . . ."

"One of?" He placed his hand over his heart and feigned a wounded expression. "Why, Suzanne, I'm hurt. You've always told me I was the best-looking man ever. I always suspected that was just a line."

She rolled her eyes. "And you are." She grinned impishly.

"How do you suggest I use that asset?"

"I've noticed quite a few women watching you . . . with longing in their eyes. I think you should start a poker game for women only. And you, of course. I'll drop some hints to those women that you might be gambling with more than money. I bet you'll have quite a few takers."

"Your mind works in strange and wondrous ways, Suzie Q."

"And you love me for it." She spun away. "Go to the desk and ask for some cards and chips, then go to the Passion Flower conference room. I'll go round up some victims."

About ten rounds had been played and Ty, who could easily read the faces of these novice players, won consistently. The problem was, the pots were tiny. The other players, seeing Ty's success, were becoming skittish. He saw the restless fidgeting and knew if he didn't do something, and fast, he'd lose them.

In any kind of dealing with people, the best strategy was to go for a win-win scenario. If everyone was happy, things went much more smoothly. It was also the way Ty liked to live his life.

He tapped the edge of the cards on the tabletop, straightening them.

"Ladies, I have a proposition."

Ten lovely faces lifted toward him, their eyes bright with curiosity. He held up one of the auction dollars. "This is what I want from you. What is it you want from me?"

"Well, since you're asking," Lucy, the brunette on his left said, leaning toward him. "I think we'd all like to see a little skin."

"Strip poker?" He raised an eyebrow. "As much as I would love to see you ladies lose your clothing, I'm not sure how that helps me increase my wealth."

"Honey, you bet the clothes, we bet the dollars." Renée, the redhead across the table, winked.

Okay, now we're talking.

He stood up and removed his suit jacket and tossed it over the back of his chair. He released the top button of his shirt, then the second, noting the smoldering look in the women's eyes. He released one more button, parting the shirt enough to reveal the shadow of his chest hair, then sat back down. The women seemed to settle more firmly in their chairs, their gazes locked on his chest. A couple more women joined the table.

It was strange, in the extreme, to be eyed by women as a sex object. But, hey, he could get used to it.

"Since I don't intend to lose, I thought I should give you a freebie."

"If you don't intend to lose, then you should give us some reason to keep playing," said Emma, a petite blonde in a red dress.

"I know. How about we all still bet money, but if you win, you take something off?" Lucy suggested.

He stroked his chin. "Only if the pot goes above fifty thousand."

Murmurs of assent sounded around the table.

Rounds flew by. As soon as the appropriate amount was thrown in, all the women would fold. He wished he'd made the amount higher, but he'd been afraid of scaring them off. Even though it was only funny money, most people were reluctant to part with it. Even counting socks and shoes, he didn't have enough pieces of clothing to get all the women's money.

He lost each piece of clothing one by one until he wore only his pants and briefs. He won another hand and raked in the bills, then stood up and unfastened the button on his pants. All gazes locked on his zipper. He dragged it down an inch . . . then stopped. A disappointed murmur sounded in unison.

"How about we make it more interesting?" he suggested.

"It was just about to get more interesting," grumbled Monique, a woman with dark hair piled high on her head and deep red lipstick that matched her low-cut sequined dress.

"What do you have in mind?" Lucy asked.

"What if the woman with the best hand gets . . . a kiss?"

Emma's eyes widened. "Oh, I like that."

"Yeah, baby," chimed in Renée.

"But first, the pants," Emma insisted.

He unzipped and slid the pants down . . . slowly, to *ohhh*s and *ah-hh*s, then wild applause as his pants hit the floor with the *clunk* of his belt buckle.

His cock, encased in charcoal cotton, hardened a little at the acute female attention. He sat down.

Betting soared on the next round. This one pot exceeded the total of the previous three, at two hundred thousand. The winner, Mandy, a tall, blond goddess, stepped toward him. He stood up and opened his arms to her. She pressed her long, lithe body against him and slid her arms around his neck. His lips met hers in a soft caress, then he dragged her tight against his body, crushing her generous breasts against his naked chest, and thrust his tongue past her lips. She tasted sweet, like icy mints. She gasped, then melted against him. His cock reacted in the most natural way possible. It grew an inch. She undulated her hips forward, pressing hard against his groin. His cock grew another inch.

Their tongues tangled for a good two minutes, then he drew back. He continued to hold her for a couple of seconds, his hand securely on the small of her back, then he released her. She smiled at him, batting her eyelashes in a demurely feminine way. She was extremely sexy and any man would want to toss her into bed without a moment's hesitation . . . but all he could think about was Melissa. The pot of gold at the end of the rainbow. He wanted Melissa.

And that thought disturbed him. Sure his goal was to buy Melissa in the auction and ensure she enjoyed herself—so much she wouldn't, or couldn't, make Suzanne's resort the target of a negative news segment—but he realized it was much more personal than that. He'd been fantasizing about touching her, holding her . . . making love to her. He wanted the woman badly.

Right now he was in any guy's idea of heaven. He should be enjoying the attentions of the sexy women around him, and contemplating the exciting activities he might share with them, not obsessing about one woman, no matter how attractive she was.

"Thank you, Mandy."

"Thank *you*." She returned to her chair, her smile broad and her eyes glittering.

More women had joined them. There were twenty-five or so now. Over the next couple of hands, more drifted in. His cock ached with need as body after soft, womanly body pressed against him, breasts cushioned against his chest, full lips compressed under his.

After several more rounds, he noticed a couple of the women murmuring unhappily.

"Is there a problem?" he asked.

"Well, the kisses are nice for those who win, but the rest of us . . ." Emma's words trailed off.

"We want to . . . see you." Lucy stared at him with longing in her eyes.

A longing he yearned to see in Melissa's eyes.

Suzanne glanced around the ballroom, trying to decide how best to help Ty get money together. Her gaze caught on Shane Woods standing by the bar. He saw her and smiled, then held up a glass. She nodded, assuming he was offering to get her a drink.

He might be the one sent here to report on the resort, so spending some time with him, ensuring he was having a good time, wouldn't be a bad idea.

She strolled toward him as he spoke with the bartender. As she approached, he turned from the bar with two drinks in his hand, smiled when he saw her, then handed her the martini glass.

"I noticed you were drinking a Cosmopolitan at dinner. I thought you might like another."

The light brush of skin on skin as she took the glass from his hand sent tingles through her.

Her mouth turned up in a seductive smile. "I'd rather have a Screaming Orgasm, but this will do for now."

He blinked, then his smile broadened and he leaned close to her ear.

"Whatever the lady wants, the lady gets." His murmured words whispered against her ear, sending goose bumps along her neck and down her arms.

Her heart rate sped up as she realized she might be getting in over her head. She sipped the drink. The tangy taste and the heat of the vodka swirling down her throat revived her confidence and she nudged her head sideways as she started to walk, signaling him to follow. His hand brushed down her back and settled below her ribs as he accompanied her. She led him out the door and down a hall, into one of the rooms set aside for guests to go and talk in private. Several upholstered chairs circled a low table, and a couch sat along one wall. But no bed. She closed the door behind them.

"I was getting tired of all the noise. I thought it would be quieter talking in here."

He nodded and leaned against one of the chairs. He sipped his drink, clearly waiting for her to take the lead.

"Are you enjoying the gambling?" she asked.

"I did a little, but it's not really an interest of mine."

"You know there are prizes to be bid on at the end of the evening."

He shrugged. "I'd rather spend my time in the company of a beautiful woman."

She raised her eyebrows. The germ of an idea occurred to her that would both help her get more money for Ty and help show Shane what a great place this was. On top of that, it had her hormones sizzling into high gear.

"If you won't be bidding on the prizes, you don't really need the money you won, do you?"

His eyebrow arched upward. "What do you have in mind?"

Ty checked his watch and realized the gambling time would be ending in under an hour. The women said they wanted to see him.

"How about if you can get a pot together for . . ." He did a quick calculation. Suzanne had suggested he make his target five million dollars. He only had a little over three and a half million now. He had to step this up. "One and a half million, then I'll get totally naked and . . ."

"And what?" Lucy's eyes were wide.

"It doesn't matter." Emma shrugged. "Most of us are tapped out. We couldn't get a tenth of that together."

"Except that most of you are here with husbands. You could always get it from them," Ty suggested.

Monique sighed. "They will have gambled it away by now."

"Someone's winning it," the woman standing behind Renée said.

"Honey, this is fun gambling." Lucy smiled. "Everyone's winning."

"Still . . ."

"I want to know what we get," said Emma, staring at Ty.

He shrugged. "What do you want?" He didn't want to suggest something that might scare them off.

"I want to touch . . . it." Mandy's cheeks flushed red.

"I want to more than touch it." Renée's gaze trailed down his stomach and locked on to his crotch.

"How about I let the lucky winner . . ." He winked. ". . . do more than touch it?"

"Oh, I am so in," said Jenny, a lovely auburn-haired beauty with curls cascading past her shoulders.

"Not one winner. Five," Lucy suggested.

"Seven." Renée still stared at his crotch.

"Three," Ty stated firmly. He had to think about time. And energy. He wanted enough left to spend on Melissa.

"But not based on the bids." Renée leaned back in her chair. "I think you should draw names from everyone who puts money in."

"Draw from the top ten bidders. Otherwise, someone could drop only a thousand," Monique chimed in.

"Then what do the rest of us get?" Emma asked.

Renée planted her hands firmly on her hips and smiled. "You get to watch."

An *ohhhh* sounded through the crowd.

"Agreed," Ty said.

"Yessss."

The women scattered. Over the next fifteen minutes, they straggled back in, tossing money onto the table. Finally, Lucy counted the bills scattered across the table.

"One million, seven hundred thirty six thousand." She thumped the stack of bills on the table.

The ten highest bidders wrote their names on a slip of paper and dropped them into a bowl. Lucy, not one of the ten, drew three names. They weren't even pretending to play poker anymore.

Mandy, Jenny, and Emma stood up and stepped toward him.

Mandy stroked her hand along his chest and down his belly, to the waistband of his briefs. Her finger slid under the elastic and she tugged a little. His cock lengthened at her warm touch so close to his hardened flesh. Jenny tugged the elastic and his cock lurched forward. The women in the room, an audience of at least forty now, sucked in their breath. Jenny pulled the briefs down and dropped them to his ankles. He stepped out of them and kicked them aside.

Mandy took his hand and drew him to a large, open space in the room, then urged him to the floor. He sat on the thick, soft carpet. Mandy stroked his chest, easing him onto his back, while Jenny slid her hands along the inside of his thigh. A second later, Emma stroked the tip of her finger along his shaft. He sucked in a breath at her delicate touch. His eyelids fell closed as he enjoyed the situation. A warm mouth covered the head of his cock, a soft, wet tongue circling around the underside of the crown.

Damn, but it felt great.

But he couldn't help thinking it would be even better if it was Melissa's mouth.

He opened his eyes to see that Mandy had shed her dress, leaving her large breasts covered only by shear black lace. The other two women were shedding their clothing, also. Soon the three of them gathered around him dressed only in sexy bras and thongs. He longed to reach out and touch those breasts, to suck them into his mouth, but that wasn't part of the deal.

Mandy licked his cock head and then swallowed him whole. His already rigid cock grew rock hard. A moment later, she climbed over him, tugged the crotch of her panties aside, and slid down on him, capturing his pulsing erection in her hot, wet pussy. He sighed, concentrating on keeping control. She shifted up and down twice.

"Hey, leave some for us," Emma insisted.

Reluctantly, Mandy slid off him and shifted forward. Emma sat down on him, capturing his cock inside her sweet, warm pussy. Mandy sat right in front of her, their two bodies together, Emma's front to Mandy's back. After two bounces, Emma shifted off him and moved forward, pushing Mandy farther up his chest. Jenny slid onto his cock and glided up and down twice. The three of them were giggling like crazy. They began moving back and forward, shifting their bodies enough to pass his cock from pussy to pussy. Mandy, Emma, Jenny, then change direction. Emma, Mandy, then change direction. Emma, Jenny, then change direction.

"Hey, Emma's getting it more often," Mandy complained.

"Yeah, that's not fair," Jenny agreed.

Ty's cock was aching and their argument had stopped their movements. He twitched inside Jenny.

"I'll solve this."

He grabbed Mandy's hips and pulled her forward, toward his face. He drew her close and parted her sexy, lower lips and licked the moist flesh. She got the idea and settled over his mouth, leaving him a little room to breath. He pulled Emma forward to sit on his stomach, then slid his thumb into her pussy. His fingers stroked the little puckered opening of her anus. Jenny remained on his cock.

He dabbed at Mandy's clit, while working his finger inside Emma's hot opening. Jenny shifted, then glided up and down, once.

He used his free hand to part Mandy's flesh, then sucked on her hard little clit. She gasped. He slipped his index finger into Emma, alongside his thumb, while continuing to stroke her other tight hole. Jenny shifted up and down again.

He slipped two fingers into Mandy. He swirled his finger inside Emma, then drew it back to her anus, slowly pushing the lubricated digit into her. Jenny started moving in a fluid up and down motion. His cock pulsed with need. He couldn't last much longer. He swirled his tongue around Mandy's clit while thrusting his fingers inside her. He pushed against Emma's anus, his finger slipping farther inside, then he began to move his thumb along her moist opening in parallel to the slow thrusting motion of his finger in her ass. She clenched around him, tight and hot, moaning.

"Oh, oh, I'm close." Jenny moaned as she bounced up and down on him.

He felt his balls tighten, ready for release.

"Oh, baby, that feels so good." Mandy undulated on top of him.

Emma simply groaned and clenched around his thumb and his finger. She let loose first, moaning, then wailing loudly. Mandy next, adding her wails of pleasure, then Jenny. The song of three women in orgasm sent him over the edge. Their orgasms went on and on as he filled Jenny with his seed.

As he erupted into the hot embrace of her body, he thought about Melissa riding his cock, wailing in ecstatic pleasure as he brought her to orgasm. As he intended to do several times over the course of the evening.

Finally, they all collapsed together in a tangle of bodies. Emma's face, next to his, beamed with a bright smile.

"Wow, that was great. I get your cock this time."

Oh God, they wanted him to do this two more times. He glanced at his watch and realized he only had a half hour left. There was no time to gather any more dollars. Not that it mattered. He safely had his target.

Melissa would be in his arms tonight.

Melissa peered into the Passion Flower room. She had been looking all over for Shane or any of her other dinner companions for the past half hour. A number of women were standing watching something. She stepped into the room and moved forward, trying to catch a glimpse of what they were seeing.

Shock pulsed through her as she saw Ty lying on the carpet with three women undulating on top of him.

What had she expected from a man who attended a swingers' club? Despite the fact he had a beautiful wife, he was here to have sex with other women. Even though she'd known what kind of man he was when she'd met him, disappointment burned through her.

She wanted to turn and leave, but the sight of his long, hard cock sliding in and out of the sexy blonde, while his mouth worked on the redhead and his fingers stroked inside the brunette, held her frozen. The passionate sounds of the women washed through her, and her rate of breathing increased.

Melissa's hormones danced through her in a wild passion dance. She yearned to have his cock thrusting into her, even if it meant sharing him with two other women.

All the women wailed, their faces contorted in bliss, then they slumped together. A moment later, they pushed themselves up and, to Melissa's complete surprise, they switched positions and settled on him again. Her eyes widened, watching the blonde suck Ty's cock to life, then grasp his big shaft and direct it inside her.

Melissa felt a tap on her shoulder and she jumped.

"Ms. Woods." A man dressed in the crested jacket of the resort stood beside her. "It's time to change into your costume."

Chapter 10

SUZANNE WATCHED AS SHANE LEANED TOWARD HER. HIS WARM mouth covered one hard nipple reverently. The heat and moisture sent her blood boiling. His tongue moved slowly over her nipple, then he drew it deep into his mouth.

Their flirtation had turned bolder and she'd decided to have some fun with it while furthering her mission to get Ty more auction dollars. She'd offered to let Shane kiss her for some of his auction money and he'd asked where. His hungry gaze on her cleavage had told her exactly what he'd hoped for.

She hadn't been able to resist the temptation.

He released her breast and she almost cried out, but he quickly covered her other nipple. She sucked in a breath at the intensely divine pleasure.

This man was *hot*!

She wanted to grab his hands and hold them against her breasts. She wanted to press her throbbing nipples against his hard, muscular chest while his hot cock thrust deep inside her.

But she'd only agreed to let him kiss her breasts.

He leaned back, gazing at her hard nipples, then shifting to her face.

"Thank you." His smile and the boyish glint in his eye took her breath away.

"Thank *you*." She leaned toward him and their lips touched. The contact blossomed into a passionate kiss.

Their lips parted and she stared into his simmering blue eyes for a long moment, debating whether to obey her hormones and fling off her dress, then pull him on top of her.

The lights flickered, signaling time for the show. The guests would be returning to the dining room.

She sighed as he pushed himself to his feet, then helped her up. Maybe later she'd get a chance to experience everything this sexy man had to offer.

As she rearranged her dress, he pulled out his dollars and slipped all of them into her evening bag.

"But . . ." It was more than they'd agreed on.

"That's okay." He tucked his hands around her waist. "It's just play money. No big deal."

"Thanks." She smiled. "Ty will be thrilled."

He pressed his hand to the small of her back as they walked toward the door.

"Is there something special he wants bid to on?"

She nodded.

Yes. Your wife.

Melissa wrapped her hand around her martini glass, trying to quell the butterflies fluttering in her stomach. Why had she volunteered to be in this show?

Her gaze slid to Ty as he chatted to his wife. Part of the reason had been to show him that she could be adventurous, but why did his opinion matter? She was nothing to him but the possibility of a little sex on the side. He had a beautiful wife and, based on what Melissa had witnessed a few moments ago, a bevy of beautiful women willing to screw him. As soon as he realized Melissa wasn't interested, he'd totally forget about her.

Suzanne laughed and kissed Ty's cheek. Her finger toyed with the top button of his shirt and Melissa imagined unfastening that button, then the next, slowly revealing the hard, male muscles beneath.

Okay, it's not that she wasn't *interested*. He was a gorgeous, sexy man and there was an undeniable attraction between them. And she had enjoyed their time together yesterday. More than that, he had touched something deep inside her when he had acted as her protector. Never before had she felt so cared for. Even with Shane . . . and that disturbed her. What was it about Ty Adams that affected her this way?

Her stomach coiled tightly as she realized she really didn't want to know. Her good sense warned that if Ty wasn't married, she could find herself wanting him too much. Needing him too much. And that was far too dangerous to her emotional health.

Memories of the loss she'd felt after her mother left, of the all-encompassing pain, flashed through her, nearly knocking her over. She hadn't thought about that in years—hadn't allowed the feelings to surface . . . ever.

Loving someone that deeply meant loss . . . and unimaginable pain. She would not allow herself to . . .

Her gaze shifted away from Ty.

"Melissa, are you okay?" Giselle asked. "You look a little pale."

Melissa glanced at her. "I'm just . . . a little nervous. About the show." Anxiety about her upcoming performance gave focus to her churning emotions.

"Don't worry, honey. You'll be great." Suzanne sent her a reassuring smile from across the table.

"Melissa, I love your costume." Giselle smiled at the waiter and thanked him as he set a tall, cocktail glass full of a frothy pink drink in front of her, then turned her attention back to Melissa. "Tell us a little about the show."

"I can't. It's a surprise."

The butterflies began again. Her fingers reached for her heart necklace but it wasn't there. She remembered she'd taken it off because it didn't fit with her peasant costume. She reached into the pocket in the front of the skirt and drew out the necklace.

"Shane, would you keep this? I don't want to lose it."

"Sure thing." He slipped it into his inside jacket pocket.

Melissa plucked at the ribbon at the neckline of the white peasant blouse. It left her shoulders totally bare. She'd left off her bra because the straps would have shown otherwise. The full skirt, gathered at her waist, fell to her ankles. They'd told her to leave off her pantyhose and shoes, wanting the effect of a barefoot peasant.

Melissa sipped her drink. She wished she hadn't volunteered for this show. She hated speaking in front of a group, let alone performing, but the staff had assured her she would be fine. Since she wasn't taking part in the more . . . erotic aspects of the show, she would be led by the three professional actors rather than being teamed up with other volunteers.

Four of the volunteers were married couples who had chosen to swap partners for the performance and the others were couples who had chosen to stay together. They must get a sexual thrill out of being exhibitionists, but Melissa really couldn't understand it.

She tipped her stemmed martini glass again, glancing surreptitiously toward Ty as he whispered something to Suzanne and again Melissa remembered the three women riding him to sexual bliss. A flash of heat blazed through her, an echo of her response to watching him pleasure those women—and wishing it was her. He hadn't minded performing in front of a crowd. What kind of man did that sort of thing? Now that she had her chaotic thoughts under control, she knew she would never consider a relationship with a man like Ty Adams, even if he wasn't married. Shane, to her left, laughed at something Giselle said to him and Melissa's cheeks burned as she realized her hypocrisy. Shane had enjoyed performing with those women their first evening here and Melissa had taken it in stride. In fact, she admired Shane because of it. In her eyes, it showed how comfortable he was with himself and his sexuality. That was a great thing.

Her gaze returned to Ty Adams as he chuckled at something Suzanne murmured to him. Of course, Shane wasn't a married man.

The band began to play music and the conversations around the ballroom faded. An announcer strode to center stage. The music stopped and he launched into his introduction to the show. Melissa hardly heard a word he said over the drumming in her ears. Her stomach clenched as she waited for her cue. The satirical production he described was a diversion so the audience would be surprised when—

One of the waiters shouted, then ran onto the stage and whispered in the announcer's ear. Melissa stiffened.

"Ladies and gentlemen, please stay calm," the announcer said in a taut voice. "I've just been told that there are—"

A loud blast filled the room, like a cannon being fired. The audience gasped and glanced around nervously. The waiter pointed toward the doors behind them.

"Pirates!" he shouted.

Several shouts pierced the uproar from the audience and everyone stared toward the back of the room.

This was her cue. She glanced at the pirates swarming into the room, all but two the male volunteers for tonight's show. A man with long dark hair drawn into a ponytail and a large gold earring charged toward her, grabbed her wrist and dragged her to her feet. She struggled, as she'd been instructed to. Shane grinned at her and winked.

She staggered along with the pirate as he led her up the stairs to the stage, on the tail of the other captives. Within seconds, she found herself center stage. The curtains had opened, revealing a pirate ship with the mast looming behind her. The other women were being bound to various props around the stage, the pirates leering with obvious sexual intent. The women, although they tried to look fearful, appeared more turned on than anything else, gazing at their partners with a sweltering heat.

"What have we here, mate?" A second pirate, with blond, shoulder-length hair, approached her, a lascivious leer in his eye. "You seem to have the fairest of the fair."

Both the man who'd captured her and this man were professional actors. Two of the three in this performance. During the ruckus, the announcer had disappeared backstage so he could change. He would reappear shortly as another pirate.

"Aye, she's a pretty one."

Melissa stiffened as his hand stroked across her bare shoulder, then her stomach did a somersault as the second stroked her other shoulder, then slowly tugged the fabric lower.

This wasn't supposed to happen.

"No," she protested, but the first man tugged her into his arms and smothered her words with a kiss.

Such a strong, good-looking man—and with an actor's charisma. She felt herself reacting—wanting him to kiss her, to caress her. The other man moved in close behind her, stroking his hand down her arm, sending goose bumps quivering across her flesh. The heat of both their bodies enveloped her, exciting her.

The man behind her grasped her arms and panic raged through her. This wasn't supposed to be happening. Would they force her into this? Given the scenario, no one would realize it was against her will, believing it to be part of the captive tale being performed.

"*Ahrrr*, me maties. Stop or I'll chop you into shark food."

The men stepped back, glancing at the newcomer.

"Captain, we were just—"

She glanced around to see the announcer, now dressed as the pirate captain, in a wide-legged stance, hands on his hips.

"I know what you were doin'! I'm no fool, man." He strode toward her, his gaze raking her up and down. "She's a lovely lass, 'tis true, but you'll be keepin' yer hands t' yerself." He tilted his head toward the mast behind them. "Tie 'er up."

The men dragged her to the large wooden mast and fastened her hands behind her with manacles.

"This one is a virgin and, as such, will bring us a pretty penny when we put into port." He drew a dagger from his waist and held it under the taller man's chin. "She's untouched now. Make sure she stays that way."

"If she's innocent, she shouldn't be seeing this." The other pirate smiled as he glanced around the ship at the other captives.

Melissa kept her focus on the three men in front of her, trying to ignore the clothing fluttering to the floor as the pirates stripped women, and themselves.

The captain nodded.

"Yer right about that." He tugged a cloth from his pocket as he strode toward her, then blindfolded her with it.

The black satin cloth blocked out the disturbing images of sexual foreplay going on all around her with the audience smiling and watching intently. She felt enfolded in a cocoon of darkness, safe from the goings on around her.

"Maybe we can't touch her," the blond pirate said, "but at least let us look at her."

The captain grunted. "I suppose that's fair."

A second later, Melissa felt her blouse ripped from her body. Her nipples tightened from the sudden rush of cool air. Her skirt deserted her body as quickly, leaving her in only a brief, white thong—and the blindfold.

She could imagine the gazes of the pirates on her . . . gliding along her body, spiraling around her breasts . . . coming to rest on her nipples. Those traitorous buds of flesh hardened even more. She imagined the audience staring at her.

She imagined *Ty* staring at her.

Her knees felt weak. She jumped as a hand stroked along her waist to her hip.

"Captain, are you sure we can't touch?"

A loud *bang*, like a gun firing, startled her.

"Do you want to question my orders, too?" he demanded.

"N-no, captain."

"Wise."

Melissa felt someone close to her, leaning toward her.

"Don't worry, my pretty. You'll be safe." The captain chuckled. "For now."

She heard his footsteps against the wooden floor, as he traveled a few paces.

"Now to enjoy our plunder, mate."

"Aye, captain."

She could hear the sound of heels clomping on the deck as two of the men strode away. Jaunty music played and the sounds of sex surrounded her. Clearly, the other couples had progressed in their foreplay while Melissa and the actors had been commanding the focus of the play. Now she heard women moaning. One gasped and wailed in orgasm. Another begged for more and yet another demanded her captor to fuck her now. A man groaned, telling his partner how good her mouth felt, telling her to keep sucking him deep. The sounds melded together into one mass of sexual energy thrumming through her. Although she was certain the audience would be totally enthralled by the sex around her, she felt as though every eye were on her. Caressing her naked flesh. Stroking her to arousal.

Another woman moaned, and a man grunted in climax.

Melissa felt herself grow wet with need, and she couldn't understand why. This whole situation was extremely uncomfortable yet it seemed to turn her on. Confusion swirled through her as the players around her took their pleasure. As in a dream, she listened while her insides swelled with excitement.

Things quieted on the stage and she could tell that the lights grew dim. The music softened and lulled for a few moments, then the lights came up.

Ty and the others watched as the stage lights came up, signaling that a new day had dawned on the pirate vessel. The naked bodies of the volunteers so recently in the act of sex, lay slumped on the floor, as if in sleep.

Ty's gaze remained locked on Melissa, totally naked except for a brief, white thong, and tied to the mast.

Good God, he wanted her. His cock throbbed with the need. Why did she have this intense effect on him? Maybe once he had her, this obsession would fade. Surely it was just the challenge of conquering her inhibitions and allowing her to embrace her sensuality.

Whether his body still craved her or not, he would never see her

again once she left the resort on Sunday. He didn't want an entangle-
ment with her, married or not. He didn't want a woman in his life, pe-
riod. Most wanted to control a man, like Celia had. Melissa seemed
like the type who expected commitment. Those kind never knew when
to let go. Like so many of his clients who hung on, even knowing their
spouses had started sowing greener pastures.

"Land ho!" one of the actors shouted.

The captain leaned close to Melissa, and Ty wished it was him so
close to her sinfully sexy body.

"Well, me pretty. 'Tis almost time."

The volunteers roused and skittered off stage. Two pirates—the
actors—moved to center stage and stared across the audience. The captain strode toward them.

"There're a lotta people here, Cap'n," the one with the eye patch
said.

The captain nodded. "Good. We'll draw a fair coin for our treasure. He strode forward, and struck a pose before them, his hands on
his hips, and addressed the audience.

"Are ye ready to buy pirate's treasure?"

Applause, mingled with hoots and shouts, greeted his question.

He swung his arm wide, gesturing broadly to his men. "Bring 'em
on, swabs."

The volunteers returned to the stage, the men dressed again as pirates, the women wearing nothing but manacles.

The captain winked at the audience. "Ye weren't thinkin' gold now,
were ye?" Then he laughed with a pirate's cheer, and stepped to the
side of the stage.

One naked woman, a blonde with waist-long hair, stepped to the
center of the stage.

"Now how much do I hear for this fine lass?"

The bidding started fast and soared, until finally the pirate in a red bandana, acting as auctioneer, declared the winner at $560,000. One of the volunteers, Ty was pretty sure it was her husband, accompanied her from the stage and handed her over to the winner, who led her away.

Bids ran fast and furious as two more women were sold. Ty watched as two pirates unfastened Melissa from the mast then chained her hands together in front of her and led her to the side of the stage.

Next, two women were led forward.

"Now these two . . ." The captain stroked his chin. "They want to be kept together . . . and I saw no reason to turn down their request." He glanced around the room. "What man here is up for the challenge?" He chuckled. "O' course, don't be worrying too much about it. If ye get tired I'm sure they can amuse themselves for a bit."

This time bidding rocketed in a burst of shouts. Five hundred thousand. A million. A million and a half. All in the blink of an eye. At three million, the bidding died down, then trickled to 3.8 million, more than triple the previous highest bid.

The man who'd won the pair walked away with a broad smile and a glazed look in his eye, the two women pressed tight to his side, his arms around their waists.

"Now, my friends, time for the highlight of the evening. The virgin slave." The captain's gaze shifted to Melissa.

Ty felt heat in his groin as they led the blindfolded Melissa forward. Bidding started at a hundred thousand. Ty jumped in at two. It rose rapidly to two million, then the other bids began to die off. By three million, Ty had only one rival. Clearly, from the disappointed faces and the mild curses, the others simply didn't have that much money. Ty's competitor matched every bid Ty made. By four million, the other man paused and Ty thought he had it, but people at the other table tossed money in the center, which Ty's opponent collected, then bid again. Ty kept bidding, but every time the other man ran out, someone else tossed him some money. Since Melissa was the last prize, the others couldn't use the money anyway, so they used it to keep the auction going—to extend the fun.

"Five million, five hundred thousand," the auctioneer said, glancing to Ty. Ty stared at the money in his hand. Damn it, he didn't have enough.

The auctioneer started counting off, and Ty was sure he'd lost, when someone tugged on his arm. He turned to see two of the women he'd played poker with.

"Here." One handed him a wad of money. "We collected it for you. There's two hundred thousand there."

Ty smiled his thanks and raised the bid, then watched as the other man scrabbled around, imploring those around him for more money. A few people searched their pockets and tossed bills on the table. He scooped it up, doing a quick count, then raised the bid to $5,800,000 . . . a hundred thousand above Ty's.

"Going once . . ." The auctioneer glanced at Ty. "Going twice . . ."

"Oh, wait." Suzanne grabbed her small evening bag from the table and opened it. "I forgot about this. Here, Ty."

She handed him a wad of bills. A quick count told him there was just enough.

He raised his arm, snagging the attention of the auctioneer.

"Five million eight hundred and fifty thousand!"

*Ohhhh*s and *ahhhh*s emanated from the crowd. The other bidder glanced around and, when no further funds came forward, he shrugged.

"Going once . . . going twice . . . sold!" The auctioneer pointed at Ty.

Adrenaline thrummed through him at his victory—and the thought of what was to come. He and Melissa alone. Her naked. His cock strug-gled against the constraint of his pants.

The crowed broke into a cheer. The captain removed Melissa's blindfold. Her wide-eyed gaze shot straight to Ty.

Ty watched as a pirate led Melissa down the stairs. He took the chain from the pirate and let his gaze wander over her delectable, naked body, more than ready to claim his prize.

Chapter 11

MELISSA SHIVERED AS TY'S GAZE RAKED OVER HER NAKED BODY. Heat shimmered through her and goose bumps raced across her skin.

He tugged off his jacket and threw it over her shoulders. She grasped the lapels from the inside and pulled it closed, hiding her naked breasts. *He's protecting me again.* The thought skimmed through her consciousness.

Ty pulled on the chain and led Melissa toward the door. She fell in step behind him, holding the fabric of his jacket close to her. The heat of his body still emanating from the garment, and his uniquely masculine scent, warmed her.

He led her down the hall and into the elevator. Away from the crowd. He pushed the button for the next floor up and the elevator started moving. Neither of them said a word. It was such a strange situation. Melissa felt like she was in a trance.

Where was he taking her? Somewhere quiet where she could collect herself?

The elevator stopped and the doors parted. He stepped forward and the chain grew taut, tugging her after him. At the end of the hall, he opened a door and led her inside, then locked it behind him.

She glanced around. The room was lit by torches mounted on the gray stone walls. Several long, thick chains hung from the ceiling. Attached to one wall were several pairs of chains, each about eight inches long, with clasps dangling from the other end. They looked like the clip her youngest sister, Ginny, used to attach her car keys to the outside of her purse, but bigger and thicker. Stronger.

The place had the feel of a dungeon. Why had he brought her here?

Ty unlatched the chain from each of the metal bands at her wrist, freeing her wrists from each other at the same time. Good, she would feel more like herself when these darned metal bonds were off her.

But instead of freeing her wrists completely, Ty wrapped his hand firmly around her wrist and led her forward. She couldn't shake herself out of her trancelike state as she followed him. He grasped a chain hanging from the wall and lifted her arm upward, then flicked the clip onto the ring of her wrist strap.

The sharp *chink* of metal against metal cut through her daze.

"What are you doing?"

When he grasped her other wrist, she tried to back away, but he held her firmly. He lifted her arm as he eased her around to face him and his jacket slipped from her shoulders and fell to the floor, leaving her breasts naked. The nipples hardened, more because of his fervent, masculine gaze than because of the cold. He pressed her back against the stone wall, cold and hard against her naked back.

The blatant hunger in his eyes frightened her a little, yet at the same time, excited her.

"No," she protested as he clamped a chain to her other wristband. The metal links clanked together as she tugged her hands forward, pulling against the restraints. "Let me go."

"You're my slave." His deep voice rumbled through her. "I just purchased you. Why would I let you go?"

My protector has become my captor. Excitement quivered through her, but she ignored it.

"This is ridiculous. It's just a game. I don't intend to play."

His gaze slid down her body, swirling around her naked breasts, sending the nipples puckering, then continued down to her pelvis and resting on the triangle of thin white fabric covering her golden curls, then traveled back to her breasts. Adrenaline raced through her.

"I intend to play," he said, his voice husky.

She held her breath. Shock cascaded through her as she realized she wanted him to play. She longed to feel his hands caress her body. Despite her earlier conviction that he was the wrong kind of man for her, a powerful yearning burned through her.

But she couldn't just let him chain her up against the wall . . . take her like a slave he'd purchased to satisfy his sexual need.

Could she?

With her hands chained about a foot away from either side of her head, her arms spread wide, she felt supremely vulnerable. He could touch her body anywhere he wanted and she couldn't stop him. Her nipples tightened and her vagina ached. Would he touch her now? Would his hands caress her, stroke her breasts, seek out the intimate folds between her legs?

Her knees felt weak at the thought. Or maybe he wanted to pull out his long, rigid cock and thrust it into her immediately. She imagined his cock pushing into her, driving between her legs, his body ramming her against the wall.

Her vagina filled with moisture. She wanted to feel his cock inside her, wanted him to bang her hard and fast against the stone wall until she screamed.

The fact that she wanted it . . . so badly . . . shook her more than anything else. Especially with this man. Why did he have such a powerful effect on her?

"Let me go," she demanded.

"No." His eyes twinkled in amusement as he uttered the single word. Quiet and relaxed.

Her eyes widened. He stroked her hair back, tucking it behind her ear. His gentle touch triggered a cascade of tumultuous emotions within her. Dangerous and alluring

She sucked in a breath, steadying herself.

This was all a game. Surely he didn't intend to proceed against her protests.

"You can't just chain me up and . . ."

He smiled lazily, running his finger down her temple, then along her neck.

"And what, Melissa?"

His touch played havoc with her hormones.

She pursed her lips. "Exactly what do you intend to do now?" she asked.

He eased closer, only inches from her naked body and dragged his finger along her collarbone, then down her chest, ever so slowly, gliding over the swell of her breast.

"I'm going to touch you. All over." His low voice rumbled through her, sending her thoughts scattering.

She started to shiver, her insides fluttering wildly, her body longing for his touch.

"Slowly, and gently," he continued. "Stirring you to new levels of arousal. Your breasts will swell. Your nipples will grow hard." He kissed her earlobe and she jumped. "I'll cup your breasts and gently caress them, then I'll draw your nipple into my mouth and lick and suck on it until you gasp with pleasure."

"No." The word slid from her lips like a moan. Her hard nubs burned with need.

"I'll kiss down your stomach, then part your legs and kiss your long, sexy thighs and move closer and closer to your pussy . . ." He paused, watching the effect his words had on her. "But not touching it. Making you wait. Making you want me to touch you there so badly you'll open your legs for me. You'll ask me . . . beg me to touch you there. To kiss you and lick you. To suck on your clit." He smiled. "If you're very good . . . I will. Do you know what I'll do if you're bad?"

She gazed at him, mesmerized, shaking her head.

His voice lowered. "I'll make you wait. I'll kiss down your legs, I'll lick your calves, then I'll kiss up your thighs again."

Her legs parted a little.

"What then?" Her voice came out hoarse and needy.

"Then I'll wait to see if you open your legs for me."

Her thighs parted a little more.

"And then?"

He slid his finger down her belly, catching on the elastic of her thong, tugging it down. He glided past the slick flesh hidden by her curls . . . so close, but not touching her there. A whimper escaped her lips. She wanted him to touch her there. To stoke the fire his words had ignited. To show her the meaning of true desire.

He stroked her inner thigh, an inch or so from her hot opening. Her legs opened more.

"What would you like me to do?" he asked.

He leaned in and kissed her earlobe, breathing into her ear. She sighed.

Oh God, she needed him so badly.

"I want . . . I want you to touch me," she admitted.

"Where?"

She arched her pelvis forward.

"There."

His eyebrows arched.

"Where?"

Oh, don't make me say it.

"There." Her voice strained with her desperation.

His fingers slipped under the elastic of her panties and he tore them away, exposing her golden curls to his intense gaze—which made her burn all the hotter.

"There?" he asked, stroking his finger up her thigh again. Getting close. Oh, so close.

"Yes," she wailed.

She bent her knees, trying to slide down onto his finger but he drew his hand back.

"Oh, you naughty girl. You've been bad. Now I must make you wait."

"Nooo."

Her mournful moan transformed to one of pleasure when she felt his hot mouth cover her nipple. She sucked in a breath. He flicked his tongue over the tip of her nipple, teasing. It felt incredible.

"Yes." She wanted more. So much more.

He sucked her into his mouth. Her nipple was so hard it ached. He switched to her other nipple and it swelled in response.

His hand, still caressing her thigh, slid upward. She made no move, wanting to feel his touch on her wet, sensitive flesh. He slid along her slit.

"Yes."

One finger, then two pushed inside. He moved them in and out. He sucked on her nipple, drawing it deep into his mouth. His fingers caressed her inside passage. Exquisite pleasure spiraled through her . . . then slowly faded as he withdrew his fingers. His mouth released her nipple, leaving it cold and wanting. And hard as rock candy.

"What . . . ?" She stared at him.

"You asked me what I'm going to do to you. I didn't finish telling you."

"Tell me," she pleaded.

He leaned close to her face, his lips less than an inch from hers. So close. She wanted to feel them press against her, to feel his mouth move on hers in a seductive kiss, to meld their tongues together in a passionate dance.

"What I'm going to do," he murmured in her ear, "is . . ."

She held her breath while he lingered there, his breath sending electric tingles dancing along her neck.

"What?" she pleaded, risking the punishment of delay.

He tilted his head to glance at her, a smug smile crossing his face. He nibbled her earlobe.

"I'm going to fuck you." His soft, seductive words rippled through her, triggering electrifying need. He eased closer, pressing his body against her, holding her against the wall. "I'm going to thrust into you, hard and deep, banging you hard against this cold, stone wall."

She could feel the stone against her naked back, contrasted against the hard heat of his body. She almost moaned as she imagined his long, hard cock gliding into her, thrusting faster and faster, making her come in an explosive climax.

"I'll drive my cock into you so deep . . ."

She couldn't believe how intensely turned on his coarse description made her.

"Yes."

"So hard . . ."

She moaned in need.

Somehow she knew being with Ty would surpass anything she'd ever experienced before. Even with Shane. Because here, with Ty, she felt something wild rising from deep within. Something reckless, and totally uninhibited.

His finger swirled over her clit.

"Oh God. Please."

"Please what, Melissa?"

"Please do it."

His finger dabbed her clit and the sensitive nerve endings burst in tiny explosions of pleasure.

"Do what, my love?" he murmured against her ear.

"Drive your hard cock into me. Fuck me against the wall."

Oh God, she couldn't believe she was saying these things. What was he doing to her? Whatever it was, it was incredibly erotic.

She felt his hands fumble, then something hard and hot press against her flesh.

"Oh yes . . ."

His cock. The head nudged into place against her slit. She desperately needed him inside her.

"Oh God. Fuck me."

He slid in a little, his cock head stretching her, gloriously opening her to his invasion . . . then pulled back.

"Noooo," she wailed.

He stepped back and smiled. She glanced down to see his erection jutting out of his pants. Long. Hard. She longed to touch it. To taste it.

She stared at him, wide-eyed.

He wrapped his hand around the shaft and stroked its length, a half smile curving his lips. She felt light-headed . . . staring at his rigid cock. . . .

"Do you want to touch it?" he asked, as if reading her mind. He stroked his rigid rod again.

She nodded.

He released his cock and leaned forward, nuzzling her neck, then lightly kissing her mouth. He drew her lower lip into his mouth and nibbled lightly, then sucked. His tongue teased the insides of her lips as he stroked around them, then slid inside her mouth. She drew on his tongue, sucking softly, pulling him a little deeper. Their tongues tangled and curled together, then his slipped away. Her wrists strained against the metal bands in frustration. He kissed down her neck then along her shoulder. His mouth traveled downward, then captured first one nipple, then the other. She moaned softly. He slid farther down, pulsed his tongue into her navel, then lapped at her belly. A moment later, the tip of his tongue caressed her pubic curls, then dabbed lightly over her clit. She gasped, then moaned as glorious sensations burst through her.

He sat back on his heels and glanced up at her.

"You seem to want something, but I wonder what."

"I want you to lick me. There."

"Where?"

"My . . . pussy."

He leaned forward and licked along her slit. He stopped short of her aching button, then licked her again. Still, he stopped short of that needy bundle of nerves.

"My . . . clit. Lick my clit."

He dabbed his tongue against it, then sucked lightly.

She gasped as an orgasm slammed through her.

"Oh God . . . oh yeah . . . oh God!!!!"

She gasped for breath, again and again, as he sucked and prodded, driving her higher and higher.

Finally, she slumped against the wall, sucking in air to fill her aching lungs.

Just as she'd found release from the tremendous need he'd awakened in her, he began to suck her nipples again. One after the other, stoking the flame of her desire yet again.

"I want you to do something you've never done before. Something you'd like to do." He kissed her, stroking the inside of her mouth with his tongue.

She sucked lightly on it, then flattened her tongue against his. He eased away. The movement of his hand drew her gaze downward. His fingers, wrapped around his rock-hard cock, stroked up and down. Her mouth watered.

"What would you like to do?"

"I want to . . . touch your cock." She gazed at him intently. "I want to suck it."

"Tell me more."

"I want to lick the tip. I want to take it in my mouth and suck it deep inside. I want to suck it so deep, I can lick your balls."

Oh, it felt so naughty talking this way. It gave her an intense rush. She'd never behaved this way with anyone before.

His midnight eyes darkened and he stroked her cheek.

"I'd like that." His deep, lust-filled voice sent tremors through her. His lips nibbled her earlobe. "But I bet you've sucked cock before." He kissed along her jaw line, then under her chin. "I want you to do something new."

"I've sucked cock, but never yours," she pointed out persuasively, "and . . ."

"And?"

"I've never swallowed."

A smile spread across his lips and he unclasped one of her wrists, then the other. He drew her a few feet to the left and drew her arms down, then attached both of them to a single ring on the front of a cushioned bench. She watched Ty strip off his clothes, baring first his broad, muscular chest. He tossed his shirt aside, then dropped his pants to the floor, briefs and all, revealing the glorious length of his rigid cock. His testicles hung like counterweights below it.

He sat down on the comfortable bench seat, which placed her hand within inches of his balls. She stroked them.

"Mmmm." His eyelids fell closed. "That's right, honey. Touch me."

She stared at the big, beautiful head of his magnificent erection as she tucked her right hand under his balls and cupped them in her palm. She stroked them with her left.

"I really want you to suck my cock, sweetheart. But first, lick the end."

She leaned forward and licked it.

"Yeah, now stroke your tongue around the head."

His words rippled through her, melting her insides. She'd never been so intensely aroused.

She lapped her tongue around the ridge of his purple cock head, dipping under the crown. She dragged the back of her tongue down his shaft, lapped lightly at his balls, then licked up to the head.

"Oh yeah, baby. That's great."

His hands cupped her head, then stroked gently through her hair. She opened her mouth and captured the very tip of him in her mouth, swirling her tongue around and around the scant territory of flesh, wanting to tease him like he'd done to her.

"Yeah. Now suck it deep into your mouth."

She drew more of him in, until his entire cock head was in her mouth. She swiveled her head from side to side as she rotated her lips around his enormous shaft, teasing the underside of the crown. He moaned loudly.

She dove downward, taking him as deep as she could, while her hands stroked and teased his balls. He dragged in a deep breath. She sucked on his cock, pulling and pulsing her mouth around him, squeezing him, then releasing. She drew back, gliding along his cock, her mouth squeezing him firmly.

"Oh God, Melissa."

She dove down again, then drew back. Her head bobbed up and down as she fucked him with her mouth. Tight and hard. Stroking him. Sucking him. She felt his body tense and she knew he was close.

She released his cock and it bobbed back and forth, the kid-leather flesh drawn impossibly tight. He groaned.

"Are you going to come?" she asked, her voice sultry.

"I almost did."

"Really? Maybe I should stop now."

He growled and drew her head forward until her lips barely grazed his straining member. She smiled and kissed his shaft, then dropped her head down to his balls. She lifted them in her hands and nibbled one with her lips, then slowly drew it into her mouth. She licked it and pushed it against the roof of her mouth with her tongue, squeezing it gently.

"Oh, yeah. Honey, that's incredible."

He sat back, raising his lower body to give her better access. His hand wrapped around his cock, keeping it out of the way as she drew the other sac into her mouth. She squeezed it within her mouth, then caressed each in turn with her tongue. Finally, she released them and licked up his shaft. Ty's hand dropped away as she nibbled the tip of his cock, then swallowed him deep.

She glided up and down in earnest, feeling his body tighten once again. This time she kept on sucking and squeezing, bobbing up and down.

"Oh man. I'm going to come. Yeah, honey. That's it."

She sucked hard and hot liquid erupted into her mouth. She swallowed, but more kept coming. She gulped and sucked continuously as he filled her. The salty-sweet taste lingered on her tongue as she licked his drained cock, then released him.

He leaned forward and brushed her lips in a sweet, gentle kiss.

"That was just . . ." He shook his head. "Incredible."

He kissed her again, this time cupping her face tenderly in his hands.

He stood up and released both her hands then turned her around and sat her on the padded bench. He clipped each of her wrists to chains attached to the bench.

He reached for her, curling his hands around her face and kissing her, then drawing her into an embrace. Her hands hung limply in front of her as he held her close, his mouth exploring her in a heavenly show of passion, his tongue curling inside her, stroking her tongue. He released her mouth and kissed along her jaw to her temple, which he nuzzled. Goose bumps fluttered along the flesh of her arms at the delightful sensations.

He eased back, his dark eyes simmering with desire.

"I want you to do something for me."

He dabbed the tip of his tongue against one nipple, the barest hint of a touch. He dabbed the other in the same way, then returned to the first. He dabbed gently, and lightly, igniting a deep yearning within her. She arched her back forward, but he shifted away, keeping his touch light and maddeningly unfulfilling, but with the promise of so much more.

He dabbed again, then drew her into his mouth. Briefly.

"Ohhhh . . ." she wailed in disappointment.

"Will you do it for me?"

"What?" she asked, her head nodding despite not having a clue what it was.

He shifted to his knees in front of her, his semi-erect cock bobbing up and down.

"Touch yourself."

She flushed at the thought, but as he watched her with intense desire, she realized she wanted to. For him.

This wicked man lit a fire inside her, making her want to do wild, sexy things. Things she'd never wanted to do before.

Her hands couldn't reach her breasts, so she stroked along her opening. His eyes glazed in lust. She slid her finger inside and swirled around. He watched her every movement. Her other finger slid to her clit and she dabbed the end.

Oh God, that felt good.

But she would prefer his touch.

Her breathing accelerated as she stroked her sensitive clit. She leaned back against the alcove wall, arching her breasts forward as her finger vibrated on her tiny mound, sending wild pulses of pleasure jolting through her. Her breathing accelerated and she raced toward release.

He grabbed her hands and tugged them away, then wrapped her fingers around his cock. Hard and heavy in her hands. Fully erect again. She squeezed and stroked, then pulled him toward her, nudging his cock against her hot, wet slit.

He groaned, then jerked forward, impaling her in one clean, smooth thrust. She squeezed him inside her. His long cock filled her so incredibly full. She wanted him to move now. He would easily drive her to another orgasm in a few strokes.

"Fuck me," she demanded. "Fuck me hard like you promised."

A devilish grin claimed his face.

"Chained against the stone wall? Where you'll be totally vulnerable to me?"

"Yes, now. Do it!"

He flicked her chains free, then wrapped his hands around her waist and drew her forward, off the seat. As he shifted her sideways, his cock slipped free and she moaned in frustration. He flattened her against the wall, his body holding her fast against the cold stone. Within moments, he'd attached her wrists to the chains again, and she stood before him, her arms spread wide.

"Tell me again what you want."

"Fuck me. Please. I want you to—"

He moaned and thrust forward. His cock impaled her in one sweet, long thrust. She was so turned on she could barely remain still. She felt the familiar waves begin.

"Fuck me hard," she urged. "Ram it into me." She couldn't believe the words coming out of her mouth.

He drew back and thrust forward again. The waves crested higher.

"Harder." She whimpered, feeling them swell. "Oh, please. Fuck me harder."

He groaned and thrust again, then again, harder and faster. She wailed as the intense pleasure swelled around her, robbing her of air. She sucked it in, deep and fast, then moaned long and hard, the orgasm sweeping her away.

Still he pounded into her. Another orgasm pummeled though her. Then another.

"Oh my . . ." She sucked in a breath. "Oh God."

Consciousness cracked wide as she plummeted into the most explosive orgasm she'd ever experienced.

She slumped against the wall, letting her wrists fall loose against the chains. His hands stroked gently up her sides.

"Oh, you are a dirty girl." He nibbled her ear. "What else do you want, dirty girl?"

She sighed.

"I think I'm pretty much done."

"No, I think there's something else you might like."

Her brow furrowed. She couldn't think what he might be alluding to.

"Something else you've never tried before."

He unclasped her wrists, turned her around, then drew her to the bench again and clasped them to the front of it, with her facing the wall, forcing her to lean forward with her derriere pointing upward. She had to grasp the edge of the bench seat to keep her balance. His hands caressed in circles over her buttocks, then he spread her cheeks.

"Oh, no. I don't think so."

But the movement of his hands was soothing.

"I think you'd like to try it."

She strained her head around, glancing at his enormous cock. Fully erect. Dangerous looking.

"There's no way your huge cock is going to fit in *there*."

He slid his arms around her waist, drawing her back against his hard, muscular body. His lips caressed the side of her neck.

"I won't hurt you, Melissa."

He didn't have to tell her that. She knew. Deep down inside.

His hands stroked over her breasts, then cupped them. They felt incredibly warm in his big, strong hands.

"You won't mean to, but it's just too big."

He smiled and stepped back. He opened a drawer in a cabinet a few feet away. She watched him open a tube and spread lubricant over his cock. She longed to stroke it herself. He returned to her and his slippery fingers stroked along her ass, then concentrated on her puckered opening. He worked the warm gel into her opening, then slid one finger inside, then another. It felt odd at first then, as he rotated them around, first one way, then the other, stretching her, it started to feel . . . erotic. He squeezed more gel onto her ass, then pushed another finger inside.

A moment later, he drew his fingers out and his cock head nudged her opening. Immediately, she stiffened. His other hand stroked along her spine and he kissed her ear.

"Relax, sweetheart."

She forced her muscles to relax a little.

"As I push inside, you push out with your muscles. That will open you."

He eased forward, his cock forcing her opening to stretch around him. She started to tense, until his hand slid around and glided over her clit.

"Ohhh."

"Push out," he reminded.

She pushed and his cock head slid into her.

"Oh." She froze.

His finger stroked her clit again and pressed against her pelvis, bringing her ass back against him. He pushed deeper into her and she sucked in a breath as her body stretched around his huge, rigid rod. He held her tight against him, his cock fully immersed in her.

It felt . . . incredible. Her anal passage was stretched tight around his amazing cock. The thought was intensely erotic. His finger quivered on her clit and she wailed. He held her tight, his cock simply filling her.

He kissed her ear, then one of his arms slid away, then returned seconds later. A whirring sounded and something bumped against her slick folds. Something stiff and vibrating. Her insides trembled as he slid it inside her.

Oh God, this was so extremely erotic. How did he know she'd longed for two cocks?

Another something brushed her clit. It was one of those vibrators with a clitoral stimulator. The delicate, trembling sent pulsing sensations ricocheting through her. Her nerve endings quivered in blissful surrender. He began to glide the vibrator in and out of her vagina, at the same time sliding his cock in and out of her other passage.

"Oh . . . yes . . ."

She had never felt so full. As the vibrator thrust inside, the clitoral stimulator brushed her clit and her nerve endings sparked like fireworks.

"Oh . . ."

In and out. His cock stretched her. The vibrator pulsed into her.

". . . my . . ."

Front and back. Thrusting . . . pulsing . . . quivering . . .

". . . God . . ."

Ecstatic pleasure swelled over her as he erupted inside her. The sensation of his semen filling her set off a chain reaction of bursting, pulsing pleasure catapulting through her. Every nerve ending seemed to contract then explode in rapturous abandon. She moaned, riding the blissful waves of delight.

Finally, she slumped forward, gasping for air, and he hugged her close.

"Melissa, you are incredible."

He kissed her neck, then drew the vibrator from inside her. A moment later, his cock slipped free of her ass.

He released her wrists and turned her to face him, then drew her into his arms and kissed her deeply. The warmth emanating from him filled her heart.

Ty held her against his body, amazed by the effect she had on him. Her warmth, her ultra sexy femininity, her sweetness . . . he never wanted to let her go.

"Um . . . Ty. I'm getting a little stiff."

"Isn't that my line?"

She glanced up at him, her lips pursed.

"I bet the only thing you could get right now is a *little* stiff."

He chuckled. "Is that a challenge?"

Her eyes widened and she shook her head, a small, tinkling laugh escaping her lips.

"Oh, no. Not at all. I would not question your male prowess." She smiled. "Not after that."

He laughed, then kissed her ear. He felt almost giddy, full of a joyful happiness that could only be explained by being with this wonderful woman. Everything about her delighted him. Her sweetness. Her femininity. Her stunning sensuality.

"I take it you enjoyed your time as my slave."

"It was . . . definitely interesting."

He kissed her. "Interesting? You had so many orgasms I lost count."

She grinned. "Me, too."

He hugged her again. He couldn't resist.

He realized he really enjoyed being with her. She was funny and she'd shown an impressive willingness to embrace new experiences. He remembered how apprehensive and inhibited she'd been when she arrived at the resort, and now look at her. She had blossomed.

He released her, then tugged on his pants.

"I don't have any clothes," she pointed out.

He gazed at her, drinking in her gorgeous body. "Yes, and it suits you."

He picked up his shirt and she snatched it from him, laughing, then slipped it on.

"I guess this will have to do."

She buttoned it up as she followed him to the door. He pulled it open and they stepped into the empty hallway, but a second later another door opened and a swarm of people pushed into the hallway. When they saw the couple they cheered loudly.

Melissa's eyes widened and she clung to Ty's arm. Shane rushed forward and draped a blanket around her shoulders, then tugged her away from Ty.

"What's going on?" she asked him.

Shane pointed into the second room. Ty glanced in with her and saw a large video screen with a view of the dungeonlike room they'd just exited. *Damn*. He hadn't realized it was one of the viewing rooms.

"You mean, all these people were watching?" Shock laced her words.

Shane nodded.

Melissa's gaze, blazing with fury, locked with Ty's. He watched helplessly as her husband stole her away. Ty wanted to drag her back into his arms and carry her up to his room, to make love to her again, then hold her in his arms all night long. Maybe longer.

Damn it. He had never felt like this about a woman before. Why in hell did he have to start with another man's wife?

Chapter 12

NUMBLY, MELISSA FOLLOWED SHANE AS HE GUIDED HER AWAY from the room where she'd just shared the most incredible sex of her life . . . with Ty.

Melissa was shaking by the time Shane led her into their room and closed the door behind them, blocking out this strange world of upside-down mores. Here, in this resort, it was okay to sleep with another person's spouse, to have sex in front of a crowd of people—even to make love to a woman in front of a camera without telling her. Like Ty had just done.

It was a strange place and it frightened Melissa. It was too far from what she considered normal. Yet here she had found a part of herself that had been locked away for a long time. A part of her that reveled in this newfound freedom.

A part that frightened her more than this resort and all the people in it.

She couldn't hide from herself. She couldn't walk away and forget. She was terrified that this hidden side of her would no longer be silent. It would insist on freedom, and acknowledgment.

What would that mean when she returned to her normal life?

Shane stepped up behind her and placed his hands on her shoulders. Shudders wracked her body.

"I didn't know . . . all those people . . . watching."

She sucked in a shaky breath, suppressing a sob. She had bared more than her body. Her wantonness had been displayed to the world—or at least this world of lecherous sex addicts.

"It's okay, Liss."

She twirled around. "No, it's not. Don't you understand? All those people saw me. Watched me have sex with that man."

"No one judged you, Liss. Any of the other people here would have loved to be you . . . or him. What you two did was sexy and exciting."

She shook her head back and forth, trying to shake away his words. All she could think of were those people focused on her, some of them probably masturbating while Ty . . . while he . . .

Oh God, Ty Adams had fucked her in public. And she'd begged him to do it!

"Liss, you have nothing to be embarrassed about."

Anger flared through her. "That's easy for you to say. You're happy to go off and fuck a bunch of women in front of everyone without a second thought." Like on their first night here.

His brow furrowed. "Are you angry at me for fucking other women, or for doing it in public?"

"I . . ." Her anger deflated. She wasn't mad at Shane for being with other women, or for being open enough to do it in front of others.

She rested her hand on his shoulder.

"I'm sorry. I shouldn't have said that." Her lips compressed into a tight line. "I don't understand, though. Why didn't you stop it?"

"You went with him of your own free will. And you certainly seemed to be enjoying yourself. Why would I stop it?"

"But you know me. I would never . . . in front of other people . . ."

His eyebrows arched.

"And yet you volunteered to go up on stage and be part of the show."

"But I told them I didn't want to take part in any sexual activities."

"And then got tied to a mast, stripped naked, then auctioned off as a slave. Not once did you tell them to stop. If you had given any indication that you wanted out, they would not have forced you to continue."

She stared at him, her cheeks burning hot, aware of every breath she sucked into her lungs.

He clasped her shoulders in his big, warm hands. "Liss, I think you wanted to be out there. I think there's an exhibitionist inside you begging to get out." He smiled warmly. "And I think it's great. Letting go of your inhibitions and trying out new things is good for you."

"But . . ." She sucked in air so she could continue. "What if I can't go back to . . . being a good girl?"

He chuckled. "I hope you don't."

She frowned and thumped him on the shoulder.

"Liss, you're always a good girl. You follow all the rules and take your responsibilities seriously. You aren't about to toss everything aside and turn into a hedonist." His eyes twinkled as he grinned. "But I hope you continue to allow yourself to be a bad girl sometimes."

Confusion swirled through her. It was all too much too soon.

She shivered and Shane took her in his arms and held her close. She clung to him, losing herself in his embrace . . . in the warmth of his friendship.

He led her to the shower, then unbuttoned the shirt she wore—Ty's shirt—and removed it from her body. He ran the water until it was warm, stripped down, then drew her into the stall with him. After their shower, he patted her dry, then slid her nightgown over her head. She slipped her arms into the sleeves, then lay down on the bed. A moment later, he climbed in behind her and held her close.

Her confusion turned to numbness as she stared into the darkness. Minutes ticked away on the clock beside her bed, then hours. And Shane held her, close and warm, his strength reminding her she was not alone.

She didn't know what she was becoming, how she was changing, but one thing helped her through the long hours. Shane would always be there for her. He would accept her, no matter what she became. He was her best friend. And that would never change.

Ty awoke to the classical melody of Suzanne's cell phone.

"Yeah, hello?" Suzanne's sleepy voice turned businesslike. "You're kidding me. Where?" She glanced around. "Yeah, send it to me."

She skittered out of bed and across the room to the computer. "Ty, I'm going to use your laptop, okay?"

"Sure. What's up?"

She tapped at the keyboard. "Give me a minute." She clicked the mouse, then clicked again.

She drew in a breath and exclaimed, "Oh, my God!"

Ty bolted upright. He strode to the screen and shock catapulted through him as he saw Melissa's face, contorted in pleasure, her erotic moans surging through him, setting his hormones on fire.

"Melissa's in a viewing room?" Jealously raged through him at the thought of another man making love to her.

"She's in a viewing room, but not right now. This is from last night."

As if on cue, the picture zoomed out and he saw the man thrusting into Melissa. It took him a moment to recognize the man as himself.

"I thought the video feed was live only. No recordings."

"That's right. The video is fed to the TVs around the resort and to many of the video viewing rooms we have, but never recorded. Whoever took this recording not only took it illegally, they've posted it on the Internet."

Suzanne grasped Ty's arm. "Ty, if this gets out, I'll be ruined. No one will risk coming here or to any of my clubs if they think their activities might be made public. Discretion is vital in this business."

The sight of Melissa, fully exposed on the screen, in full orgasm in his arms, sent his cock throbbing. But the thought that others could be watching, men using this as a fantasy to masturbate to, set his blood boiling in a different way.

His fists clenched. He would find out who did this and throttle the life from them. But first, he'd get this disaster off the Internet as soon as possible.

Melissa sat cross-legged on the blanket and watched the seagulls gliding lazily overhead. A handful of guests sat on colorful towels sprinkled across the wide, white beach. The waves washed softly along the sandy shore; the steady pulse of the ocean was soothing.

No one stared at her. No one seemed to notice her at all. Not like she'd feared.

"Music?" Shane asked.

"Sure."

He pulled his MP3 player from the backpack along with a small speaker stand, then he set the unit into it. He pushed a button and soft music began to play.

Shane opened the picnic basket and drew out containers. He opened several and handed her a croissant packed full of chicken salad. He popped the cork on a tall, green bottle then poured bubbly white wine into two plastic wineglasses. The sandwich was delicious and the wine even more so. By the time she'd finished the last bite, Shane had refilled her glass twice. She felt more relaxed than she had been the whole trip.

Maybe she had made too much of a fuss over what had happened last night. Although the thought of all those people watching her making love—or rather, having sex—with Ty had mortified her when she'd first found out, right now she didn't feel that way. Her thoughts slipped back to last night, to when Ty held her in his arms. She thought about Ty's body tight against hers, his big cock deep inside her, and all she could think of was how much she still wanted him. She would do it again, she realized. Under the same circumstances.

Despite the people watching.

From deep inside her subconscious, a thought curled through her, surfacing as an astonishing certainty that the people watching would not just be endurable, they would be desirable. Knowing people—strangers—had watched them actually made it more exciting.

Was Shane right? Did she enjoy being an exhibitionist? Or, rather, would she if she allowed herself to be?

She glanced around the beach and noticed several of the men had shed their bathing suits, and one or two women had bared their breasts. It reminded her of last night and how her clothes had been stripped from her body. Her skin flushed at the thought of the audience gazing at her naked body.

She glanced around to see Shane watching her intently.

"If this is making you uncomfortable, we can go back to the room," he said.

She smiled and shook her head. Shane was so sweet. He'd brought her out here, where there weren't many people, so the two of them could enjoy the afternoon without her feeling she was a spectacle.

"It's fine. I'm getting used to the nudity and . . ." She glanced at a naked couple sitting on beach towels several yards away and noticed the man's hand stroke over the woman's breast. ". . . the public displays of affection."

Everyone here seemed so free and relaxed, with an easy acceptance of each other. Melissa actually found it quite appealing.

She wanted others to accept her like that. She wanted to accept *herself* like that.

If that's what she really wanted, this resort was the perfect place to take the first step.

She smiled and reached behind her, unfastening the hook of her bikini top. A mischievous smile curled her lips as she locked gazes with Shane. His gaze dropped to her chest as she drew the slim strap of her bikini halter top over her head. She released the skimpy, turquoise garment and it fell to the ground.

Shane grinned, his gaze caressing her naked breasts. "I see you're feeling a little more relaxed."

She grinned broadly and stretched her arms high in the air, then tucked them behind her head, luxuriating in the feel of the sun and the soft ocean breeze caressing her breasts.

Shane's eyes glittered as his gaze fluttered over her breasts, then settled on her face. Her nipples pushed forward, proud and hard.

"Melissa, you are an incredible woman."

"You got that right."

Melissa started at the sound of Ty's voice. Behind her.

She turned around, lowering her arms, resisting the urge to cover her breasts. The sun, behind him, set him in silhouette. She couldn't make out his expression, but she could sense the exact moment he became aware of her state of undress.

"I'm sorry, I . . ."

Melissa was absolutely amazed. The confident Ty Adams actually at a loss for words? Nonplussed by the sight of her naked breasts?

She held her head a little higher, feeling a power pulsing through her. She could strike a man mute by simply thrusting her naked breasts in his direction.

"I didn't mean to intrude. I was hoping to talk to you for a few minutes."

"Well, I was thinking of going for a swim. Want to join me?"

Ty glanced toward Shane, who lifted his spy novel and wagged it back and forth.

"Don't worry about me." Shane lay back, resting his head on a rolled up towel. "Have fun."

Melissa pushed herself to her feet and strolled across the hot sand alongside Ty. She was very aware of her naked breasts bouncing slightly as she walked—and of every male eye watching them. Including Ty, though with surreptitious sideways glances.

Her nipples pushed forward and she felt her insides tighten. Good heavens, this was turning her on.

They reached the water's edge, the sand damp beneath her feet and warm water washing over her ankles. She waded deeper, Ty by her side. The water washed over her calves, her thighs, her waist, until it swirled across the underside of her breasts. She shivered, despite the hot sun beating down on her shoulders and back. Her nipples puckered impossibly tight as the water washed over them. Not cold, by any means, but cooler than the air.

"Melissa, I came out here looking for you. To apologize about last night. I didn't know about the audience. I never would have—"

"I know. It's fine."

His eyebrows drew together. "Last night, I would have sworn you were angry with me."

"I was, but I've thought about it and realize you have nothing to apologize for. Even if you had known about the audience, it wasn't your responsibility to watch out for me."

"That's true, but I would have. If I'd known you didn't know."

At the tender look in his eyes, her breath caught.

"Just like you watched out for me the first day," she said softly. "In the numbers room. I really appreciated that, you know."

Ty realized he liked to watch out for her. It didn't mean she was dependent. It just made him feel needed.

They stood in silence for a moment, the pulsing of the ocean waves rocking them back and forth.

She stepped toward him, her naked breasts bouncing in the water. She cupped his face in her hands and kissed him.

His arms slipped around her waist and he drew her against his body and claimed her lips with a tenderness that startled them both. She tightened her arms around him and her nipples pushed into his chest, hard as pearls. He hardened immediately.

God, he couldn't keep holding her like this, her naked skin teasing his, making his groin ache with need. Not when he couldn't slide into the warm embrace of her body. And he wouldn't do that out here in public. Not with her. Not after last night.

He released her.

"Melissa, I need a little distance here."

She grinned. "Or you'll ravage me right here in the water?"

He smiled, but uncertainty shuffled through him. "That's right."

Her grin widened and she dragged a finger across his shoulder. "Maybe I'd like that."

Her hand slid down his stomach then he felt her hand encircle his straining cock. She stroked him, her gentle hand gliding over his length, driving him crazy.

"Melissa, if you keep doing that I'll . . ."

"Yes?" Her eyes glittered. She kissed him again, thrusting her tongue deep into his mouth.

Her nipples pressing into his chest were driving him wild. He wrapped his hands around her buttocks and lifted her. Her legs wrapped around him, the heat of her pussy pressed against his cock.

Their lips parted and he sucked in a breath.

"Melissa? Out here in front of all these people?"

As an answer, she guided the tip of his cock to her hot opening. She pushed the crotch of her bikini bottoms aside and, before he knew it, his shaft slid inside her. She opened her legs wider and he thrust into her by rocking her body forward and back. They bobbed rhythmically in the water, the sun warming their skin and the sea breezes caressing them.

She kissed along his jaw, then murmured in his ear, "Yes, Ty. Go in deeper. Fuck me hard."

The dirty words, coming from sweet little Melissa, burned through him, blazing a trail of pure, lusty need. He slammed into her hard.

He thrust faster and faster.

"Oh, Ty." She sucked in a breath. "Please . . ."

He could feel the orgasm shudder through her body.

She whimpered. "More . . . yeah . . . yeah."

She moaned loudly, which changed to a long, languorous wail.

"Oh God, Ty." She slumped forward, her head resting on his shoulder.

He held her like that—his cock embedded inside her, her body snuggled against him—until he couldn't hold her any longer. He released her and she slid to her feet. He felt cold as his cock slid free of her warmth.

"That was pretty incredible," he said. "I take it you've decided you like being watched."

"You think people were watching?" She grinned impishly.

He glanced around and noticed dozens of spectators eyeing them from the beach. "Oh, yeah."

She grinned. "I guess I'm . . . opening up a bit. Being in this environment . . . at this resort . . . makes you learn a lot about yourself."

He was amazed. And to think he'd once thought she couldn't stand on her own two feet. She might balk at a new situation at first, but she quickly adapted—allowing herself to grow.

Melissa really was an impressive woman. A woman he could see himself spending a lot of time with. Under other circumstances. If only she weren't married.

He squeezed her hand. "Does that mean we'll have to do it in front of an audience for the rest of the weekend?"

She smiled up at him. "Oh, I think the novelty of being in a private place . . . for us . . . could be quite a turn-on."

Chapter 13

TY STROLLED DOWN THE HALL TO THE ROOM HE SHARED WITH Suzanne, feeling like he was walking on air. He would be meeting Melissa in a couple of hours for the game they had signed up for this evening, but he would love to turn around right now and go find her again. He just couldn't get enough of her.

It was too damned bad she was a reporter who held Suzanne's future in her hand—and a married woman at that. Ty kept telling himself she had come around, that there was no way she would trash the club, but the fear still spiraled through him.

He opened the door and stepped into the room.

"Hey, stranger. Did you straighten things out with Melissa?" Suzanne, who'd been curled up in the easy chair reading, put her book down on the table beside her.

His lips curved into a smile as he remembered the delights he'd enjoyed with Melissa.

"Oh, yeah."

She grinned. "I see. So, have you two signed up for the games tonight?"

"Yeah." He could hardly wait. He had sensed Melissa's interest in a ménage à trois and had suggested they sign up for a game with another couple—or more. "What about you? Got plans this evening?"

"Yeah, I'm going to spend some time in the management office. I want to see if they've come up with anything on that video of you and Melissa. This morning, I told them to check all the video feeds to see if any had been tampered with. Hal suggested that someone might have just pointed a video camera at the television and recorded that way. Then there'd be no way of tracking it."

Ty's gut clenched at the thought of that video circulating around the Internet.

"That's true, but the quality of the video seemed better than that," he said. "Do you want me to hang around? I could be of help."

"No, way. I need you watching Melissa."

"But—"

She pushed herself to her feet and lightly whacked his arm, a big grin on her face.

"Get over it, Ty. So I'm paying you to get your rocks off with a pretty lady? What are friends for?"

He didn't remind her that he wasn't going to take her money. Knowing Suzanne, she'd find some way to make him take it.

She strolled to the door.

"Have fun." She grinned, then closed the door behind her.

Ty sat down at the computer. He had work to do, too. He signed on to the administrative account Suzanne had given him access to and sorted through the e-mail records. He could check e-mails sent by any guest over the resort's wireless network, but the only ones of interest to him were Melissa's and Shane's. So far, Shane had not accessed e-mail at all and Melissa had read and responded to a few messages. Ty had learned that Melissa had two sisters, one with three kids, and that she'd be joining them for dinner the Sunday after she returned. They'd asked her how her vacation was going and one had expressed surprise at Melissa going on vacation again so soon after a trip to Hawaii with Shane.

Ty pushed down the jealousy that arced through him at the thought of her alone on the beautiful, romantic islands of Hawaii with another man—even though that man was her husband. *Especially* since that man was her husband. Ty felt a sickening pull inside his stomach at the fact that she was married to someone else. At the knowledge that he could never have her as his wife, to come home to every day, to kiss and cuddle in front of a roaring fire on a cold winter's day. To have kids with. To grow old with.

Shock jolted through him as he realized the direction of his thoughts. He'd never even contemplated any kind of commitment with a woman let alone kids and retirement. What the hell had Melissa Woods done to him?

And why the hell did he like it so much?

He perused the computer screen and realized that Melissa was currently on an online chat with someone. His stomach churned as he clicked open the chat session in progress from Melissa's room. He didn't want to spy on her, but it was his job. He had an obligation to Suzanne.

He quickly read over the log showing the messages exchanged to this point.

JANET_RUNS_WITH_SCISSORS: *Melissa, you there?*

MELISSA_w: *Hi, Janet. How was your vacation?*

JANET_RUNS_WITH_SCISSORS: *It was great. Lot's of food on the ship and, more importantly, lots of fabulous men. I've got some stories that'll curl your toes. LOL. But right now, what I want to know is, are you really at The Sweet Surrender in St. Haven?*

MELISSA_w: *Yeah.*

Ty could almost sense Melissa's hesitation as she'd typed the single word. Hell, had her friend seen that damned video? He had to hold himself back from flying to her room, then scooping her into his arms and holding her close.

JANET_RUNS_WITH_SCISSORS: *Way to go, girl. I never figured you for a swinger. Why didn't you ever tell me? With all the stuff I've told you . . .*

MELISSA_W: *It's not like that. I'm just here to . . . look around.*

JANET_RUNS_WITH_SCISSORS: *Yes! Finally. You're going to pitch a story, aren't you? Bob will absolutely love this. It's sexy and controversial and will absolutely bring in the viewers. What's your slant?*

Ty's gut clenched. He realized he'd pretty well convinced himself Melissa wasn't the type to pitch some sleazy story to a news network just for ratings. Now seeing evidence in black and white—

MELISSA_W: *No slant. I'm not pitching a story. I'm here because*

Ty had finally caught up to their exchange and the sentence hung before him.

JANET_RUNS_WITH_SCISSORS: *Because what, Melissa?*

Yeah, what? Ty stared intently at the screen. Waiting.

MELISSA_W: *Because my sister is planning to go there and I wanted to check out the place. I want to talk her out of going.*

JANET_RUNS_WITH_SCISSORS: *Ginny?*

MELISSA_W: *No, Elaine and Steve.*

JANET_RUNS_WITH_SCISSORS: *I think Ginny's a little young for a place like that, but Elaine is in her late twenties and married. Aren't you being a bit overprotective?*

MELISSA_W: *You can never be too protective of someone you love.*

Ty smiled. Melissa had come here to protect her sister, not to pitch some sleazy story.

JANET_RUNS_WITH_SCISSORS: *Okay, but you're there. Why don't you take this opportunity to put together a proposal? It would be good for your career here at the station and they might even pay for your trip.*

MELISSA_W: *I don't want to pitch this story. There are some really nice people here. They aren't hurting anyone and I don't want to be responsible for ruining this for them.*

Ty felt proud of Melissa at that moment. She might have come here with a set agenda, but she'd quickly opened her mind to new ideas and she'd accepted the people around her and recognized their right to their own actions. How could he not love a woman like that?

His chest ached as he realized the feelings careening through him. Love. He loved the woman. A married woman.

No, it wasn't love. Maybe some kind of infatuation. Nothing more.

MELISSA_W: *As for paying for the trip, I don't have to worry about that. Shane paid for it.*

JANET_RUNS_WITH_SCISSORS: *You went with Shane?*

MELISSA_W: *Sure. Why not? I didn't want to come alone.*

Ty stared at the words on the screen. Why would her friend be surprised Melissa had come here with her husband? Could it be that

Melissa and Shane were separated? Was it possible Ty really did have a chance with her? Yet it seemed that she and Shane got along just fine. That didn't make sense for a couple contemplating divorce.

No, he was reading too much into her words. And whether she was married or not, he would end his involvement with Melissa at the end of their time here. He knew that he was in real danger of losing his heart to Melissa—and suffering the painful consequences. Because, somewhere along the way, one of them would fall out of love—and then the other would get hurt.

Suzanne had gotten nowhere tracking down the video. Frustration surged through her. It was bad enough that her resort would be condemned in the swingers' loops, causing business to plummet, but for it to hurt Ty and Melissa in the process was just totally unfair.

She sat down at a table in the lounge, wondering what to do with herself. Ty would be off enjoying himself with Melissa, and he deserved it. She'd never seen him so happy.

Her thoughts turned from Ty and Melissa to Shane. What would he be doing while Ty fucked his lovely wife this evening?

"What would you like to drink, ma'am?"

Suzanne glanced up at the young waiter standing beside her table. Young, well built, and sexy. His black pants encased muscular thighs and large biceps bulged from his short-sleeved black T-shirt. She'd bet that shirt hid tight abs and killer pecs.

"A Sexy Stud, please." She'd love the real thing, but one of the two house specialty drinks would have to do for now. The other, a Wanton Woman, was a favorite with the men. That's what she felt like right now. A very wanton woman. And what she wanted was sex.

He tossed her a charismatic smile, winked, then turned and walked away. Her gaze followed his tight rear end as he hustled that thing right to the bar.

Ah, to hell with it. She was hot and horny. She needed to get laid. It should be easy enough to find a willing guy, even though most of them would be involved in the games tonight.

Like Ty. He was off enjoying the couple's game with Melissa. Man, he sure had it bad for that woman. It was truly a shame she was married, because she did Ty a world of good.

With Melissa busy with Ty, Suzanne wondered what Melissa's good-looking husband was doing tonight. At the memory of his lips on her breasts, she realized that right now, she'd love him to do her.

Man, she really needed to get laid.

Hmm. She glanced at her watch. It wasn't too late to sign up for Blind Man's Lust. It was one of her favorite games, and the one for any guy left on his own—which was a lot since most couples wanted another woman in the mix, not another man. Women were so much more open to sex with another woman than men were with another man. Men often liked the idea of seeing their wife with a second man, but were too intimidated with the idea of accidentally touching another guy, or another guy touching them, while pleasuring the woman.

She smiled as the sexy young waiter returned with her drink. She signed the bill and added a hefty tip, then headed for the door. The resort only allowed as many men to enter the Blind Man's Lust game as there were women. She'd be doing the first guy on the waiting list a favor by joining the game.

Twenty minutes later, she sat in a comfortable leather armchair waiting for her man to enter. She closed her eyes and Shane's gorgeous face smiled at her. No doubt about it, the man was hot! She imagined him leaning toward her, his lips drawing closer. She could imagine his breath on her cheek, then his lips gently brushing hers. His kiss, tender and sweet, grew more passionate as his tongue slid into her mouth. She could almost taste him. Minty male. The distinctive scent of his musky aftershave filled her nostrils.

"Excuse me, Ms. Fox."

Her eyelids flipped open and she saw a hostess standing in the doorway.

"Are you ready for your guest?"

Suzanne smiled.

"Definitely."

"Jean will bring him in directly. Would you like another drink? Any props?"

She had a pitcher of cold water on a side table and a bottle of champagne chilling on ice. As for props . . . He'd be here in a moment.

"I'm fine."

The woman disappeared out the door and Suzanne tipped up the fancy stemmed glass with the last of her cocktail, drained it, then set it aside. Her fingers tapped absently on the table beside her chair. She sucked in a deep breath, trying to focus on what was to come, rather than slipping back into her daydream about Shane. She could still smell his aftershave from their imagined kiss. Another hostess appeared in the doorway, guiding a tall man with a black satin blindfold over his eyes.

Tall, with wavy sandy blond hair, broad shoulders, and full lips.

Suzanne smiled.

Shane!

"Um . . . Ty. Don't look now, but I think someone is flirting with you."

At Melissa's words, Ty glanced toward the bar to see a tall, shapely blonde eyeing him. When she caught his eye, she smiled seductively.

He escorted Melissa to an empty table and sat down, surveying the room the whole time. A couple standing on the other side of the lounge, who had watched him and Melissa with great interest when they had entered the room, approached their table. The woman, petite and curvacious, smiled brightly and the man, tall with shoulder-length sandy brown hair, offered his hand.

"Good evening." The man wore a crisp white shirt, open at the neck, and a casual jacket. Intelligence gleamed in his dark eyes. "I'm Brand and this is my wife Juliette."

Ty shook Brand's hand. He noticed a smooth, stainless steel ring on the little finger of his right hand. An engineer.

"This is Melissa," Ty gestured toward her, "and I'm Ty."

Brand nodded at Melissa, his smile broadening to reveal straight, white teeth, his gaze traveling over her in an appreciative manner.

Ty stamped down the jealousy rising in him.

"May we join you?" Juliette asked.

Ty glanced at Melissa.

"Yes, of course," she offered.

Brand pulled out a chair for his wife and she sat down, her gaze locked on Ty. Brand leaned in toward him.

"We were hoping you and Melissa would like to join us for the evening."

Ty stared at the man. This was the activity he and Melissa had chosen, but faced with this man, who wanted to make love to his Melissa, he had the urge to grab Melissa by the hand and drag her back to his room. Keep her totally to himself.

He glanced at Melissa and saw her watching the man with fascination, curiosity in her glittering eyes. He could tell she was thinking about what it would be like to have this man touch her, make love to her. Her hard nipples showed clearly through the thin fabric of her slinky, royal-blue gown. An image of the man kissing her naked breasts, his hand gliding down her flat stomach then sliding between her legs, made Ty's cock jump to attention. His jealousy swirled away.

"Juliette saw you with several ladies during the Monte Carlo night and she . . ." Brand said.

Juliette glanced down at her hands, her cheeks flushing a rosy red.

He grinned. "Well, she liked what she saw and would love to . . . be with you."

"Actually," a new male voice behind him said, "so would my wife, Yana. And I'd like to watch."

Ty turned around to see the lovely blonde from the bar, beside a dark-haired fellow in a black shirt and pants.

"My name is Trent and I would be extremely happy," his gaze fell on Melissa and he smiled, "to entertain your lovely partner."

Although Brand was a good-looking man, this newcomer was exceptionally handsome. Classic features, glossy sable hair with burnished gold highlights, styled fairly short, and a tall muscular frame. With his manicured fingernails, Italian leather shoes, and well-cut, expensive suit, Ty could tell the guy had money.

Brand looked a little intimidated.

Melissa placed her hand on Ty's arm and whispered in his ear. "This doesn't have to be a problem. I wouldn't mind sharing you with the two women if you don't mind sharing me with the two men. That way we could watch each other."

Ty smiled at her then turned to the others. "Our interest this evening was to allow Melissa to try something a little different." He glanced from Brand to Trent. "Being pleasured by two men—and it seems one of them doesn't have to be me."

Brand's eyes widened slightly and Trent smiled knowingly.

Trent's wife glanced at Juliette, then leaned in to her husband and whispered something. His smile broadened.

"I, too, saw you with the women at the poker game," the blonde said, a slavic accent coloring her words. "I think it would be very exciting to reenact the situation with this other, quite lovely, lady." Smiling, she glanced at Juliette, then back to Ty. "And, perhaps, your companion would be willing to be the third." She glanced at Melissa. "Before she has her pleasure with both our husbands."

Ty slid his arm around Melissa's waist and whispered in her ear, "What do you think?"

"They're very attractive, but . . . Do you really think we should go ahead with this?"

He could see her nipples straining against the fabric of her dress, could see the flush on her cheeks. A little encouragement was all she needed.

"That's your decision, sweetheart, and I'm okay with whatever you decide, but the thought of Trent kissing your lovely, soft lips, while Brand touches your naked breasts, really turns me on." He took her hand and slid it over the growing bulge in his pants. "I can imagine Brand's cock sliding into your pussy while Trent slowly works his way into your ass, then the two of them—"

"Okay," she murmured, breathless. "Yes. Let's do it."

Ty kissed her temple then took her hand and drew her to her feet.

"Let's go find a room."

The staff set them up with a specialty room. Mirrors along all the walls, which Ty confirmed were simple mirrors, not two-ways. Not that it mattered, since Melissa had discovered her exhibitionist tendencies. Two beds faced each other, and two couches and a couple of chairs lined the walls.

Trent wasted no time. He unzipped Yana's strapless black gown and the silky fabric dropped to the ground, pooling around her feet. Her very full breasts and jutting nipples showed clearly through her sheer, black bra, which Trent disposed of in a flash. She tucked her thumbs under the elastic of her thong and wriggled as she slid it down to her ankles.

Juliette untied her teal halter gown and dropped it to the floor, revealing lovely, naked breasts that would nicely fit in a man's hand. She disposed of her teal silk panties.

Across the room, Ty watched Melissa shift her gaze from the two women undressing to the men. They seemed in no hurry to shed their clothes and, knowing Melissa, she saw no reason to strip down if they weren't.

Yana and Juliette stepped toward Ty.

Chapter 14

TY FELT THE WARMTH OF JULIETTE'S DELICATE FINGERTIPS AS they traveled along his chest releasing the buttons of his shirt. His pants tightened for a second as Yana unfastened his belt, then she released the button. He kicked off his shoes as Juliette tugged off his shirt. Yana tugged on his pants, then pulled them over his feet. Juliette's warm hand slid inside his briefs and her fingers wrapped around his erection. Yana disposed of his briefs, staring at Juliette's hand around his cock with great fascination.

Yana licked the head of his cock with her hot tongue, then Juliette did the same. They both leaned down and began sucking his cock head from each side, facing each other. The warm, moist mouths nestled around him drove his pulse up a notch. They pivoted their heads and slid down his shaft, then wrapped their lips around him until their mouths touched. They slid upward in unison, then kissed each other. His cock twitched at the sight.

Oh, man, this was heating up fast. The problem was, Melissa and her guests might get too hot and begin while he was preoccupied. He wanted to see the men touch Melissa. He wanted to witness her pleasure. It would be a fantasy he would carry with him forever. Since he couldn't have Melissa at least he would have that.

"Brand and Trent, if you undress, Melissa might feel inclined to follow suit," he suggested. "I'd love to watch the two of you kiss her breasts while I entertain these lovely ladies."

The men undressed quickly, then settled on the bed facing the one Ty and the women occupied.

Melissa watched the men strip off their underwear, revealing two lovely large cocks. Her vagina clenched as she thought about the fact she'd be experiencing those two cocks inside her very soon. She unzipped her dress with trembling fingers, then slowly peeled it from her body. The two men watched her every move, their glittering eyes telling her they found her attractive. Her hard nipples thrust out over her demi-bra. She moved to the bed and turned around, her back to Brand.

"Would you get this for me?"

As she felt his warm fingers work at the hook of her bra and release it, she was amazed to see Ty gazing at her with unconcealed lust, despite the two women currently licking his rigid cock. Her black, lace bra fell to the floor and Ty winked at her. She dragged her fingertips over her nipples, then pinched them lightly, knowing the effect it would have on him. His charcoal eyes grew darker.

She stripped off her panties and climbed onto the bed, settling between the two naked men, their thighs pressed against hers. Trent gently stroked her shoulder while Brand leaned in and kissed her collarbone, but her attention remained on Ty as she watched the two women lick the length of his cock. Yana slid her mouth over the tip and down on him, swallowing him deep into her throat.

Melissa felt a warm hand cup her breast—Trent's—and she settled back into the pillows. Brand stroked her nipple as Juliette sucked Ty's cock-head into her mouth. Watching her pretty mouth move up and down on Ty's big cock fascinated Melissa. Ty watched her watch them and smiled. She felt Brand's mouth settle on her right nipple, then Trent captured her left. She groaned and slumped back. Despite the arousing situation on the other bed, her eyelids fluttered closed. Knowing Ty watched her, lusted after her, even while two beautiful women pleasured him, intensified her own pleasure. She wanted this, and she wanted him—and tonight she would have both.

Ty watched the two men suck on Melissa's breasts and his cock grew impossibly hard. He reached for Juliette's breast and stroked it, feeling the bead of her hard nipple against his palm. Yana leaned forward, dangling her enormous breasts over his face, so he captured a nipple in his mouth and sucked.

"Ohhhh." Yana's fingers settled over her other breast and she stroked it, then tweaked the nipple.

Melissa arched on the bed, both breasts covered by hot, moist mouths, driving her wild. The men's hands stroked down her thighs.

"Melissa, why don't you join us?" Juliette suggested. "Otherwise, Ty will be too busy to enjoy the show."

Trent and Brand sucked deeply and Melissa moaned, then they withdrew. Her pussy dripped with her arousal. They drew her to her feet and led her to the other bed. Yana and Juliette knelt over Ty and each offered a breast. He took first one in his mouth, then the other, alternating back and forth. Brand and Trent sat on the bed, Brand beside Yana and Trent beside Juliette. Each man took the neglected breast of the woman beside him in his mouth while Ty continued to alternate. Yana slid away and shifted down, settling on Ty's thighs.

"Come, honey. Sit in front of me." Yana urged Melissa onto Ty's stomach.

The heat of Ty's hard muscular stomach burned through her pussy, igniting a deep need within her. Oh God, the man was so hot.

Juliette shifted onto his chest. They all rose on their knees and Yana guided Melissa to cup Juliette's breasts. The soft, warm flesh conformed to her hands, the nipples pressing into her palms. Yana cupped Melissa's breasts and her nipples tightened. Juliette shifted forward and settled over Ty's mouth. Melissa imagined his lips pressing against her own pussy, his tongue teasing her slit. A second later, Yana swallowed his cock inside her pussy. Melissa almost groaned at the thought of his large cock pushing its way inside her own pussy, stretching her vagina on its pathway upward.

Melissa felt delicious sandwiched between the two women, Yana caressing her breasts, Juliette's puckered nipples pushing into Melissa's palms. She felt Ty's hand, hot as a branding iron, slide up her thigh, then two fingers slip inside her pussy. She moaned, an echo to Yana's and Juliette's soft murmurings. Ty's thumb stroked over her clit, and her vaginal muscles clenched around his fingers, squeezing them, trying to draw them deeper inside.

She felt herself moved up and down with the other women's movements, led by Yana as she pumped Ty's cock deep inside her. She could hear Ty's groan, muffled since his mouth was full of Juliette's pussy. His finger stroked gently but insistently on Melissa's clit, sending sparks flashing through her. Yana tightened her hold on Melissa's breasts and moved faster, up and down. She began to wail.

"Oh God, Yana's coming," Juliette cried. "I'm so close. Make me come, too." Her hands covered Melissa's hands and ground them into her breasts. "Oh, yes . . . oh, yes. Ohhhh . . . ," she moaned.

Melissa felt waves of pleasure wash through her as Ty's thumb swirled and his fingers stroked inside her. The pleasure he brought the other women intensified her own. As if his tongue swirled over *her* clit, his cock thrust inside *her* pussy.

"Yesssss. Oh, yessss." Melissa arched into Yana's hands as the orgasm pulsed through her.

Ty groaned.

"Oh yeah, give it to me, honey," Yana declared in a throaty voice. "I can feel your hot cum spurting into me."

Melissa could imagine Ty's hot semen spilling into her own womb and another orgasm exploded within her.

A moment later, feeling very sated, Melissa felt Yana shift, then dismount Ty's cock. Melissa felt a strong urge to climb onto it, but that was not on the agenda just yet. Juliette collapsed on the bed, arms and legs wide. Trent immediately climbed on top of her and nudged his huge cock against her pussy. He raised his eyebrows and she nodded. He thrust forward, filling her with long, hard cock. Melissa ached with need as she watched his shaft appear and disappear as it thrust into her.

Yana pushed Brand down on the bed and sucked his cock into her mouth. He groaned as she deep-throated him just like she had Ty.

Ty's hands slid around Melissa and she nestled back against his chest, watching the other two couples pleasuring each other. Excitement thrummed through her, knowing those two hard cocks would soon be hers—then later, Ty's cock would fill her.

Juliette cried out in climax and Trent slid from her wet pussy, his cock wilted. Yana immediately pushed him to the bed and sucked his limp cock into her mouth. Within moments, he was hard again.

"Sweetheart, I think you're on." Ty kissed her temple and she watched the two men stand up, their hard cocks bobbing up and down. "Time to experience two cocks."

Two. She gazed at them and her mouth went dry. Brand and Trent each took one of her hands and led her to the other bed.

"Both of you sit down," she instructed.

They sat in front of her, their cocks sticking straight up, staring at her.

She dropped to her knees and lapped at Trent's long, purple cock. She wrapped her lips around him and dove down, then up.

She shifted to Brand's cock and licked his red, full cock head, then swallowed it. She licked the shaft, narrower than Trent's but slightly longer. She slid down, then back to the tip, dabbing her tongue against it as she released him.

Trent's cock filled her mouth more with its broader girth. Brand's twitched when she dragged her tongue under the ridge of his crown. Trent moaned when she sucked his head, pressing it against the roof of her mouth with her tongue.

She moved into a rhythm, sucking Brand's cock to the hilt, then Trent's. One stroke each. When they were both solid as steel, she stopped and smiled at them, then stood up.

"What now?"

"Here, Melissa." Ty tossed a tube of lubricant to her.

She opened the tube and squeezed the gel onto her fingers, then grasped Brand's lovely cock with her other hand. She spread the slippery gel over his long, hard cock, applying more to the head, gliding it around under the ridge. He twitched in her hand.

He stood up and turned her around to face the bed, then stood behind her. His hands stroked over her waist and slid up to cup her breasts. He leaned her forward and spread her cheeks. She felt his cock nudge her ass. As he pushed into her, very slowly, she remembered what Ty had told her before and she pushed against him with her muscles. He continued to ease forward, past the tight band of muscles. His hands curled around her waist.

"You are so tight." Slowly, he slid forward, until his entire shaft filled her.

Ty couldn't believe how turned on he was getting watching that long cock slide into Melissa's sweet, beautiful ass. He could almost come right on the spot. His fingers curled around his cock and he stroked. The two women sat beside him, their fingers finding their own sweet spots.

Trent sat down on the bed beside Melissa. She shifted sideways, Brand holding her firmly against his body. Slowly, she tried to climb over Trent, but Brand's cock slid free. Trent grabbed her waist and pulled her on top of him. She straddled him and mounted his cock.

His long, shaft slid into her and Ty thrust back the intense need to ejaculate. He wanted to enjoy every second of this. He watched Melissa's face in the mirrored wall at the head of the bed as Brand crawled up the bed and positioned his cock against her puckered opening. Melissa stared at the mirror and her gaze caught on Ty's—and held. Brand eased forward, his cock disappearing inside her.

He was fascinated by Melissa's fascination with watching him—his pleasure intensified by her being there. A tiny part of him objected, insisting she was becoming too much of an obsession, that he wanted her too much. She was getting under his skin. He could learn to care for her and that direction led to disaster. Relationships didn't last. He'd seen that a hundred times with his clients. And his own past relationships.

But he wanted her, and there was nothing wrong with that, as long as he kept it in perspective. He wouldn't allow himself to fall for her. The fact that she was married helped. This was a brief affair that would end Sunday night when they left this sexual haven and returned to their normal lives. She would forget him. And he would forget her.

She moaned again and his insides convulsed in intense need. He wouldn't forget this, though. This would be his fantasy for a long time to come. Watching her writhe under the hands and mouths of two lovers, then accepting both their cocks into her hot, sexy body. After that, he would drive his own cock into her slick opening and blast off to sensual heaven.

He would release his obsessive feelings for Melissa, knowing they were just an infatuation that would fade with time, but he would never forget this extremely erotic scenario.

Melissa stared into Ty's reflected eyes and gasped as Brand's big, iron-hard cock stretched her rear opening again.

"Oh my God." Melissa couldn't believe the intense stimulation of having two, hard, real cocks inside her, magnified by Ty's hot gaze burning through her. Black spots flashed in front of her as she felt faint with pleasure. She sucked in a deep breath, steadying herself.

"Oh, please, push those cocks into me."

They started to move, slowly at first, one in each opening.

Ty's eyes darkened and she felt as if it were his cock gliding into her vagina, and stretching her tight back opening in an exhilarating, electric invasion.

"Yes. Deeper. Fuck me with those two hard cocks."

She said it to Brand and Trent, but more she said it to Ty. He was fucking her with his hard gaze, gliding through her body and swirling over her nerve endings like a wet, hot demon of pleasure.

They pushed deeper. In, then out. In. Deeper. Then out.

"Oh God, yes." Every cell in her body throbbed with need. "Fuck me. Fuck me hard."

In the mirror, she saw Ty's face tighten, his hand gliding up and down his cock. Watching her get fucked by two men was turning him on immensely. In a moment, she knew, he would burst with his building climax. Because he was watching her. Wanting her.

She felt pleasure flood her, washing through every crevice of her existence. They thrust. Harder and deeper. She clenched around them, loving their hardness. Loving their length. Her body pulsed with exquisite delight.

"Oh my God. Oh yes. Oh yes." She moaned, then her orgasm hit like a solid brick wall, blazing through her, searing every nerve ending. "Ohhhhhh . . ."

Brand groaned first, then Trent, as they filled her with hot semen, flooding into her in heady spurts.

She collapsed on top of Trent, then Brand on top of her. A moment later, Brand slid out of her. His soft cock dragging along her backside tickled and she began to giggle. Trent twitched inside her, reminding her he was still rigid, but she released him, still giggling, as he flopped to the side.

She fell back on the bed between them, all three of them chuckling and laughing. A second later, she became aware of Ty's gleaming black eyes staring down at her.

"My God, you are sexy." He climbed over her, ignoring the two men on either side of her.

The sight of his familiar, endearing cock, standing fully aroused, rock hard and ready to go, recharged her libido. Somehow, he had held off his release. Kept himself ready for her. Despite having been fully satisfied—by two hunky men no less—only moments before, she now felt more desperate to be fucked than ever. By Ty. Only he could satisfy her intense craving.

She wrapped her hand around his cock and nestled it against her opening. He drove into her immediately. She wrapped her arms around him as he thrust. Deeper and faster, chasing away her need. Fulfilling her desire. Satisfying a need in her beyond the physical—as if they shared a deeper connection.

She wailed and clung to him as he fucked her fast and hard. His mouth captured hers in a tender kiss—so sweet she melted into a boneless mass, just as the first orgasm slammed through her. He slowed, still kissing her, his tongue stroking the inside of her lips.

His finger pushed between them and he stroked her clit.

Her mouth pulled free from his as she gasped for air.

She wailed, long and hard, as the pleasure blasted through her in a massive eruption, bliss exploding through every cell.

His cock pounded into her, then heat flooded her womb. The sensation skyrocketed her into another orgasm.

Finally, she collapsed on the bed, Ty on top of her. A moment later, he slid to her side, his drained cock sliding out of her. She relaxed in the glow of the incredible closeness she felt to him.

Applause filled the room. The other couples thanked them, then left, each with an arm around the other's spouse. Melissa murmured her good-byes, then curled up against Ty and succumbed to sleep.

~

Ty sat staring at his inbox on the computer screen, but he couldn't focus. Memories of Melissa in his arms snuggling close still haunted him. The warmth of her body. The softness of her skin. Her face angelic in the soft lamplight.

He stretched his fingers, then curled them into his palms. Damn it, he was falling in love with the woman, which was complete folly. First, the woman was married. Second, even if she wasn't, love didn't last. He'd learned that the hard way with Celia. He'd fallen for her hard and fast, but after they'd married, he'd discovered she had a jealous streak a mile wide—and she'd always used sex as a way to manipulate him. He'd always given in to her demands to save the marriage, until the day he'd walked in on her in bed with another man. After that, something inside him had died, and he'd closed off his heart forever.

Ty clenched his fists. He didn't want to be some jerk who always let a woman control him. He had more pride than that. Yet Melissa was different. The memory of her warm body snuggled close to his bored through him. If he started a relationship with her, would he be strong enough to leave her if his feelings were no longer returned? His chest constricted in pain. In fact, he had no idea if she even shared his feelings.

He stood up and paced. Damn it, he was in love with her. And he wanted to spend the rest of his life with her. He raked his fingers through his hair. But he couldn't, for God's sake. The woman was married.

Of course, married people could take part in extramarital sex and still have the marriage work—that's what clubs like Suzanne's were all about. Could he satisfy himself with continuing a relationship with her based on sex alone? Would it be better than no relationship? Most men would be thrilled with that—hell, a week ago he would have been, too—but now Melissa had triggered feelings in him he'd never known before.

He slumped back in the chair. Even if he could live with it, the problem was a relationship based on swinging required honesty— that's why it worked—but honesty was something he and Melissa hadn't shared in abundance. He'd deceived her about being married, hidden the fact he was a private investigator, and . . .

He thumped his fist on the desktop. *Damn.* What would she say when she found out he'd been spying on her? Because if he planned to continue any kind of relationship with her, he'd have to tell her.

His cell phone chimed and he snatched it up, glad for the interruption.

"Adams."

"Hi, boss. I've got something interesting."

"What is it, Ash?"

"Shane Woods is the buyer."

"What?"

"He's the one who's buying the resort," she continued, unfazed by his snapping response. "And his name isn't Woods. It's Mason."

"So they were only posing as a married couple?"

"That's right. She's just an old friend of his, though maybe more than friends. Neither of them is actually married."

An old friend. That made sense. She cared for the guy, but not enough to marry him. In fact, it was possible they'd never even been intimate.

He snorted at the thought. No way. The guy had been sharing a room with her. Ty would bet they'd been intimate. The guy would have to be a monk not to drag her into his arms and . . . Whatever. From what Ty had seen, the guy was no monk.

"What was that, boss?"

"Huh? Oh, nothing. Good work, Ash."

He hung up and clicked the mouse, a smile spreading across his face as the fish screen saver disappeared to display his inbox again.

Melissa wasn't married. That changed everything.

Suzanne closed the door behind her and kicked off her sandals. Ty glanced up from the computer where he was busily working away. She headed for the mini-fridge and grabbed a bottle of water.

"It's hot out there." She held up a bottle. "Want one?"

"Sure."

She tossed it to him and he caught it in one hand. She took a long sip from her bottle. The cool, refreshing liquid washed down her throat.

Ty swiveled in his chair and leaned back.

"I've got some interesting news."

She sat down and crossed her legs, noticing with amusement the flicker of interest as his gaze glided along her calves, then skimmed over the swell of her breasts, pushed up by her red, underwire bikini top.

Men. So easily distracted.

"Your potential buyer didn't send an investigator to check out the resort."

"Really?"

"He came himself."

She uncrossed her legs and leaned forward.

"Do you know who it is?" Since Ty had said "he," it obviously wasn't Melissa.

This was huge. If Suzanne knew who it was, she could spend some time with him and get a handle on how he was enjoying the resort. Maybe find out any reservations he had and address those concerns. Without letting him know she knew, of course.

"Shane," Ty answered.

"Melissa's husband?"

"Actually, they're not married. They're just posing as a married couple."

Of course, because he wouldn't have been able to come as a single man. Same as Ty. The reason she'd asked Ty to come here was so she could find out who was representing the potential buyer of the resort so she could ensure things went along smoothly and that the buyer's representative would come out with a positive view of the resort. She believed in the resort and all it had to offer, and now that she had access to the man actually interested in buying it, she intended to give him a little more personal attention. Which was an especially attractive idea given it was the hottie Shane.

She glanced at her watch. Two o'clock. "You're meeting Melissa for dinner, right?"

"That's right."

She'd better work fast before Shane made a date for dinner. She had some arrangements to make, and some shopping to do. She wanted to look fabulous tonight.

She grabbed her purse and headed for the door.

"Where are you going?" Ty called after her as she tugged open the door.

She glanced at him and grinned. "To do a little shopping."

As she pulled the door closed behind her, she saw Ty shaking his head with one of those "I just don't understand women" expressions on his face.

Chapter 15

THE SWEET FLORAL SCENT WAFTED INTO THE ROOM AS SOON AS Shane opened the door. The bellman held a dozen long-stemmed red roses.

"Melissa, someone sent you flowers," he said as he signed the delivery receipt and gave the man a generous tip.

"Actually, sir, the roses are for *Mr.* Woods," the bellman said, as he handed the flowers to Shane.

"Really?" Melissa stepped beside him and breathed in the scent of the blossoms as Shane closed the door. Her lips curled up in a mischievous grin. "I wonder who sent them."

She plucked the tiny envelope from the flowers and dodged out of Shane's reach. He dropped the roses on the table and tackled her, his hands around her waist, sending her sprawling on the bed, then he tugged the envelope from her fingers and pulled out the card.

A top hat rested on a pair of ladies long, black gloves, crossed by a single red rose. He opened the card. His eyebrows rose at the words written in elegant script in hot pink ink, surrounded by several hearts.

Meet me for an exciting evening of erotic sex.
Wild Rose room. 8:00 P.M. this evening.
Your Secret Admirer

Melissa stared over his shoulder. "Wow. Hot stuff. Are you going?"

Hot stuff all right. His heart thrummed, wishing—no, hoping in some impossible twist of fate—the note was from Suzanne and he would enjoy the delights of her delectable body tonight. He'd been yearning to hold her close again ever since the Monte Carlo night.

No matter who had sent the flowers, how could he pass up such a delightful invitation?

"Are you kidding? I wouldn't miss it." He kissed her on the cheek. "You don't mind, do you?"

"Oh, I think I can find a way to occupy myself."

"Right this way, sir."

Shane followed the sexy hostess, dressed in a tailored black suit, into the Wild Rose room.

Ever since he'd received the flowers and invitation, he couldn't seem to wipe the silly grin from his face.

A secret admirer. How cool was that?

The hostess's blue eyes glinted in amusement as her pink-glossed lips curled up in an understanding smile.

"There's champagne over there." She gestured toward a round two-person dining table beside the sitting area. "The bottle is open."

Two tall flute glasses stood beside a black bottle of champagne in a glass ice bucket. Very elegant.

"Is there anything else I can get you?" she asked.

"No, I'm fine."

She clasped her hands together.

"If there is anything else you need, don't hesitate to call." She gestured to the phone by the bed.

He sat back in the comfortable easy chair, his gaze glued to the door. He felt a little like a kid at Christmas. Any minute now, his secret admirer would come through that door.

A knock sounded.

"Come in." He watched the door as it swung open, revealing a tall, shapely woman with straight, glossy black hair and bangs.

As she sauntered into the room in a fluid swirl of black satin, she smiled with deliciously sinful red lips, set off to perfection by her pert chin and high cheekbones.

"Hello." Her deep, sultry voice melted through him, sending his hormones into a rage of heat.

Her exotic herbal scent seemed familiar. This could be the delicious woman he'd made love to during the Blind Man's Lust game. But then he took in the soft glow of her skin, her delicate, high cheekbones and full heart-shaped lips . . .

"Suzanne." He grinned. "So you're my secret admirer."

She smiled warmly. "I didn't think you'd recognize me right away."

The straight, black hair and bright red lips, which were a dramatic, and highly sexy, change had distracted him, but only for a moment. The memory of her nipple pebbling under his tongue sent his hormones raging.

She wore a black satin jacket and long, skin-tight black leather pants, showing every curve of her shapely legs. With satin-gloved hands, she released the three rhinestone buttons down the front and slowly drew the jacket open, then dropped it over her shoulders, revealing only the naked, tanned flesh of her upper arms. His heartbeat accelerated. She was so incredibly sexy!

"It's a little . . . hot . . . don't you think?" Her voice was as smooth and silky as the satin she wore.

She turned around, dropped the jacket lower, then let it glide to the floor. Her back, totally bare, triggered images of this woman lying naked on the beach, her bare, round ass glowing in the sunshine. He drew in a deep breath, wanting to touch that smooth golden skin. Her black gloves, extending several inches above her elbows, hugged her arms. When she turned around, his gaze snapped straight to her nipples—totally naked, peering out of quarter-sized holes in the form-fitting, black leather halter she wore.

She took three steps toward him, the sway of her hips mesmerizing him. He wanted to reach out and stroke one of those lovely, dusky pink nipples, but she stood two yards away. If she wanted him to touch, no doubt she would let him know—and he wouldn't rush this for anything in the world.

She sat down in the chair across from him, crossing her long, lovely legs.

"So how do you like the resort?" she asked.

"I've been having a great time." He grinned as his gaze glided over her. "And it just keeps getting better."

She smiled. "I really liked the games night the other evening. Did you take part?"

Ah, was she hinting that she'd been the woman? The more he breathed in her lovely scent, the more he realized it must have been her.

Damn, he had wanted so badly to see the sexy woman as she'd moaned beneath him. Now it looked like he'd have that chance.

"I signed up for the Blind Man's Lust game . . . and I was paired with an incredibly sexy woman."

Her cherry-colored lips turned up in a smile. He longed to taste that mouth of hers again.

"I remember her delicious scent." He winked and drew in a deep breath. "Very reminiscent of yours."

"Really?" A sense of feminine satisfaction vibrated through Suzanne. She must have made quite an impression on him.

"I was with a pretty sexy guy, too."

His smug look told her he knew she was talking about him.

She settled back in her chair, resting her arms on the cushioned armrests. Her movement drew his attention back to her exposed nipples. Goose bumps danced along her flesh and her nipples pebbled.

"So do you enjoy the place enough that you'll probably come back next year?" she asked.

"There's no doubt in my mind about that."

His enthusiasm for the resort encouraged her. Hopefully, that enthusiasm would make him buy the place and all her problems would be solved. She would miss the resort terribly, but at least if she had to sell it, it was good to know it was going to such a nice guy.

"Would you like some champagne?" She rose and stepped toward the table.

She tugged the bottle from the ice bucket and poured the bubbly wine into the two glasses. The way his gaze stole across her body made her blood boil.

Shane watched as she took a sip then drew an ice cube from the bucket and, watching him with a seductive smile, dragged the ice over her nipple. He watched the nipple harden and protrude, liquid dripping from the tip as her hot flesh melted the cube—just as she was melting him to a boneless mass of need. She dragged the cube over the other nipple and he licked his lips, his mouth watering to taste one of those hard nubs of flesh.

She sauntered toward him, holding out one of the flutes. As he accepted it, her damp, gloved fingertips brushed his hand. Damp from the ice, which had touched those lovely nipples.

"Cheers." She held her glass toward him and clinked it with his, then they both sipped.

The bubbles danced around his mouth, then down his throat. He took another sip, watching her.

"What do you like best about the resort, Suzanne?" he asked.

Her eyes glinted. "Meeting sexy men like you."

She stepped away, her perfectly round, firm ass swaying. She stopped, her hands working in front of her, then her pants dropped to the floor, leaving that glorious ass naked, with only a triangle of leather at the top and a strap encircling her waist. A sexy, black leather thong. She turned around and the sight of her, wearing only long black gloves, a tight black leather bodice with her naked nipples peeking out, and a narrow triangle of leather covering her pussy, sent his heart rate skyrocketing.

She smiled and stroked her hands up her sides, then over her breasts. Her damp, gloved fingertips toyed with her hard nipples. His cock strained painfully against his zipper.

She swayed toward him, a half smile curving her lips. She leaned forward, her puckered nipples pushing out from the black leather, and brushed her lips against his cheek, then took his hands and drew him forward. He rose to his feet, his gaze locked on those tantalizing nipples. She stroked her hands over his chest and around his neck, tipping her face upward. He eased closer and gazed into her eyes, dark and simmering with pure lust.

He captured her lips and drew her against his body. Her full breasts crushed against him. He could feel her hard nipples poking into his chest through the thin silk of his shirt.

His arms tightened around her. His tongue stormed past her lips and ravaged her mouth with overwhelming passion.

Suzanne melted against his strong, muscular chest. God, this man was sexy.

Her heart thudded against her chest as she stroked over his bulge. She longed to feel that long, hard cock in her hand . . . in her mouth.

She pushed him onto the chair and knelt in front of him, a smile curving her lips. The zipper of his pants slid down easily and she grasped his big, rigid cock in her hand, stroking it within her satin-clad fingertips. But she wanted to feel the heat of him. Flesh on flesh. She tugged off one glove, then the other, and tossed them aside. He caressed her cheek as she wrapped her bare hand around his hot, steel rod and stroked.

Oh, wow, he was gorgeous. And being with him made her heart flutter.

She wrapped her lips around him and stroked downward, engulfing his cock-head in her mouth, lapping at the bottom of the crown with her tongue. She stroked his balls as she sucked.

"Honey, you're going to embarrass me if you keep that up. I want you so much I'm going to blow like a geyser."

He drew her forward onto his lap and kissed her, then eased around until she sat in the chair and he knelt facing her. He smiled as his gaze danced over her body.

"That's quite an outfit you've got there."

He stroked one nipple, then leaned forward and licked the other. They throbbed with need. He licked and sucked and she murmured her approval. As he drew hard on one nipple, she gasped, drawing near orgasm. He toyed with the other and she moaned, pleasure spiking through her. One more tug and she exploded in orgasm, gasping for breath.

He leaned back and gazed down at her, a smug, satisfied smile gracing his lips.

He tucked his fingers around the strap of her thong and drew it from her body. She parted her legs, ready for his attention, her pussy aching with need. He leaned forward and licked her, then dabbed at her clit. She whimpered.

He tucked his hands under her buttocks and lifted, then dove into her damp folds with enthusiasm. His tongue dipped into her opening and he thrust several times, then slid upward and swirled over her clit. Then he sucked lightly and every nerve ending exploded with pure pleasure. She clung to him, riding the wave of another orgasm.

She stood up and twirled him around, then pushed him onto the chair. She knelt on the chair, her legs arching over his lovely, steel erection and she grasped it and positioned it against her soaking wet pussy, then collapsed down on him. The feel of his giant cock thrusting into her nearly set her off again. His hands cupped her bottom as she lifted herself, then dropped again. They moved in a steady rhythm. Up and down, driving him into her. Thrusting her to another mind-shattering orgasm.

"Oh yes." She bobbed up and down, grasping him within her. Hot fluid filled her womb as he climaxed.

Shane watched her ride him to completion, continuing to thrust as she wailed in a long, continuous orgasm. Finally, she slowed and snuggled against his chest, his cock still buried deep inside her.

He held her close, stroking her silky cheek, enjoying her soft, warm breath on his skin. There was something very special about this woman. Something he'd love to explore in more depth. What startled him was that he found himself wishing she was not married.

Ty led Melissa into the restaurant. The theme was a drive-in movie where the booths were car seats—with a front and back seat, the back offering a little more privacy. The front dash served as a table for food and drinks, allowing a great view of the large screen in front of them, which currently showed a popular music video.

Ty had been yearning for Melissa all day and he knew it was deeper than lust. He wanted to touch her, to hold her close. To be with her, because that made him feel complete. She enhanced his life in every way and he hoped to convince her to be a part of it permanently.

But he couldn't ask her yet. First, he'd have to find a way to admit he'd been spying on her without having her turn tail and run. Before he risked it, he wanted to enjoy this one last night at the club.

He slid his arm around Melissa's waist as she stepped into the metallic blue fifties-style car. He sat down beside her and she snuggled close, her soft curves pressing against him.

"What'll you have?" A waitress stood by the side of the car, chewing gum and wearing an old-fashioned uniform.

"Sex with a Stranger for the lady and I'll have a draft."

She jotted on her pad, then hustled away. Melissa smiled at him and he smiled back, wanting to capture those sweet lips with his own, but forcing himself to wait.

The waitress returned with their drinks, then went on to the next car. He grabbed his beer and took a deep drink.

Melissa took a sip of her frothy pink drink. A little foam clung to her upper lip and he wanted to lick it from her lips, but instead he brushed his thumb over her mouth. Her gaze caught his and the heat simmering in those blue-green depths took his breath away.

He wanted the quiet intimacy of spending some private time together. Just the two of them in a romantic setting.

"We should order." He handed her one of the glossy menus that stood on its end between the sugar shaker and the napkin dispenser. He opened the other menu and studied it.

The waitress came by and took their order, then they watched the video—clips of old drive-in movie favorites—while they held hands under the table. Ty knew that the video would change from B movies to erotic in about an hour and he intended to hustle Melissa out of here before that, otherwise her newly discovered exhibitionist tendencies would kick in and he'd probably lose his opportunity to have her to himself.

"Where is Suzanne this evening?" she asked as their meals arrived. The waitress set the fancy burgers on the tray in front of them.

"Actually, she's with your husband." He watched her face, looking for any sign of jealousy. "Does that bother you?"

She might not be married to the guy, but that didn't mean they weren't involved. He wanted to know how big a competition Shane Mason would be—because Ty intended to win Melissa. As far as Ty was concerned, Shane and Melissa weren't married, so she was fair game.

"Does it bother you?" she asked.

He grinned. "I don't mind him playing with my wife as long as he doesn't mind me playing with *you*."

Her eyebrows furrowed. "But what about the whole thing? Being in a place like this, sharing your wife in such an intimate way with other people?"

The thought of Melissa as his wife going off somewhere with another man made his chest clench. Hell, the thought of her going back to the room she shared with Shane every night drove him crazy.

He could share her like he did last night, but only because they did the sharing together. Participating with other people had heightened their arousal and attraction to each other, like a potent aphrodisiac.

Melissa's skin tingled as he cupped her face with one hand and leaned close, as if he were going to kiss her, and her heart thudded at his intense gaze.

"If you were my wife, I'd never let you out of my sight."

His startling comment knocked the wind from her. *If you were my wife . . .* She sucked in a breath as she realized just how much she wished that could be true.

She expected him to capture her lips in a passionate kiss, but he didn't. He returned to eating his hamburger.

As much as she cared for Shane, she realized it was Ty she wanted to be with and her heart ached at the thought that after this weekend, she would never see him again.

They had barely finished their meals when the waitress came by and cleared their plates away, then brought them another round of drinks.

"Melissa, these past few day have been pretty spectacular. You and I seem to have something special."

Oh God, she didn't know where this was leading. The guy was married, so the only direction she could honestly see it going was him asking her to fool around with him on the side.

"I was wondering. If you weren't married to Shane, and if I wasn't married to Suzanne . . . do you think you'd—"

Her cheeks drained of blood as she stared at him, trying not to show any sign of a reaction. Did he want to leave his wife? For her?

"Ty, you're married to a wonderful woman. I couldn't be responsible for . . ." She shook her head, not wanting to utter the words out loud.

His hand covered hers.

"Relax, Melissa. I'm just talking theoretically. I wouldn't hurt Suzanne for anything in the world."

He tightened his fingers around hers and gazed into her eyes with a deep tenderness.

"Just tell me . . . If we lived in a different world, where we were both single, do you think you might . . . ?"

At his hesitation, she held her breath.

"Might what?" she finally prompted.

But he just shook his head. "Never mind. It's not really something I can ask."

Damn. Ty clenched his fists under the table. What kind of fool was he? He couldn't just come out and ask the woman if she'd fall in love with him.

Since he'd found out she wasn't really married, he'd asked himself some tough questions and he'd come to the conclusion that he loved Melissa. She was strong, yet she wasn't controlling and manipulative like Celia. Not that he'd even place his sweet Melissa in the same category as Celia.

Melissa, on the other hand, hadn't had that opportunity, so even if she had feelings for him, she would deny them. He might even scare her off. He'd seen the panic in her face when he'd broached the subject. Clearly, she'd thought he wanted to divorce his wife and run off with her. Melissa wasn't the type of woman who would break up a marriage.

Ty opened the door to the room he'd booked for this special night with Melissa. The soft light of candles, dozens of them, set the room aglow, and vases of long-stemmed red roses perfumed the air. The large, four-poster bed was turned back and the white sheets strewn with red rose petals.

The staff had followed his instructions to the letter. He smiled at the look of awe on Melissa's face.

"Oh Ty, it's . . . beautiful."

Melissa couldn't believe he'd arranged all of this. Romantic music played in the background and a bottle of champagne sat chilling on a side table.

Ty closed the door behind them.

"I'm glad you like it."

His hand slid over her shoulder, then he stroked her hair behind her ear and kissed her.

"I wanted tonight to be special. I want to make love to you in a quiet, romantic setting. No other partners, no spectators. Just the two of us."

Her heart swelled at his words. It sounded so wonderful . . . so intimate . . .

So dangerously like a normal relationship.

Despite the clanging of warning bells inside her head, a desperate longing for him pulsed through her.

His lips settled on hers and she wrapped her arms around him, her tongue surging forward to meet his.

"Oh Ty, I want you so badly."

He scooped her up and carried her to the bed, then placed her on it. Red petals swirled around them as he settled down beside her.

She dragged her hand over the bulge in his pants. She'd been longing for his touch all day and now that she had him alone, she could hardly wait. The proof that he wanted her, too, thrilled her. Melissa tugged his zipper down and slid her fingers inside, stroking over his thin cotton briefs. A second later, she found his hot, hard flesh. She grasped it in her hand and stroked.

"Oh, honey."

The need in his voice delighted her. His hand stroked along her inner thigh and her sex dampened as she anticipated his touch, but he bypassed her aching womanhood and unfastened the buttons of her bodice, exposing her breasts. She'd worn no bra tonight, choosing instead to let her breasts be free under her thin top, in deference to the newfound exhibitionist within her.

He leaned toward her and his mouth covered one hot, hard nipple and he sucked deeply. She moaned, a sharp pang of need darting from her breast to her vagina and it contracted. He licked her other nipple, while his finger toyed with the first.

She threaded her fingers through his hair as he kissed down her stomach. He pulled off her panties, then his hot firm tongue licked her slick opening. It felt so good as it curled into her, then slid toward her clit. When he found that hard, hidden button, she almost gasped.

His hands cupped her buttocks securely as his tongue stroked and swirled over her clit and a magical heat bore down on her, swelling inside her, exploding in tiny bursts of pleasure throughout her body.

"Come for me, Melissa," he murmured against her hot, slick flesh.

His tongue darted against her in a rapid-fire pulse.

Intense pleasure tore through her.

"Oh God, yes," Melissa wailed.

She clung to Ty's head as she catapulted into orgasm. His blazing charcoal eyes watched her as his mouth worked its magic. The heat pelted through her, blazing in intensity, then slowly faded to a simmer.

He pushed himself upward, then embraced her. His arms felt so warm and secure around her. She wanted this man so badly, and for more than sex, but she refused to think about that right now. At this moment, she focused on how desperately she wanted to feel his cock inside her.

"Make love to me, Ty," she murmured.

Ty loved hearing those words from her lips. It's not that he didn't love to hear her talk dirty and ask him to fuck her, but hearing her ask him to *make love* to her stirred him in a very different way.

He kissed her passionately, longing to tell her how much he loved her.

Instead, he gazed deeply and tenderly into her eyes and said, "I'd love to, sweetheart."

He stood up and released his belt then pushed his pants to the floor. She pulled off her dress and flung it aside. He prowled over her and captured her lips in a passionate, loving kiss.

His cock nudged her opening, then he slowly eased into her, enjoying every inch of her tight, hot vagina as he pushed inside. She felt so incredible wrapped around him. He pulled back and glided forward again.

He could definitely get used to this kind of heaven.

He moved within her in slow, deep, potent thrusts, her gaze locked with his. Within the simmering blue depths of her eyes, he could see intense longing, and his heart swelled. She threw her head back and moaned and he felt the orgasm quiver through her, setting off a chain reaction in him. He exploded into her hot depths, clutching her close to his heart.

"Oh God, Melissa. I love you."

Chapter 16

MELISSA HELD TY CLOSE TO HER, BLISSFULLY SATED. BUT MO-
ments later, disturbing thoughts assailed her.

My God, he can't love me. That wouldn't be fair. He just can't. . . .

If he loved her, where did that leave his wife?

She thought about the fact that Suzanne was probably snuggled
tightly against Shane right now, and pushed away the thought that
maybe Ty's wife was exactly where she should be—and all the disturbing possibilities set off by that thought.

She sucked in a breath and released it slowly. Calmer now, she realized Ty didn't really love her. He'd said those words in the heat of passion. Why had she even considered he might have meant it?

Because, she realized in despair, she wanted him to mean it. Because
she loved him.

Damn it. How stupid could she be falling in love with Ty Adams?

Here was a man who happily gave his wife over to another man,
and who made love to that other man's wife, without a second
thought. Either commitment meant nothing to him, which meant he
was the wrong man for Melissa, or the commitment between him and
his wife was so strong, having sex with other people was no threat. Either way, Melissa was left with a broken heart.

Remembering his disturbing question earlier this evening, the one he'd never finished asking, made her wonder again if he was ready to leave his wife for her. . . . Her heart compressed. She wouldn't even consider that possibility.

Oh, Shane, why didn't you and I fall in love? That would have made life so easy . . . and safe.

~

As Ty waited for Suzanne to finish up in the bathroom, he undressed and wrapped a towel around his waist. He glanced at his watch. He had about fifteen minutes before Melissa arrived to go to breakfast. He sat down in the desk chair and started up his laptop. In his inbox, a message from Ashley told him she still couldn't access the link he'd sent with the video clip of him and Melissa. Apparently, she'd tried several times, thinking it was a Web site problem, but still couldn't access it.

Damn, he needed to resolve this. It wasn't that he wanted his assistant to see him in all his naked glory, and he definitely didn't want others to see Melissa, but he needed Ashley's help to find out who owned the Web site and how to get that damned video off the web.

He clicked on the link and Melissa's delectable, naked body appeared, undulating in sexual bliss. His cock began to rise and a deep yearning took hold of him. He couldn't take his eyes from the video, remembering that night, remembering her delicate gasps against his cheek, his cock buried deep inside her.

A knock sounded at the door.

Melissa!

He clicked the pause button on the video player, then flicked on the screen saver.

~

Melissa hesitated in front of Ty's door. This was very weird. She was about to knock on her lover's door—at the room he shared with his wife. Suzanne might even answer the door and invite her in, knowing she was having sex with her husband. In fact, if Melissa suggested it, Suzanne would probably join them. An image of Suzanne, with her bobbing breasts, her slender waist tapering to long, elegant hips as she'd waded into the water at the pool that first morning reminded Melissa how incredibly sexy the woman was.

Yet Ty wanted to make love to Melissa. Of course, if someone has chocolate cheesecake everyday, vanilla pudding might be considered a treat.

She sucked in a breath and knocked. The door opened and Ty smiled broadly, wearing only a towel slung low around his hips, showing off his tightly ridged stomach, his muscular chest, and arms bulging in all the right places. He tugged her to him, pushing closed the door behind them. He pressed her against it, his mouth devouring hers. His kiss—along with the bulge pressing against her belly—left little doubt that he definitely considered her a treat.

Her hands stroked over his strong back, then slid upward to his shoulders. She forked her fingers through his hair, becoming breathless as his tongue aroused and caressed her mouth. She arched her breasts against him, wanting to be closer, wanting him to push his enormous cock into her here and now right against the door. She slid one hand to his waist, toying with the corner of the towel tucked snugly underneath, easing it from its secure position.

"Hi, Melissa."

Suzanne's sudden appearance surprised Melissa and her fingers dodged away from the thick, terry cloth. Ty drew back, releasing her from his delicious embrace. To her horror, the corner of the towel slipped free and dropped to the floor, leaving him totally naked. His long, hard cock pointed straight at her. Suzanne laughed and grabbed up the towel then tossed it over Ty's shoulder.

"Here you go, dear." She smiled at Melissa. "I'm going out for a swim. You two have fun."

She winked, then slipped out the door.

Wide-eyed, Melissa stared at Ty. His cock, bobbing free and proud, twitched under her gaze.

"Keep looking at me like that and we won't make it to breakfast."

Her gaze flew back to his face. Chuckling, he leaned forward to give her a quick kiss, then wrapped the towel around his waist again.

"As you can probably tell, I was just about to take a shower. Back in a flash." He disappeared into the bathroom.

Melissa glanced around, then sat in the chair in front of the desk. She picked up Ty's watch, sitting beside the open laptop. She glanced at the digital readout: 10:33. They had a little under a half hour before the dining room stopped serving breakfast. As she put the watch down, her hand accidentally brushed across the mouse and the screen flickered to life. Replacing the fish swimming around on the screen was a full-sized picture of Melissa. Totally naked. Her mouth open. Her head arched back. And Ty—visible only from the back, but definitely Ty—caressing her breasts, his hips thrust forward.

Her heart raced in her chest as she glanced to the bottom of the screen. From the controls visible, she realized this was a video. She clicked on the play button. The sound of their lovemaking, low but audible, shocked her, almost as much as the sight of their bodies writhing in the throes of sexual intercourse.

"My God," she murmured. With shaking hands, she clicked the pause button, then minimized the screen. Behind the video was an open e-mail from someone named Ashley saying that she couldn't access the link he'd sent her to the Web site with the video. Melissa called up the video again and found the link in the e-mail matched the one on the open video screen.

She lurched to her feet. Oh God, this thing was on the Internet?

Had Ty arranged to have this video taken of them making love? Had he posted it on the Internet? Her whole body flushed and she felt faint.

Oh God, how could he do this to her? What kind of man was he?

With a sinking feeling she realized she had no idea what kind of man Ty Adams was—or what kind of deceit he was capable of.

She flew to the door.

Ty towel-dried his hair, then entered the bedroom.

"I'll be ready in a minute, honey." He dropped the towel from his head and glanced around.

Melissa was nowhere to be seen. He shook his head, wondering where she'd gone.

He dressed quickly, then headed for the door. As he opened it, his cell phone chimed.

Maybe that's Melissa.

Ty closed the door as he flipped open the phone.

"Adams."

"Hi, it's Ash. Boss, I have a hunch about that link. Are you at your computer?"

Ty sat down at the desk.

"I am now."

"Good. Try something for me, would you?"

"Shoot."

"Find the name of the link and copy everything up to the first slash."

He clicked the mouse and Ashley's e-mail displayed.

Alarm bells went off in his head. The video had been the front window open on the screen. His gaze darted down to the task bar at the bottom of the screen. He clicked on the video player and it jumped to full size.

The video was further along than he'd left it. His gut clenched.

Damn it. Melissa had seen it.

"Boss, you still there?"

"Yeah, sorry." He pulled up the e-mail again and highlighted the text Ashley had specified. "Got it."

"Click on start, then on the command window icon."

"Uh-huh."

"Now type *ping* and paste the name of the link. It'll display an IP address."

A series of numbers displayed.

"One nine two, dot, one six eight, dot, one, dot zero three two," he read from the screen.

"Yesss! That's what I thought."

He didn't know why she was excited, but it encouraged him.

"Okay, so what does that mean?" he prompted.

"Well, since I can't seem to access the link and you can, it means the video is probably only accessible on the resort's local computer network."

"So that means only people here at the resort can see it?"

"That's right. But," she cautioned, "they could make it accessible on the Internet at any time."

Relief flooded through him. The key was, it wasn't accessible now. That meant Melissa was not being displayed to the entire world, including her friends and family, in a compromising video.

The gears in Ty's brain started churning. "Why would someone make this available to the resort only?" he wondered out loud.

"Well, I've been thinking about that. If the video was splashed all over the Internet, it would kill the resort's rep, right? So whoever did this wanted it to appear that the resort's rep had been dealt a death blow, without actually killing it."

"Which would make anyone at the club who saw it believe that the value of the club had dropped substantially."

"As I see it, the main suspect is this Shane Mason guy. Since he wants to buy the resort, he'd love to push the price down."

Shane. Would he sacrifice Melissa's reputation to make a buck?

The guy might not be in love with Melissa but clearly they shared a deep friendship. He cared about her.

"I'm sure it's not him, Ash."

"One of your gut feelings?" She paused. "Hmm . . ."

He heard a clicking on the other end of the line, probably Ashley tapping her pen on the side of her computer monitor, as she tended to do when she was thinking.

The tapping stopped. "I've got an idea."

"What is it?"

"Well, you told me your friend is selling because the cost of maintaining the place is too high. Several expensive repairs and some big-ticket equipment replaced, right?"

"Yeah . . . ?" His words trailed off, as he began to see where she was going with this.

"Okay, so send me the repair log and whatever info you have on who did the repairs, along with a list of the new assets and where they were purchased."

"What's in that wicked little mind of yours, Ash?"

"Well, I'm thinking maybe the current managers of the place want to be more than that."

Ty's fists clenched. Could Hal and Vanna be behind this whole thing? It was plausible.

"I'll get on that. Anything else?" he asked her.

"Nope, I'm good."

He hung up and glanced at his watch. Almost eleven. If Suzanne didn't return from the pool soon he'd go find her. He wanted to get that information to Ashley as soon as possible. But first, he had to go after Melissa. See if she was okay. But what would he tell her?

A knock sounded on the door. Maybe that was her.

He pulled open the door. Before he could react, a solid male fist slammed into his eye. He crashed to the floor.

"Shane, what in heaven's name are you doing?" Suzanne, halfway down the hall, rushed past Shane and into the room, then knelt beside Ty.

His head ached and his eye stung sharply. Suzanne lifted his head and rested it on a soft towel. Gently, she prodded at his swelling eye. Ty pushed himself to a sitting position.

Shane glared at Ty, his eyes filled with murderous intent.

"Your husband is some kind of sleaze bucket. If you weren't here, I'd break every bone in his body."

She stared at him, wide-eyed. He turned on his heel and marched away. She turned to Ty.

"I've only been gone twenty minutes. What could you have possibly done to get him so mad?"

He pushed himself to his feet and slowly walked toward the desk.

"I assume it's because Melissa saw the video on my laptop."

He slumped into the chair.

Shane probably thought Ty had posted it, which meant, so did Melissa.

⁓

"Ty, you know pacing a hole in the carpet won't make her call any faster."

Ty glanced at Suzanne. She'd gathered together the information Ashley had requested in under twenty minutes, without tipping off Hal and Vanna. Now all he could do was wait for Ashley to get back to him.

He desperately wanted to go to Melissa to explain, but he knew it was better to finish up this business, then he could explain the whole story.

"Come lie down, and put the ice pack back on your eye."

He lay on the bed, but fidgeted as she positioned the sack of crushed ice on his black eye.

His cell chimed. He bolted upright. The ice bag dropped to the bed. "Adams."

"Got it, boss. The repairs were all made by one maintenance company. I checked it out and it doesn't have any other clients and, get this, no employees. None registered anyway. When I checked out who registered it, it seems it's this Hal guy's brother. What I can't figure out is, why wouldn't they try to hide it better than that?"

"Simple. They didn't think anyone would suspect them. They've been friends of Suzanne's for years. She trusted them."

"Some friends. It's the same with the purchases. A different company, but registered to the same guy. No assets, no employees."

"Thanks, Ash. You deserve a raise."

"I'll hold you to that."

Ty hung up and turned to Suzanne. Her grim face told him she understood the gist of what had happened.

"What now?"

"We've got them on charges of fraud. Before we call the police, though, we have to get that video off the network so they don't release it to the world in revenge."

Suzanne picked up the phone and dialed.

"Hi, Vanna. It's Suzanne. Look, I leave tomorrow and I so rarely get to see you and Hal. Are you free for lunch today? No, I was thinking in town. Yeah, okay. Fifteen minutes."

She hung up the phone. "I'll give you whatever passwords you need to get on the network admin account and whatever else you need so you can lock those bastards out of everything of importance on this resort. I assume your assistant can walk you through what needs to be done?"

"Absolutely."

Suzanne's eyes blazed with anger, hiding the pain he knew she must feel at their betrayal.

"Call the local police as soon as you're done."

He nodded.

"We'll be at the Half Shell restaurant in town." She strode to the door. "I'll keep them there until the police arrive." Her fists clenched at her sides. "They will not set foot on this property again."

The phone rang and Melissa glanced toward Shane as he lifted the receiver.

"We'll be right there." He hung up and glanced at her. "It was the manager's office. They want us to come down there. Something about the video."

He took her hand and together they walked down to the lobby. A tall man at the front desk accompanied them to an office down a side hall to a large outer office with three desks, then through the door labeled MANAGER.

"Please take a seat. Someone will be right in."

Melissa sank into one of the four chairs facing a round table off to the side of the main desk. She stared out the window at the view of the ocean as Shane sat down beside her.

A knock sounded at the door and they glanced up as Suzanne entered the office.

"Suzanne!" Shane stood up. "I'm sorry about hitting your husband but—"

She held up her hand, stopping his explanation.

"I know what you thought and I understand."

"So do I." Ty stepped into view and Shane's eyes flared in anger. "I would have done the same thing."

"Get the hell out of here before I—"

Suzanne grasped his arm. "Shane, please listen for a minute." She glanced across the room at Melissa. "You, too, honey."

Warmth and sincerity glittered in her emerald eyes.

"Melissa, I know you saw that video of you and Ty. What you must understand is that Ty didn't record the video, or post it online."

"Why the hell was it on his computer? A little souvenir?" Shane demanded.

"No, he was trying to find out who posted it. To get it off the Internet."

Melissa's chest tightened.

"So it was posted to the Internet?" she asked.

Ty stepped forward. When Shane moved to stop him, Suzanne clutched his arm. At her pleading expression, he backed off, but kept his gaze firmly on Ty as he strode toward Melissa.

He sat in the chair next to hers and spoke directly to her.

"It was never posted worldwide. It was only accessible to the local network here at the resort."

Relief swooped through her. So she wouldn't have to contend with leering men recognizing her on the street. It was one thing to perform here in the safety of the resort, in front of people who understood and shared in the sexual openness, but quite another to be displayed on the Internet as a piece of pornography.

" 'Was'?" she asked

"I removed it from the network and deleted it." He took her hand in the warmth of his. "No one can see it now."

"Why are *you* telling us this and not Hal or Vanna?" Shane demanded. "We have no reason to believe what you say is true."

"It is true," Suzanne said.

"I am a private investigator and I was hired by the owner of the resort," Ty continued. "Hal and Vanna aren't here to tell you about this because they've just been arrested." He tightened his fingers around Melissa's, his warmth soothing her. "They were the ones who posted the video."

"What?" Melissa didn't understand. "But why would they want to embarrass me . . . or you . . . like that?"

"It wasn't about embarrassing us. It was about scaring off a buyer who'd come here to check out the resort. They wanted to ensure that the owner believed the resort's reputation had been trashed and that the clientele would disappear because videos of clients were being posted to the Internet. That way, the owner would panic and drop the price, then they could buy the place for a song—going from managers to owners. They'd already been siphoning off most of the profits."

"But if the video is only accessible at the resort, why would the owner believe it? If he's not at the resort, then he wouldn't see it on the Internet."

Ty released Melissa's hand and turned to face Shane.

"The owner is at the resort, because she knew that you, Shane Mason, owner of the Mason Group, were here to check out the resort before making an offer."

"To be totally honest, I only knew that you were sending someone to check on the resort. I didn't know you were coming yourself," Suzanne said.

"You're the owner of the resort?" Melissa asked.

Suzanne nodded. Shane's mouth flattened into a thin line as he glared at her.

His glower seemed to unnerve Suzanne and she kept talking. "Actually, at first we thought you had been sent here to investigate the resort, Melissa. Then when Ty found out you worked for a news station, he thought you might be doing an exposé on the place. Especially since you hid the fact you're a reporter."

"I'm not a reporter. I work as a production assistant," Melissa said, puzzlement cascading through her. "And that's why I said I was a freelance writer, because I was afraid people here might be nervous around someone working for a news station."

Melissa turned to Ty. "So you're a private investigator and you're married to the owner of the resort?"

"No," he responded.

"But you said—"

"I mean, yes, I'm a private investigator, but I'm not married to Suzanne. I'm her friend."

Her *friend*. *Not* her husband.

"As Suzanne said, she believed the buyer . . . Shane . . . would secretly send someone to evaluate the club," Ty continued, "and I was here to identify that person and keep an eye on them. To ensure things went well."

Melissa's face flooded with heat. *To ensure things went well.* He certainly had gone above and beyond the call of duty there! Had he intended to have sex with her all along? To gain her trust, then draw her into his sexual web, mesmerizing her with his potent masculinity? Had he anticipated her falling for him, too?

Her stomach burned and her heart compressed. He must have known it would be easy to manipulate a woman smitten with him. To convince her this was a fabulous place when in reality it was a place that stripped a person of all self-respect.

She opened her mouth to speak, to deride Ty for tricking her. For making love to her. But no words would come. She sucked in a breath of air and clamped back on the tears pushing at her eyes, spun on her heel, and strode out.

Shane's first instinct was to follow Melissa, but his gaze stayed fixed on Suzanne. He had to ask.

"How long have you known I was the buyer?"

"Since yesterday afternoon."

"Before or after you seduced me?"

"Before." Her eyes widened. "You don't think . . . ?"

He turned his back on her, then strode from the room.

"No, Shane. Please."

He kept walking. Despite her plea. Despite the desperate pain inside him. She had only been using him to ensure he would buy her resort.

He should have known better than to trust any woman aside from Melissa. She was the one woman he knew he could trust with his heart.

Why had he been so blind for so long?

Chapter 17

TY HELD SUZANNE'S ARM, PREVENTING HER FROM RACING AFTER Shane.

"He won't listen to you now. Give him time to take it all in. He'll come around."

Her head shook back and forth. "No, he won't. I can feel it."

He took her in his arms and held her close, stroking her back, comforting her.

"If he doesn't, he's an idiot."

He felt her tears on his collar and her small sobs as her chest vibrated against his. He stroked her hair.

"Suzanne, it'll be all right. I promise."

Now all he had to do was find a way to make that promise come true. And he would. Suzanne was very important to him and he would ensure she got her happy ending.

His lips compressed at the image burned into his brain of Melissa's betrayed expression when she'd stared at him, believing he'd callously used her.

Since he would have done what he did whether he'd fallen for her or not, he couldn't see any way to convince her otherwise. So the fact he *had* fallen for her didn't change a thing.

This was better anyway. Their relationship had already gone too far. It was smarter to end it now and avoid more heartache down the road.

If only it didn't hurt so bad.

~

Melissa and Shane spent most of the cab trip to the airport in silence. Once they'd boarded the flight and it had taken off, Shane finally turned to her. "Melissa, I'm sorry about how this turned out."

She nodded, trying to stop the tears from welling up.

"I just feel like such an idiot. The things I did . . ."

He rested his hand on her arm. "Liss, you enjoyed yourself, something you rarely allow yourself to do. There's nothing wrong with that."

She gazed at him. His warm sea-blue eyes, his familiar smile, reassured her. The tightness in her stomach released a little.

"You don't think I turned into a slut-monkey?" Her eyes glazed with tears but she blinked them back.

He smiled warmly. "I don't even know what a slut-monkey is, but whatever it is, you're not it. You're a woman who indulged in some sexual fantasies and awakened something special inside yourself. It took a lot of courage and I think it's made you a more well-rounded person."

He slipped his arms around her and she leaned close to him, loving the comfort of his embrace.

"You have a novel way of looking at the world, Shane."

He kissed the top of her head. "And you love me for it."

That was true. That was one of the main reasons she loved him. And there were many others. But that love was from one close friend to another. She was not *in love* with him. And that, she realized, was the real reason their relationship had never evolved into something romantic. True, since making love at the resort, they shared a closer bond, but it was still friendship.

No, she was not in love with Shane.

She was in love with Ty Adams.

"Ms. Fox."

Suzanne glanced up from her papers and gazed at her assistant, Gina, peering in the door. She only called her Ms. Fox when there was someone important in the office.

"What is it?"

It had only been a week since she'd returned from the resort and she was still dealing with the aftermath of the financial damage done by Hal and Vanna. It seemed the resort had been doing quite well, but none of those profits had made it to Suzanne and now she might have to sell anyway.

"There's someone here to see you."

"Who?"

"He won't say, but he says it's very important he speak with you."

Ordinarily, Gina would get rid of anyone like that, but her uncharacteristic behavior sent Suzanne striding to the door. She pushed it open and glanced across her assistant's office to see Shane standing in front of Gina's desk, briefcase in hand.

"Ms. Fox," he said in a businesslike tone. "I would like to discuss a proposal with you."

Her heart melted seeing him standing there, so tall and handsome. She wanted to run to him and throw her arms around him.

"About the resort?"

She hoped he would throw down his briefcase and exclaim his love for her, insisting that the club didn't matter. Her deception didn't matter. Nothing mattered but their love for each other.

But he didn't. He simply nodded.

"All right," she said flatly.

She gestured him into her office. Her heart, held tightly in place by her rigid control, burned in her chest as he walked past her. Her back to him, she pushed the door closed, then turned around.

Startled, she came face-to-face with him, only a foot away. She'd assumed he'd continued to the guest chair facing her desk. His closeness set her body tingling and her heart thumped loudly.

"Suzanne, I'm sorry about what I said at the resort . . . what I thought." He rested his hands on her shoulder. "I've had time to gain some much needed perspective and I realize I was wrong."

His wonderful, deep blue eyes glowed with warmth. "Suzanne, now that I know you're not married, I want to pursue a real relationship with you."

She stepped forward, her heart swelling. "You do?"

He closed the short distance between them and cupped her shoulders. She stared into his eyes, glittering with sincerity. "Yes, I do."

His warm words caressed her then he tilted his head forward and she closed the distance, melding her lips with his, stunned by the intensity of her emotions. She realized she loved this man.

His arms encircled her and he drew her close. His lips moved on hers with a hungry passion, then he dragged her against him and hugged her so close she thought she might break. At the feel of her body pressed the length of his, their hearts thumping together as one, Suzanne's heart soared.

Shane knew he'd been an idiot thinking Suzanne had only made love with him to get him to buy her resort. She wasn't that kind of woman. He hadn't really needed Ty Adams to tell him that.

Shane realized the real reason he'd run was because he'd been afraid. When he'd found out she was not married, and therefore free to be with him, he'd been terrified. But a week without her showed him what real pain was. He'd realized he had to take that risk. Living without her would be worse than any possibility of losing her in the future.

Now, holding her in his arms, he knew he wouldn't lose her. Because this was right.

Melissa stared out the window of Shane's big country house, watching a gray squirrel prance across the lawn then scamper up the big oak tree near the riverbank. Shane had invited Melissa and her two sisters up to the place for the weekend, as he did every year for his annual summer party.

Shane hadn't arrived yet, but Melissa had gone straight to the room she always used, telling her sisters she needed a nap. In reality, she just didn't feel like socializing right now. She'd have to do enough of that over the weekend, but right now, she needed the quiet time.

She wrung her hands together. Her heart still ached for Ty. He had awakened a part of her that she'd always hidden away. A part of her that understood that pleasure was a part of life. A part of happiness. And it was something she deserved. After much soul searching, she realized she'd always denied herself what she wanted, throwing herself into looking after others.

Now she realized it was not only a person's right to pursue things they enjoyed, but it was the only way to be complete. It didn't make them less capable of giving. It filled them with joy and allowed them to give more of themselves.

How ironic that she would find that out just as the thing she wanted most in life was stolen away from her. Ty's love.

An hour had passed and she realized she couldn't hide in this room forever. She sighed and opened her door, then descended the stairs.

She could hear the murmuring of a familiar deep voice coming from the kitchen. It sounded amazingly like Ty's voice.

Oh, great, now I'm hearing things.

As she got closer, she heard it again. Her ears perked up. That wasn't her imagination. That was real!

She raced into the large kitchen to see Ty leaning against the counter, her two sisters eyeing him avidly.

"What are you doing here?" she demanded.

"Melissa, there you are." He smiled that devilish smile of his. "I was just telling your sisters about the week we spent together."

Elaine and Ginny glanced at Melissa, big grins on their faces.

"That was at the resort you went to a couple of weeks ago, wasn't it?" Elaine asked impishly.

Melissa's face burned red. She couldn't have her little sisters thinking she had gone off to a swingers' resort and had sex with a stranger . . . even though she had.

He held up a DVD, hand-labeled.

"I was just telling your sisters I have a great video of you and me at the resort enjoying ourselves."

"We'd love to see it," Ginny insisted. "There's a DVD player in the TV on the counter."

Blind panic gripped Melissa. She stared at him, her eyes demanding, *You wouldn't.*

His half smile said, *Wanna bet?*

"Excuse us a minute." She forced the words through clenched teeth as she grabbed his hand and dragged him from the kitchen and up the stairs to the only place she could be sure of having some privacy from prying ears.

She closed the bedroom door behind her.

"Don't worry about the DVD," Ty said. "It's just some photos taken by the staff photographer showing various guests enjoying themselves around the resort—all PG-rated. A service the resort provides so the guests have something to take home and show their families. I thought you might like one."

"What the hell do you think you're doing here?" she demanded, as she glared at him.

He proceeded toward her, closer than she wanted him to be.

"I came here to talk to you."

She dodged sideways, putting more distance between them.

"Well, I don't want to talk to you."

He stepped toward her again and his long reach allowed him to capture her and draw her close. His arms slid around her waist. The warmth of his embrace shocked her senses into temporary paralysis. As hard as she tried, she could not find the will to move away.

His mouth claimed hers and, damning her traitorous lips the whole time, she responded. For about a second. He released her mouth and smiled.

"Actually, I don't feel much like talking right now, either," he murmured, his hot charcoal gaze locked on hers.

She would not melt into his arms. She had to be strong. She couldn't give in to this sparking desire. He'd betrayed her and made a fool of her. And broken her heart.

She drew away.

"You have a nerve coming here. You lied to me . . . used me . . ." Her hands clenched into fists. "Had sex with me . . . as part of your job."

He stepped closer to her.

"Why are you really mad at me, Melissa? Because I didn't tell you why I was really there? Because that's the only lie I told."

"No, it's not. You lied about . . ." She bit back any further words, not quite sure what they would be, but knowing they would leave her too vulnerable.

"About what?" he prompted.

She turned around, grasping the edge of the dresser for support. Staring at herself in the mirror, she saw herself as a teenager. Knowing no one would ever love her. Believing her mother had never loved her. Always feeling the need to prove herself, to make everyone happy but herself.

Ty's hands rested on her shoulders. Gentle. Reassuring.

"What is it really, Melissa?"

"You weren't really attracted to me." *And you weren't really in love with me.* But she couldn't say that.

"The hell I wasn't." His reflected gaze captured hers. "Melissa, I did what I did to help my best friend. Suzanne has always been there for me. She's seen me through some pretty rough times. I won't apologize for that, because I'd do it again. I followed you to make sure you got the right impression of the resort. I never misled you. I helped you out of that jam the first evening, in the numbers room, because I knew you were uncomfortable, and it was the right thing to do. And I liked you."

He turned her to face him.

"I made love to you, because I found you extremely sexy and I wanted to be with you. The first time."

"The first time?"

"After that . . ." He stroked her cheek, holding her gaze with the warmth in his simmering eyes. His voice grew low and compelling. "I made love to you because I'd fallen in love with you."

She shook her head.

"I don't believe you." She wanted to—desperately—but she was afraid.

"I didn't believe it at the time, either, but when I found out you weren't married . . . and realized there was nothing standing in the way of us being together . . . then I realized. Then, when you left the resort, and I thought I'd never see you again . . . I couldn't stop thinking about you. I couldn't stop wanting you." His fingers curled around her cheek, tender and loving. "I've never loved a woman before. I never thought I would. But I was wrong."

He took her hand and stroked it with his lips, then knelt down in front of her.

"Melissa Woods, I love you more than I ever thought a man could love a woman. My life is empty without you. Please tell me you'll marry me."

Her heart pounded in her chest. Marriage? The pain of his betrayal still burned through her, but . . . He'd helped her to free herself from her inhibitions. He'd encouraged her to go after her own pleasure without guilt. He'd made her feel alive for the first time in her life.

She wanted to believe this would work . . . she really did . . . but she was afraid. How could she trust that he wouldn't hurt her?

"Melissa . . . sweetheart . . . I'm on my knees before you. I love you. Please say yes."

"I . . ." Tears spilled from her eyes. Her jaw quivered.

He stood up and wrapped his arms around her, holding her close. She felt safe and protected in his arms. Like she had always felt with Shane. But with Ty there was so much more. An awareness of his masculinity. A desire to turn her face upward and join her lips with his. An ache deep in her heart to be with him. Always.

Did she need him too much?

He tucked her head under his chin and stroked her hair. Silence hung around them as her teardrops fell to his shirt leaving round, wet splotches.

Ty had done what he'd done to protect his friend Suzanne. Just as Melissa had wanted to protect her sister Elaine. Melissa had lied, too, but Ty hadn't argued that point. He'd made his case for what he had done, not pointing a finger at her. And he'd made a good case.

She realized it wasn't about the fact he'd lied. It was because she'd come to believe he really liked her . . . had begun to hope he'd grown to love her. Learning that he was undercover had crushed that hope, along with her fragile sense of self-worth.

She gazed at him. "Do you really love me?"

His soft gaze and gentle smile reassured her. "More than life itself."

She snuffled, tears flowing more freely. As she gazed into his eyes, she realized she believed him. And, deep down inside, she knew she could trust him. He would never hurt her.

"I love you, too." The words trembled from her lips.

His mouth burst into a broad smile and he crushed her to him, then his lips swooped down on hers with a breathtaking passion.

"Does that mean you'll marry me?"

She nodded, a crooked smile claiming her lips.

He scooped her into his arms, his lips claiming hers again.

"Oh God, Melissa, you had me worried there for a minute."

"Just a minute?" The tears had stopped flowing, and her grin stretched wide.

He chuckled and laid her on the bed, then dropped down beside her. His adoring gaze and the gentleness of his touch as he stroked her cheek sent quivers through her.

She'd never been loved by a man before. Her heart swelled. She could get used to this.

He kissed her, tender and sweet. She felt his hands release the top button of her blouse, then the next. She clamped her hand down on his, stopping him.

"I can't . . . my sisters are downstairs."

His eyes glinted with mischief.

"So?"

"So? They'll think we're . . . you know . . ."

"Making love? They'll be right."

He pulled the collar of her blouse aside and nuzzled the crook of her neck.

"You know, they're grown women," he said. "They know about the birds and the bees. They've probably even figured out you've been with a man before."

As her hormones sprang to life and she relaxed into his arms, she realized she'd missed this sense of adventure, this sense of freedom. Of allowing herself to do what she wanted, when she wanted.

He kissed her, deep and long, his tongue slipping inside her mouth and caressing her tongue and lips until she quivered with need, then he drew back and gazed at her with a longing that seared her soul. His lips danced against the pulse point at the base of her neck, then skittered down to the swell of her breast. He drew her top down her shoulders and kissed along the edge of her lacy bra.

Her breasts ached for him and her sex throbbed in need. She flicked open the front clasp on her bra and peeled back the cups, exposing her naked breasts. He smiled and captured one taut nipple in his mouth. She moaned at the exquisite pleasure of his hot mouth on her hard, distended nipple. The heat of him enveloped her, quivering through every cell until her body begged for more.

"Let me see you." She gazed at him with longing.

He pushed himself onto his knees and stripped off his black T-shirt, revealing his muscular arms and chest and his ridged abdomen. Her hand stroked over his hard male flesh and she felt faint with desire. Her fingers trailed down and hooked over the waistband of his jeans. She pushed herself to a sitting position and kissed his stomach, nuzzled his belly button, while her hands worked at his belt, then tugged down his zipper. The head of his cock pushed upward, straining at his black cotton briefs.

She nipped it with her teeth, the thin cotton his only protection, then she hooked her finger under the elastic and tugged the cotton forward. Her other hand dove inside and wrapped around him.

Oh God, it was heaven to feel him in her hand again. She licked under the ridge of his cock-head, then encircled him with her lips and sucked. His hand stroked over her ear, drawing her hair back. She sucked him deeper, drawing him into her mouth. She moved her head up and down.

"Melissa, I want you so much. I'm so close, sweetie. Why don't we—"

She swallowed him down her throat and fondled his balls, then began pumping him faster.

He groaned. "Damn it, woman. You've . . . ah . . . got to have it your own . . . oh . . . yeah!"

Hot liquid spurted into her throat and she swallowed it down. Again and again as he clung to her head. When he was finally done, he dragged her into his arms and kissed her passionately, then removed her pants and eased her onto her back.

"Don't for a minute think that we're done here."

He slid his hands under her knees and eased her legs wide, then swooped down and nuzzled her pussy with his mouth. His tongue stroked the length of her slit, then he pressed it against her clit and nudged. Spectacular sensations exploded within her. His fingers stroked her wet opening as his tongue licked and cajoled. Two fingers slid inside her and stroked her vagina. Pleasure built within her, nearing that magical summit.

Then he eased back, staring down at her.

"I was so close," she complained.

His lips edged up in a smile and his eyes glittered.

"I know."

He prowled over her and pressed his long, hard cock to her opening.

"Oh, yes." This is what she'd longed for. What she'd needed.

Just as his cock slid inside her, stroking the length of her vagina, a knock sounded at the door.

"Nooooo," she wailed in a low murmur against his ear.

"Ignore it," Ty said.

His cock pulled back and thrust forward again. Sparks ignited within her.

"Liss, you in there?" Shane's voice sounded through the door.

Melissa stiffened. Ty thrust again.

"Yes," she cried.

Ty kissed her neck, sending electric shimmers quivering across her flesh.

"Can I come in?" Shane asked.

Come. She was going to come.

Ty thrust faster.

"Yes," she wailed.

The doorknob turned, but the door held shut with a thump.

"Liss, the door's locked."

Ty swirled and thrust, his hard cock stroking her to greater heights. Unable to contain herself, she wailed as the orgasm erupted through her, blinding in its intensity.

Still Ty thrust. In and out. Her vagina tightened around his long, fat cock and he swirled, sending her ricocheting into another mind-numbing orgasm. His body stiffened and his hot semen flooded her womb.

He held her tight to his body, his face nuzzled into her neck. She stirred, knowing Shane must have heard the whole thing. Her face flushed, but she reminded herself that Shane had heard, and seen, much more while they were at the resort.

"Sorry, I didn't mean to interrupt anything," Shane called through the door. "I'll come back later."

Ty pushed himself onto his arms and smiled down at her. He nudged his pelvis forward, swirling his still erect cock within her.

"No, I'll just be a second."

He kissed her, then gave her a couple of short, fast thrusts. Another orgasm pulsed through her in spasms. She panted, then moaned quietly. Ty leaned down and kissed her.

"That was great, but now . . ." She grabbed his arms and gazed up at him. "Please, just . . ." She hesitated.

She really wasn't up to facing Shane with another man in her bed right now. She wanted to break the news as gently as she could.

"Would you go into the bathroom?" she asked.

"You mean . . . hide?"

"If you wouldn't mind." She sent him her most dazzling smile.

"I do mind." He leaned down and kissed her. "But for you . . ."

He drew back and his wonderful cock slipped free, leaving her feeling empty. He strolled across the room, totally naked, then disappeared into the private bathroom.

Chapter 18

MELISSA GOT UP AND KICKED HIS CLOTHES UNDER THE BED, then grabbed a robe from her suitcase and pulled it on. She tied it at her waist as she rushed to the door, then she pulled the door open. Shane smiled at her.

"Liss, it's so good to see you."

He wrapped his arms around her in a tight bear hug, then gave her a light kiss.

He peered into the room. "You alone?"

"Uh . . . yes."

Ty was in the bathroom, so technically, it was true. Her face flushed as she realized now he would believe she'd been masturbating.

It suddenly occurred to her that her sisters knew she was up here with Ty.

"Did you . . . uh . . . talk to Elaine and Ginny?"

"No, I didn't see them. There were some towels and bags by the dock, so they're probably swimming out to the island."

He closed the door behind him.

"Liss, I . . . have something important to talk to you about."

"Okay." She glanced around the room, noticed the rumpled bed, then grabbed his hand and led him to the French doors, which led to the large balcony. "Let's talk out here."

She pulled open the left door and stepped outside. The late afternoon sun caressed her face. She sat down in one of the Adirondack chairs and Shane sat beside her.

"What's up?"

He leaned forward, resting his folded hands between his knees.

"Liss, you know you've always been very special to me. . . ."

She stared at him, eyes wide. Oh God, after progressing their relationship to the next level at the resort, was he going to ask her if they could pursue a real romantic relationship?

They hadn't been in contact much over the past couple of weeks, both licking their wounds, but she'd known they'd have to have a discussion about this sooner or later. She'd hoped he'd come to the same conclusion she had—that the best relationship for them was friendship.

As she stared at him, his eyes glowing with happiness, her heart tore in two.

How could she tell him she didn't love him? She rested her hand on his wrist.

"I know, Shane, but . . . uh . . . could you just hold that thought for a minute?"

She bolted to her feet and raced into the room. Ty stood inside the bathroom, the door open waiting for her. She shot inside and closed the door behind her.

"It's Shane. He's . . ." She gulped. "I think he's going to tell me he loves me!"

Ty stepped forward and pulled her into his arms, then kissed her with such passion she knew she belonged to him and no other. Forever.

"Tell him you're already taken."

"I can't do that."

His eyebrows arched upward.

"Why not?"

"Because I don't want to hurt him."

Ty kissed her. "Melissa, I'll go out there with you and we'll explain that you're taken. He'll be fine with it, I promise."

He slid his hand to the small of her back and pulled open the door, then urged her forward.

"No, I don't think—"

"Trust me."

As they stepped into the room, she saw Shane sitting in the upholstered chair near the bed.

"Ty." Shane stood up and offered his hand to Ty. They shook hands. "I didn't know you were here already."

"Already?" Melissa turned to stare at Ty.

"That's right. Suzanne invited him."

"Suzanne?"

This conversation was getting more confusing by the minute.

"Shane," Ty said, "Melissa was concerned about the direction of your conversation and we just wanted you to know that Melissa and I are . . ." He glanced at her. ". . . engaged."

Shane's smile broadened and he grabbed Ty's hands in both of his and shook heartily.

"That's wonderful. Congratulations."

Melissa glanced from one to the other, confusion swirling through her.

"So what's going on with Suzanne?" Melissa asked.

"First, I wanted to say that after our time at the resort, I was worried you might think our relationship had moved to a new level, but now that I know you and Ty are engaged, I see there's no problem."

"So you wanted to tell me that we're *not* going to start a romantic relationship?" Melissa asked, relieved.

"That's right." He grinned widely. "And that Suzanne and I are now an item."

"Oh, Shane, that's wonderful!" She was thrilled that Shane had found someone special.

Ty chuckled and pulled Melissa against his side, his strong arm around her waist.

And so had Melissa.

Melissa leaned back in her chair and took a sip of her coffee. It was Monday morning and all the other weekend guests, including Melissa's two sisters, had left. Over twenty people had descended on Shane's lovely, secluded country house for the weekend-long party.

During the course of the weekend, Melissa discovered that Suzanne was not just Shane's love interest, but also his business partner, since Shane had decided to invest in the resort.

Also, Suzanne had chatted with Elaine and Steve and succeeded where Melissa had failed . . . in talking them out of going to The Sweet Surrender. She had explained that people shouldn't go to a swingers' club to fix a broken marriage. She had suggested that what they needed to do was go away somewhere where they could rediscover each other. Focusing inward would help their marriage far more than focusing outward, to other people. Elaine and Steve had both thanked her and by the end of the weekend looked like they'd already started on the path to rediscovery.

Shane had invited Melissa and Ty to stay an extra day so they could all go over wedding arrangements, since Suzanne would be the maid of honor and Shane the best man.

Melissa sat with Suzanne, Shane and Ty at the oak kitchen table overlooking a gorgeous view of the river through the large picture window. Suzanne pointed at a lovely flower arrangement featuring pink roses and white lilies in a bridal magazine, asking Shane if he liked it.

Melissa's gaze shifted to Ty as he pored over a magazine showing various tuxedo styles. With his tall, muscular good looks he would be devastatingly handsome in a tuxedo. Since she'd met him, she'd only seen him in blue jeans and casual shirts—or naked.

Her mouth curled up in a smile. Right now, naked sounded very appealing.

Shane laughed at something Suzanne said, then leaned forward and kissed her. Melissa liked Suzanne and was thrilled that she would be dating Shane, knowing she would make him very happy. Shane slid his hand around Suzanne's waist, then skimmed over her breast for a second, before coming to rest on her side.

Melissa's gaze lingered on Suzanne's breast. She was not wearing a bra and the outline of her nipple showed clearly through her aqua cotton camisole. Melissa remembered those breasts naked, softly bouncing in the pool when the two of them had chatted for the first time at the resort. At the sight of Shane's hand resting on the side of her breast, Melissa remembered his hands stroking over Miss Lips's naked breasts in the viewing room that first night at the resort.

Melissa's sex ached. Her wild, uninhibited alter ego yearned to be free again. Her cheeks blossomed with heat as she realized she had shared sexual experiences with each of the three people at this table. In fact, with all of them at the same time. That thought would have horrified her only a few weeks ago. Even last week, she'd had trouble dealing with the wild side of herself that had awakened at the resort.

Right here, right now, however, she realized that all three of these people not only accepted, but encouraged, her more adventurous sexual nature.

What was wrong with sharing sexual experiences with people who loved and respected her? Her gaze slid over Suzanne's breasts, then she glanced from Ty to Shane and a tremendous desire built within her. At the resort, Melissa had experienced two men at the same time, and it had been exhilarating, but it had not satisfied a very deep craving within her. To be with both Ty and Shane. At the same time.

On impulse, her hand slipped to one nipple and she stroked it. The delicious sensations storming through her drowned out the little voice that insisted she stop before someone noticed what she was doing.

Suzanne flipped the page of her magazine. Melissa unfastened the top button of her shirt, then the second. She slid her hand inside, then under her bra to stroke her hard, naked nipple. Shane's gaze shifted to Melissa, then his eyes widened as he realized what she was doing. She smiled, then stood up. She released the rest of her buttons, then dropped her blouse to the floor. Shane patted Suzanne's shoulder and she glanced up in time to see Melissa dispose of her bra.

As Melissa stood topless in the kitchen, Shane and Suzanne staring at her, she felt sexy and very, very wicked. In a good way. She stroked her hands over her breasts, cupping them both, then grazing her thumbs over her nipples. Shane glanced at Suzanne and she smiled, then stood up and moved behind Melissa. Suzanne's soft hands slid under Melissa's and her fingers caressed Melissa's nipples. Melissa slid her hands down her stomach, and released the button of her shorts, then slid the zipper down. Suzanne cupped Melissa's breasts in her gentle, feminine hands.

"Ty," Suzanne said. "I think Melissa is trying to tell us something."

Ty gazed up from his magazine and his eyes popped wide at the sight of Melissa half-naked, Suzanne's hands stroking over her breasts.

Melissa slid her hands inside her panties and stroked herself. Suzanne slid Melissa's shorts down to her ankles, then guided Melissa to the table. Melissa sat on the edge as Suzanne stripped away Melissa's white cotton panties and tossed them aside, both men watching avidly. Suzanne peeled her camisole from her body and dropped it to the floor. Melissa couldn't help herself, she had to touch those large, beautiful breasts. They were so soft and round. She leaned forward and licked Suzanne's nipple. The aureole pebbled under her tongue. She sucked lightly, then drew it deep into her mouth. Suzanne's moan delighted Melissa.

"Oh God, you girls are so sexy." Shane had stripped off his golf shirt and his hand slid up and down the bulge in his pants.

Melissa glanced at Ty and saw his erection growing within his jeans. He smiled encouragement. Suzanne cupped Melissa's face and drew her lips to hers. The kiss, gentle and feminine, stirred a different part of Melissa than a man's strong, purposeful invasion. Melissa's tongue sought Suzanne's and stroked it lightly. Suzanne stroked back, delicate and playful. The men approached, then Shane's hand covered one of Melissa's breasts and Ty's covered the other.

Suzanne guided Melissa back onto the table and eased her legs apart. A moment later, her tongue dragged along Melissa's wet slit. As she moaned her approval, Ty took one nipple into his mouth and dabbed the end. A second later, Shane covered her other nipple and sucked lightly.

"Ohhhh, yes." She sighed, then glanced up at the men laving attention on her breasts. She stroked over Ty's denim-encased cock, then Shane's. Ty tugged down his zipper and disposed of his pants, then underwear. Melissa grasped his cock in her hand. Shane stripped down, too, and Melissa grabbed his iron rod in her other hand.

She stroked their shafts as Suzanne's hot tongue swirled over

Melissa's hard clit, sending an agony of pleasure pulsing through her. Suzanne's tongue dabbed and pulsed, pushed and cajoled until Melissa felt the pleasure sweep through her in a torrent of bliss.

"Suzanne, yes. That's so . . . Oh God . . ."

She wailed as the orgasm slammed through her, her hands tightening around the hot, hard cocks in her hands.

A second later, she lay gasping on the tabletop. The two men helped her to her feet and she wrapped her arms around Suzanne, loving the feel of the woman's round, soft breasts pressing against hers. She kissed Suzanne, a soft, delicate, affectionate kiss.

"Thank you. That was wonderful."

"Anytime, honey." Suzanne smiled and nodded her head toward their two men. "You know, it looks like a wonderful buffet. What do you think? Want to share?"

She took Melissa's hand and turned her around. The men both leaned against the table, their cocks sticking straight up, watching Melissa and Suzanne.

Suzanne giggled and leaned down in front of Ty. She licked the length of his cock, then gazed at Melissa expectantly. Melissa leaned down and licked the other side of Ty's cock. Suzanne licked again and Melissa licked. The two of them tilted their heads and wrapped their mouths around his cock as if it was a cob of corn and glided up and down. Melissa's lips grazed Suzanne's and, when they slid over his cock-head, they continued upward until their mouths melded again in a kiss.

"You two are so hot," Shane said.

Melissa glanced at him. He stroked his straining cock. Melissa winked at Suzanne and said, "Tradesies?"

Suzanne returned her smile. "You bet."

Melissa sauntered toward Shane and knelt before him, then licked his cock-head, then swallowed it into her mouth. She glanced sideways to see Suzanne beside her sucking Ty's cock deep into her mouth. Melissa sucked Shane deep, mirroring Suzanne's movements. Their heads bobbed up and down in rhythm, the men's groans forming a guttural chorus of appreciation. As Melissa sucked Shane's cock deep down her throat, she slid her hand sideways to slip between Ty's legs and cup his balls. Suzanne followed suit and reached over to fondle Shane's balls. A spasm shuddered through Shane and hot liquid flooded Melissa's throat. After a moment, Ty stiffened and groaned.

Melissa licked and squeezed Shane within her mouth, enjoying the feel of his friendly, familiar cock. Suzanne released Ty's cock and the sight of his deflated member slipping from the other woman's mouth mesmerized her. She wanted that cock inside her, but right this second, it was spent. Melissa, however, was still ready to go. She stood up and tugged Suzanne into her arms, then kissed her passionately. She kissed down Suzanne's neck, then sucked one nipple, then the other. Her fingers stroked down Suzanne's thigh, then dipped inside her pussy. The heat inside the woman was incredible, and her vagina was soft and wet.

Suddenly, Melissa hungered to taste her. She kissed down Suzanne's belly then, for the first time in her life, licked a woman's pussy. Suzanne's moan encouraged her. She eased Suzanne back against the table and eased her legs wide, then stroked her fingers along Suzanne's slit. She drew the folds apart and stared at the hard little button nestled in the moist flesh. She leaned forward and licked it. Suzanne's appreciative moan quivered through her. She covered the little button with her mouth and licked, then sucked lightly on the small bud.

"Oh, Melissa. Yes."

Shane stroked Suzanne's left breast and Ty kissed her right as Melissa continued to suck Suzanne's wet, delicious little clit. Suzanne moaned, her fingers twining through Melissa's hair. Melissa slid two fingers into Suzanne's velvet vagina and stroked the upper wall, finding a smooth, even rhythm. She alternated licking and sucking on her clit while she stroked her inner wall. Patiently, she continued, watching the men as they both sucked Suzanne's large, round breasts. Suzanne's rapid breathing turned to moans, then gasps. Still Melissa continued.

"Oh . . . Oh . . . Oh, yesssss."

Suzanne wailed, then shrieked and a wash of liquid flooded from her vagina.

Melissa kissed Suzanne's mound, then rested her head on her belly as Suzanne caught her breath. Melissa lifted her head and smiled.

"Oh God, Melissa, that was wonderful."

Melissa felt a deep satisfaction at having given Suzanne such pleasure.

Suzanne stood up and drew Melissa into her arms, then hugged her with deep affection.

"You're very special to me, Melissa."

Melissa felt warmth envelope her at the woman's words. She felt deeply accepted and loved.

"You know, fellows, I think you should show Melissa a special time," Suzanne suggested.

Melissa glanced around to see Ty's cock sticking straight up, then Shane's cock sticking straight up, and she knew exactly what kind of special time she wanted.

Two cocks. But not any two cocks.

Shane's.

And Ty's.

She almost came just thinking about it.

Ty drew her into his arms and kissed her, his tongue driving between her lips in heated passion, devouring her mouth. Shane came up behind her and stroked her hair aside, then nuzzled the side of her neck.

Ty scooped her up and carried her into the living room. Shane sat on the couch and Ty set her down on his lap. Shane guided his long cock into her wet vagina.

"Ohhhh," she moaned at the feel of Shane's steel-hard cock gliding into her.

Ty's hot, charcoal gaze burned through her as Shane wrapped his hands around her hips and guided her up and down for two strokes, then he nudged his slick cock against her ass and slowly eased her downward. His cock-head filled her, then his shaft glided inside. She leaned back against his chest, his cock embedded deep in her ass, and she gazed up at Ty. He smiled and eased her legs wide, then kneeled in front of her. He rubbed his cock against her pussy then slowly pushed inside her.

"Ohhhh." Tears formed in her eyes at the exquisite pleasure of being filled, not only by two cocks, but these two cocks.

The two men she loved.

One her best friend.

The other her lover, and soon-to-be husband.

Shane stretched her tight passage as Ty's cock glided through her vagina. It was as if the two cocks stroked each other through her. Shane's hands covered her breasts as Ty shifted out, then in. Shane twitched inside her ass and she gasped in heady arousal. Ty's cock stroked and Shane's pulsed.

She felt so full it was almost unbearable. Pleasure rippled through her. Ty's finger stroked over her clit and blissful sensations pulsed the length of her.

"Oh . . . my . . . God . . ." she wailed as intense pleasure skyrocketed through her, ricocheting off every nerve ending.

Shane's cock twitched, stretching her delightfully and Ty thrust, deeper and harder. His finger quivered over her clit, accelerating her pleasure until she burst into orgasm on a gasp. Still he thrust, riding her, pushing her pleasure higher and higher until cataclysmic joy exploded within her. Shane kissed her neck, his cock still embedded deep within her and Ty thrust. Shane stiffened and Ty groaned then, simultaneously, they flooded her with hot spurts of semen. She squeezed Ty's cock within her vagina, hugging him inside her, while Shane held her tight against his body.

Ty slid from her, then he eased her forward and Shane also slid free. She ached at the emptiness. Immediately, she pushed Ty against the table and swallowed his wonderful cock down her throat, sucking on it until it pulsed to life and grew to steel hardness.

She leaned back and admired her handiwork, then she stood up.

"Suzanne, I'd love to see Ty and Shane fuck you."

Suzanne laughed and Shane's cock hardened. Ty laid down on the floor and Suzanne mounted him. Melissa watched his long, hard cock impale her. Shane knelt behind her and Melissa watched in fascination as his cock disappeared into her ass.

The three of them moved in unison and Suzanne's moans grew louder and longer. Shane's cock slid in and out of view as he thrust deep and hard into her firm, round ass.

"Oh, God, I love your two cocks," Suzanne cried. "Oh, yeah . . ." Her voice deepened. "Oh, yeah . . . !"

She groaned, then wailed as an orgasm pulsed through her. The two men squeezed her between them, their three bodies pulsing, riding her orgasm like a tidal wave of pleasure. First Ty, then Shane, groaned as they climaxed.

A moment later, Shane drew himself from her ass and flopped back on the floor. Suzanne pushed herself to her feet, a broad smile lighting her face. Ty remained motionless on the floor.

Suddenly, Melissa's craving for his cock overwhelmed her. She shifted over him.

"Oh, babe, I don't think—"

His protest died on his lips as her hot, wet pussy glided over his cock, caressing him. His soft flesh hardened under her stroking pussy. Within moments his cock, long and hard, pulsed beneath her. She grasped it and tipped it upward, then pressed it to her opening. As she swallowed it deep inside her sex she realized that Suzanne mounted Shane beside her.

Melissa lifted her pelvis then shifted downward again, thrusting his rock-hard cock deep inside her. Suzanne followed Melissa's rhythm. Melissa moved up and down, her pleasure riding higher. Suzanne moaned. Melissa cried out. Ty's hard cock stroked her insides. His hands cupped her breasts, stroking her nipples. Pleasure swelled within her. He shifted one hand to her pussy, then tweaked her clit.

"Oh, Ty, I'm ... Yes, I'm going to ..." She wailed as a spike of sensation—thrilling and potent—erupted through her, wild in intensity.

"Come for me, Melissa. I love it when you come."

Ecstasy spiraled through her in dizzying waves of bliss. Ty thrust harder and faster, and the heat of his climax flooding her womb sent her orgasm to a higher level. She clung to him, loving him, and loving his strength flowing into her.

Beside her, Suzanne's orgasmic moan shuddered through Melissa, sending her over the edge again. Shane groaned and Suzanne rode him hard, wailing the whole time. Ty swirled inside Melissa and she cried out, a third orgasm claiming her.

Finally, she sucked in a deep breath and collapsed on top of Ty. His arms encircled her and he cradled her against his firm chest, his cock still embedded inside her.

She had never felt so loved.

Maybe the swinging lifestyle wasn't so bad. She gazed at the faces of Ty, her husband-to-be, and her two very special friends—and she realized it was better than not bad. It was sensational.

Read on for a preview of Opal Carew's upcoming erotic romance

Blush

Available from St. Martin's Griffin in July 2008

HANNA'S RELATIONSHIPS HAVE ALWAYS FIZZLED BECAUSE SHE'S never been able to shed her inhibitions and get comfortable in the bedroom. But all that changes when she meets J. M., an instructor who teaches courses in Tantra and Kama Sutra, and he offers to give her a hands-on lesson she won't soon forget. . . .

"I want an orgasm." Hanna's hands clenched into fists in her lap as she stared at her sister across the table.

Her sister, Grace, cleared her throat.

"I think the drink is called A Screaming Orgasm," Grace said loud enough for the people around them to hear.

They both knew that wasn't what Hanna had meant. She glanced around the restaurant and noticed people staring at them and her cheeks flushed hotly. She lowered her voice.

"I'm sorry. I'm just a tad frustrated."

"I'll bet. Have you tried one of those vibrators with the thing—"

"Yes, it doesn't work," Hanna answered shortly, not really wanting to talk sex toys with her big sister. "Nothing works."

She didn't really want to have this conversation at all, but she didn't know what else to do.

Grace patted Hanna's hand. "You'll find someone soon. When you're in a relationship again—"

"No, it won't matter."

"Honey, I know what you and Grey had was very special, but you'll find someone special again and with him—"

"No, you don't understand. Grey and I never . . ." She stared into Grace's intense gaze. "I mean, I've never . . ."

"Ever?"

Hanna shook her head, her gaze fixed on the water glass in front of her and the condensation beading on the crystal surface.

"Even with Grey? But he was so sexy. And considerate, and patient."

Hanna nodded. "I know. It wasn't his fault."

Grace nodded. "That's true. The only person who can give you an orgasm is you. You have to let it happen."

"You're not going to tell me just to relax, are you? If I hear that one more time, I'm going to scream."

She'd read every book she could find on the subject and they all insisted that the woman just had to relax and allow it to come. *But what if she couldn't relax?*

Grace's lips pursed as she watched Hanna.

"Why haven't you told me about this before?"

"It isn't exactly the kind of thing you want to go running to your big sister about."

Grace squeezed Hanna's hand. "It is exactly the kind of thing you can come running to me about, honey." She paused. "Is that why you broke up with Grey?"

Hanna had known her sister would ask that. After all, Hanna and Grey had seemed perfect for each other. But Grace didn't know that in the year they'd been together, he'd never once told her he loved her.

Hanna's heart had ached to hear the words, but although he'd been a hot, hungry lover, outside the bedroom he'd seemed almost . . . distant.

She had wanted to ask him outright if he loved her, but she remembered when Grace had separated from her husband and one long tearful evening her sister had confided to her that Derrick, Grace's ex-husband, had said the words of love throughout their marriage, but had only been mouthing what he'd known she'd want to hear.

Hanna didn't want false words of love from Grey. If they weren't genuine, they were better left unsaid.

She had finally decided that if he still didn't love her after all that time, he probably never would. She remembered Susan, her friend from school, who had stayed with a guy for over six years, longing for a commitment from him, only to finally break up and see the guy marry someone else within two years. Hanna didn't want to end up wasting that much time. She wanted marriage and a family, but she refused to push Grey into it. That didn't make for a sound relationship.

So she had ended it.

Even though she still loved him.

Pain lanced through her heart. She missed him every single day . . . and night. As distant as he seemed during the day, she'd always felt loved and cherished snuggled in his arms in bed.

Tears welled in her eyes and she dashed them away.

"Oh, honey." Grace pulled her into a warm embrace and patted her back.

Hanna accepted her big sister's hug, then slowly drew away, still thinking about Grey.

"We just weren't right for each other."

How could she settle for less? How could she ask Grey to settle for less?

Grace looked skeptical, but she let the subject drop.

"Okay, honey, what are you doing to solve the problem?"

Her sister, a holistic healer, was a firm believer that everyone was responsible for their own problems . . . and solutions.

"I've been reading books." She gazed at Grace. "And I'm talking to you."

Grace's eyes glowed with warmth and she smiled.

"There's a ten-week course at the college, in the evenings. I believe it starts next week. I know the guy who's teaching it and he's exceptional."

Hanna's eyes narrowed. "What kind of course?"

"It's called Kama Sutra for the Beginner, but he discusses different sexual issues and one of the things he talks about is female orgasm and the fact that a lot of women have trouble achieving it. I know the instructor and I've recommended a couple of my patients take the workshop."

"I'm already signed up."

"You are?" Grace's eyebrows rose. Obviously, she didn't believe her.

Grey had signed them up for that course, hoping it would help her with her problem. Now that they'd broken up, though, she couldn't bear to take the course. Not that she would tell Grace that.

Taking the course would remind her that she wasn't with Grey. It would remind her of the frustration they'd both shared. It would remind her how hard he had tried to make it work between them, despite her problem.

"Okay, so why don't you do something wild and different. Something you've never done before."

"Like what?"

"Well, maybe find some sexy guy—someone you don't even

know—and make wild, passionate love. If you don't know him, you can act differently. You don't have to be yourself. You can be wild and uninhibited. Maybe then you can let go of what's holding you back."

Wild and uninhibited. Hanna's stomach tightened.

"Oh, no, I don't think so."

"Why not?"

"A complete stranger? That's crazy."

"Sometimes you need to let loose. Do something crazy. But it doesn't have to be a complete stranger. It could be someone you've seen a few times. Maybe been attracted to. You could even form a relationship after . . . or not. The point is not to worry about it. That's where the freedom lies."

Goose bumps shivered down her spine. The thought actually excited her. How insane was that?

In fact, she thought about the tall, sexy man who'd started coming into the Hot Spot Café, the coffee shop she owned, a couple of weeks ago. He had eyes the color of espresso and a deep, melodic voice that sent tingles down her spine every time he spoke. And he was exceptionally good looking, with a strong, straight nose, a square jaw softened by the waves of dark curls that caressed his collar. She had found herself making an excuse to help out behind the counter whenever he came in so that she could serve him. Organic Earl Grey tea with milk and natural cane sugar. He was always warm and friendly . . . and his masculine smile melted her insides.

Maybe her sister's suggestion wasn't so crazy after all.

J.M. walked along the stone path through the campus, which was lit by the streetlights and the soft glow of an almost full moon. A light, warm breeze rustled through the trees as he stepped toward the traffic

light on the corner of Stevens Street and Main, the college campus behind him.

Ordinarily, he would head straight home this late, but he had a
craving for an Earl Grey tea with Bergamot oil. Or more, a craving to
see the attractive woman who frequently served him his tea in the coffee shop across from the campus.

The light changed and he crossed the street. It was unlikely she'd be
on duty now, since he usually saw her there in the late afternoon, but it
didn't really matter. All they'd ever done was exchange a few friendly
words while he'd waited for his tea, then he'd been on his way. Of
course, if the shop was still open—which he doubted on a Thursday
night at nine thirty—and if she was there . . . and if the opportunity
presented itself . . . then maybe he'd ask her out.

His intuition told him this could be his lucky night.

The bell over the door rang and Hanna hurried to finish clearing the
tray of dishes, wishing she'd locked the door after the last customer
had left a few moments ago.

"I'll be with you in a moment," she said over her shoulder as she
wiped the tray and placed it on the stack of clean ones.

She was already here twenty minutes after closing. There had been
a rush of people about a quarter to nine, and they'd kept coming in.
Someone had mentioned there'd been a special speaker at the psychol-
ogy building tonight and the talk had ended at eight thirty.

She turned around and stopped cold as she found herself facing the
tall, dark-haired man she'd been dreaming about ever since her sister
suggested she jump a stranger. Her cheeks flushed.

"I'm sorry. I didn't mean to startle you." He smiled. "I'm glad
you're still open."

"Well, actually, we aren't." Oh, damn, why had she said that? "I mean, I can still get you something, but . . . I'm just closing up now."

"You're sure?"

"Of course. I haven't turned off the machine yet, and there's still plenty of hot water." She smiled, but glanced toward the door, hoping no one else would come in. "An Earl Grey? I have decaf if you'd like. Naturally decaffeinated."

"That would be great."

Her gaze strayed to the large front window and a couple walking by, gazing into the shop. She grabbed the key from the drawer under the till.

"Look, would you mind locking the door for me?" She placed the key with the brass cup and saucer key holder on the counter. "It's actually past closing time and I don't want any more customers tonight."

"Absolutely."

She grabbed a tall mug from the shelf and filled it with hot water, then ripped open the foil pouch on the tea bag as he walked across the store. When she heard the click of the lock, she realized she was in the shop all alone at night with a sexy, attractive man. One she'd been having hot dreams about.

She dipped the bag in the steaming water until it reached the darkness she knew he liked and she filled it with milk and one packet of cane sugar, then placed the cup on the maple counter. He placed the key beside it, along with a couple of bills to pay for the tea.

"I was going to take it to go so I wouldn't keep you."

She stared at the ceramic cup she'd given him.

"Oh, sorry. I can put it in a take-out cup . . . or . . . you're welcome to enjoy it here, if you like. I've, uh, got some leftover banana walnut muffins I can't serve tomorrow." Great, she'd just offered him what sounded like stale muffins. "On the house."

She lifted the glass cover from the decorative plate containing three muffins, picked up the tongs and placed the biggest, fattest muffin on a plate and handed it to him.

He smiled. "Thank you. These are my favorite."

She knew that. He ordered them every time they had some. So she'd added them to the menu more often just in case he came by.

She dropped the rest in a paper bag and curled the top.

"Actually, take the rest, too. I'd just wind up taking them home and I don't need any more muffins."

He took the bag. "Are you this generous with all your customers?"

"No, not really, I uh . . ." She paused, worried he would think she was flirting with him, then realized that's exactly what she was doing. She just wasn't very good at it.

"I just hate to see them go to waste."

She *really* wasn't good at this!

"Here's to finding myself locked in a coffee shop with a cup of tea, a muffin . . . and a beautiful woman." He held up his cup. "Would you join me?"

His warm, inviting smile chased away any thoughts of refusal.

She smiled shyly. "Okay."

Someone tried the doorknob, rattling the door a little. When the man peered in, she shook her head, mouthing "we're closed."

"I . . . uh . . . need to turn down the lights so people know we're closed, otherwise that'll keep happening."

She dimmed the lights then grabbed a bottle of water from the cooler and followed him to the table with the two loveseats in the corner.

"This is nice," she said as she sat down across from him.

She watched him as he sipped his tea, her gaze straying to his lips. Full and sexy. She could imagine them pressed against the back of her hand, playing along her knuckles. Goose bumps blossomed along her arm as she thought of those lips taking a long, leisurely stroll up her arm, then nuzzling at the base of her neck. He would stroke the back of her neck, then tip up her chin and capture her lips in a firm, passionate kiss.

Oh, man, she wanted him. Maybe her sister was right. Maybe she should just jump him here and now. Have a sexual romp totally devoid of a relationship or baggage. Just consume each other's bodies in a hot, wicked flight of fancy.

But how could she be so bold? Her gaze shifted from his lips to his hot, simmering eyes, and she felt her breasts swell with the need to feel his hands on them. His lips. She wanted him. Here. Now.

"Exactly what are you thinking?" he asked.